If your Wife is so Good...

Why are You in the Bed with Me?

The confessions of a Clean-Up Woman

By Alisha Coleman

The Clean-Up Woman Chronicles
Series 1

Revealed by Alisha Coleman

Copyright 2013 Holloman

ISBN 10: 0-615-77727-9

ISBN 13: 978-0-615-77727-6

I would like to thank my children for supporting me as I wrote this book by taking on more household duties and making sure I took breaks to eat.

I want to say a special thank you to those that supported and encouraged me my brother, mother, cousin in law, aunt, editing friend, and my friend aka Blair (LOL) who wanted to be in this book.

Table of Contents

Introduction

My First Boyfriend....1

My First Normal Relationship...2

My Man Of Distinction....3

My First Experience....4

My First Husband....5

My Mocha Dream....6

My Teacher...7

My Best Friend....8

My One Week Stand....9

My Beginning To The End....10

The Story Of Me....11

The Clean-Up Woman Dies....12

The Leap....13

Introduction

The life of a cheater is simple because there are only three motivations behind the why: Selfishness, Insecurity, and Availability. I have dealt with each of these personalities in some form or fashion; whether it led to an indiscretion or not was completely up to the man. Okay ladies control your anger because at this point calling me a ho; which should be whore, is not the answer. I am not at fault for having sex with someone's man because he is the one that owes you trust. I didn't chase him and at times tried to avoid him, so I need to make this clear and understandable. I have never chased after a man but I will allow them to fall in lust with me.

In my sick reality I thought, it was only sex and I knew my place so I felt like I always respected and protected the wife. If I were to meet her face to face I would end the relationship with her husband because she became a reality to me and I knew I was hurting my sister. I would allow them to fall in love, well a lustful desire, and broke them in such a way that I thought they would never cheat again. I know what I said does not calculate, but I never wanted a committed relationship or a man of my own. I wanted companionship from time to time , so that was my excuse for doing wrong. Truth is I wanted sex without commitment and a man with an appetite as big as mine. The reality was I kept attracting unavailable men; men that were married, in a relationship, legally married but separated, or afraid of commitment and I loved it.

That was my reality until I met Malcolm Diablo Maldad. The desire for a passionate sexual relationship with him started creeping into my dreams. The warmth of his body, the touch of his hands between my thighs, and his tongue caressing and exploring my body from top to bottom caused me to explode in my dream. I would awaken full of unused passion and a desire to scream out his name as we reached a climax of passion like never before.

Earlier I stated I never chased a married man nor would I deal with a married man once I met or knew his wife. There were two more rules I followed:

1. I did not sleep with married men that always cheated on their wives.

2. I did not deal with men that insulted or disrespected his wife or women in any form. I believed it was my duty to protect the wife from any hurt during these indiscretions. I

know my logic may not make sense to anyone but me but that one summer day caused me to have a venomous hatred for women and an unexplainable disdain for men.

Each chapter details an indiscretion or life situation causing my heart to harden year after year. Until my indiscretion with Malcolm Diablo Maldad caused a startling change in my life. Consequently, the story of my life becomes confusing cultivating the start to an end of the Clean-up Woman. Names, places, details, and life choices have been changed to protect the people that hurt me, marriages, relationships, and friendships. Sex should get better over time never routine, regular, or boring. I've been told by several women that there is more to marriage than sex. Which is true but it's a big piece of the communication, trust, financial, and respect puzzle of marriage.

Ladies stop blaming everyone except for the one in the mirror for your issues. The same characteristics that you saw in him that attracted you, attracts others as well so do not get upset at the woman; he should know better than to reciprocate. This applies to male or female and straight or gay.

I didn't start out as a Clean-Up Woman, I just filled a position that women tend to leave open. Now for those choosing to be the other woman, are still cleaning, settling for less because they have low self-esteem or desperate for a man and hope he will leave her for you; live by my motto as a Clean-up Woman, "Respect the wife by knowing your place because you are just the one he is doing for fun."

This is a fictional book based on reality that speaks to women that have been hurt, don't let your past hurts dictate your future.

Remember:

You're a precious GEM protected by God

1

My First Boyfriend

Kelvin Klutz my first boyfriend and the
start of a name that was used to belittle me
but I used it to empower me. Let's go back to
my college years. I attended a school in a state
as far as I could get from my hometown, but
not too far from Papa and Grams to drive up
once a month. I thought I would be attending
school with my best friend Tommy, but his
father had other plans. He was my only friend
after that summer day and I was his best
friend in that dreadful town. Looking back I
guess the town was not dreadful, but the
people in the town made it unbearable.

Kelvin was a senior and the star basketball
player at school. He was in college on a full
scholarship and knew how to party; which I
found out later. Kelvin dated the head
cheerleader, Patricia, who was also the
chorographer for the Main Attraction girls. I
met him late one night at a Greek mixer; he
had just broken up with Patricia for the
second time that year. I did not party or hang

out much, which made me a loner and I was fine with that. My grandparents bought me a house in an older quiet middle class neighborhood the summer before I enrolled in college and I had a car, so I did not live on campus. My grandparents would pop-up once a month without notice and spend the week with me or to check on everything around the house Papa would say. He was really keeping an eye on me and Grams kept him in check.

I did not have to make friends because I didn't live on campus nor did I not want to. My goal was to do my four years, get a job and prepare for graduate school. Because I was friendly and approachable, not making friends was hard. I had very little trust for women, so I would not let them get too close. I was very active on campus; I tutored students in math, served at different events, and helped at the counseling center. That was the first time I spoke to Kelvin; he was every college girl's dream...except mine. I believe that is why he was attracted to me. I had seen him around campus and heard a few of the girls giggling about him, but he was unattractive and arrogant in my opinion.

On a warm Saturday night I was cleaning up and keeping all of the intoxicated students out of trouble, as usual, when I spotted

Kelvin. I had never seen him drunk before and tonight something about him seemed different. The party was ending but he was still here sitting in a room by himself drinking. I walked in to pick up all the empty cans, cups, and other trash when he looked up and said, "Hey loner girl what are you doing?" "I'm cleaning up behind all of you party kids." "Why?" He said as he sat up, "Why are you always doing stuff like this for us?" I looked at him and smiled, "Because it's needed."

"It's needed, but we don't even appreciate what you do?" I stop cleaning to talk because I believed if people saw my efforts it could cause them to act, maybe not today but some day. "I don't do it because you appreciate what I do, but because like I said, I know there is a need for my help." I started cleaning again as I talked. "You see some people come to college to have fun as they get an education, but I came to get an education, love others, and remind myself to stay humble through life's experiences. That's why I cleanup behind you guys and help others. My actions may help others see the light one day, causing them to help someone," I said as I threw a plate in the garbage. "You're weird but I like that." He jumped up in front of me and asked. "What do you think about me?" Pausing I took a deep breath and said, "You're arrogant, self-centered, and selfish; but I am

required to love you in spite of your flesh."
He stepped back and widened his eyes before
saying, "Dang you're brutally honest. Not one
girl on this campus would have ever said that
to me."

I turned up my mouth as I rolled my eyes.
"Well I don't march to the same beat of the
crowd and I'm not praising a man."

"Are you one of those virgin bible chicks?" He
laughed.

"No, I've never had consensual sex and a bible
chick I am not. I am saved because of grace
and given mercy when I deserve more." I
stared out into nothing and continued slowly
as I thought about that one summer day. I
knew I had lost my ability to give what I had
been given. Knowing deep down inside the
real reason I cleaned up behind everyone so I
sighed, "I should do the same for my fellow
man but I still struggle with that some times.
That is why I serve others, as a reminder that
we are all imperfect except by the blood." I
was a little uptight and self-righteous back
then, but life or living life can change a person
real fast.

"I didn't understand a word you said, so can
you bring it down for a simple brother?" I tried
to be hard but this guy was not that bad
without his entourage. Trying not to laugh I
said, "You are not simple. The blood of Jesus
is what saves us by confession, repentance,

and belief." Kelvin paused for a moment as if he was reflecting on something and with a sigh he said, "My grandmother would tell me that. I miss her because now I don't have anyone to talk to." He pushed back tears as he started to speak, "She passed a few months ago." I could hear his hurt and unbeknown to me my next statement would cause the start of a good friendship. "You can talk to me because I won't tell anybody. As a matter of fact I have my own house if you want to talk in private," I said picking up the last two cups. "Can we go now I really need to talk to you?" He walked over and whispered. "I know you helped out a buddy of mine a few months ago so this will stay between us right?" He eagerly replied.

"Yes, but you have to ride with me because you've been drinking." I threw the rest of the trash away and helped him to my car. As we drove off I never noticed that Patricia had been watching from an upstairs window.

When we got to my house I made Kelvin some coffee as he sat in my meditation room. I had a three bedroom house with a den, sitting room, living room, dining room, and kitchen but Papa considered this to be small.

After I took him in the room he said, "Loner this is cool."

"Thanks, so what did you wanted to talk about?" I said as I sat down.

"Can I really trust you?" he said with a questioning tone and a look of desperation.

"Yes my allegiance is to God." I said as I eased to the floor next to him.

"Patricia is cheating on me." He said with a sigh of relief.

I raised my eyebrows and asked, "Okay but how do you know that for sure and don't you cheat on her?"

"Yes but she burned me." He fell back as if defeated.

I was puzzled because he was known to have sex with different girls all the time, "Are you sure, because you sleep with a lot of girls?"

He sat back up, "Yes because I use condoms with everybody even her, but she gave me head and a couple of days later I was pissing fire." He covered his mouth as if he could recapture his words. "Excuse me for being so graphic."

I put my hand on his shoulder to ease him. "Have you talked to her?"

"No that bi...sorry. That girl is so trifling that it's in her mouth." He stood up and started pacing the floor. "She's the only girl I kiss. I don't put my mouth on groupie h...sorry." He screamed as he fell hard on the floor as if he wanted her to hear. "Damn!"

"Okay but why are you so upset?" I said as I stood up folding my arms.

He rubbed his face with both hands as he stood up. "She was going to be my wife after graduation." He came closer towards me and grabbed my shoulders. "It's hard for guys that are going pro to know who is real and who is not. I've got girls watching me just waiting for me to make a mistake, so I have to make sure I don't become some chick's meal ticket just because I knocked her up."

I looked him in the eyes. "Okay that's understandable, so um...do you want her back?"

"That's the thing I don't know for sure." He said as he fell back to the floor onto a pile of pillows.

I walked towards the door. "I'll let you sleep it off over here and we'll talk about it some more in the morning."

"Thanks but can I ask...never mind" I turned and asked, "What is it?" He sat up, while making himself comfortable and said, "Will you pray for me?" He said, I walked in and kneeled beside him. "Come on let's pray right now." After we prayed I went to my room and got ready for bed as I drifted in to a peaceful sleep my mind erased the negative moments of the day.

The next morning I got up and prepared breakfast. I was setting the table when I realized Kelvin was still asleep. I walked into the room and woke him up. I handed him a towel, wash cloth, toothbrush, and some Papa's old clothes. I washed his clothes as he showered. We ate as we talked. He asked with a mouth full of biscuit, "Alisha, why do you act like an old person?"

I twisted up my face and asked, "What do you mean?"

He took a sip of juice and swallowed before he continued. "You are like really hot, but you don't party or hang out." He looked around the room scratching his head before he continued. "You're beautiful and people like you hang with people like me, but you won't hang out with us." He leaned in as if he had gotten a revelation. "Do you hang out at all?"

"I hang with me." I said with a smile. "I like being by myself because you don't have any false witnesses or backstabbers in your life." I stated as a fact but knew I was telling a lie.

"Well I hang deep, got folk watching my back." He retorted sticking out his chest.

"Yeah, the same people watching your back are probably the ones that stuck a penis in your girl's mouth." I said and rolled my neck as if I had stated a fact.

"Man they wouldn't do that, would they?" he said looking up into the ceiling as if he were in

16

deep thought. I stood up and cleared the table. "You would be surprised at what people will do behind closed doors, if they thought no one would find out about the situation."

"You sound like you're speaking from experience," he said as he helped me load the dishwasher.

"I've lived long enough to see my share of this and that. That is why I try to separate a person's spirit from their flesh," I said as images of that summer day flashed into my thoughts, knowing that a part of me hadn't forgiven them. "How do you do that?" He asked taking a seat. I walked over and sat next to him. "You must spend time with God and you give yourself time to heal, while accepting why you really got upset as you examine yourself." I knew this would be painful but continued on. "You have to be honest with you about you. You have to understand your feelings and why or what caused you to be the way you are." He looked at me as if I had the answer, but I was just using Papa's belief and Gram's advice, that I never used for myself. "But I know who I am." He replied slowly.

"Do you?" I asked because I knew he didn't know or understand his purpose.

"Yes," he hesitantly replied as if he were unsure and wanted me to give him the answer as he walked away.

"Then why were you getting drunk instead of talking to your girl?"

"Because it hurts," he said looking out the sliding glass door.

"Did it hurt or was your ego bruised?" Before he could reply I questioned him again trying to show compassion. "Why is it that you don't know if you want to be with her?"

"Damn, you're right, that's why I'm mad…she embarrassed me and made me feel like a fool." He slid the door open and leaned on the door jam. I knew he was pondering my second question as I continued. "Always be honest with yourself and you won't get so angry at others, because you understand their action before you respond." I said as I looked at my hands. He turned around and walked over to me. "You're kind of wise for a youngster. I believe we are going to be good friends."

"We'll see about that" I laughed as I stood up and pushed his left shoulder gently. We hung out all day Sunday and most of Monday because he did not have class, but I did.

When I got to school on Tuesday people were whispering and pointing at me as I walked around campus and in class. Later I found out why, when the Dean pulled me out of class. I was a walking disease, burning guys and girls. Anyone that had been with me in any type of sexual manner needed to get

18

tested and treated if necessary. When I got to the Dean's office, introductions were made; he had someone from the Health Department there.

"Hello Miss. Coleman, I called you here because you have been spreading a communicable disease and have yet to be treated," he said as he sat down behind his desk. "Would you like to consent to testing and treatment?" I walked toward the door and said, "I would if I had a disease or had given it to anyone; or better yet if I were sexually active in any way." The official from the Health Department tried to scare me as she stopped me from walking out. "Miss. Coleman this is a serious matter and you could be jailed for refusing testing and treatment, but continue to have sex with these young men." I put my bag in a chair and leaned towards the Dean. "I've been falsely accused. If you force a woman that has never had sexual contact with anyone on this campus, or consensual sex in her life to be tested I will sue you! So that means, starting with me and all the way down to my great grand children's children we will attend this institute of higher learning for free."

The health official said, "Miss. Coleman we know you have had relations with a young man that was treated Friday."

I picked up my bag and replied in shock. "I

didn't have sex with Kelvin."

"Well, I didn't tell you his name, but you knew exactly who we were talking about," the Dean said.

"I know because he told me Saturday night after a party." Suddenly the revelation of what I said made me realize I sounded suspect. The Dean stood up. "Why would he disclose that information if you were not the one that gave it to him?" He walked toward me. "We have received several calls pointing to you as patient zero so we must take action."

I calmed down and said. "Well if you had common sense you would see that the only people infected are the popular students and the phone calls were from females, that didn't give a name."

The Dean stuttered and said, "Well yes, but men are ashamed of these things." He picked up some papers off of his desk. "How did you know that...never mind."

"Dean, men usually know first and if a female doesn't pay attention to her body then she could be infected and not know it." I put on my book bag and walked to the door saying, "I'm not your patient zero. As a matter of fact, the males that were infected were the star athletes, but you don't have to answer."

"We know a young lady such as you desires to be accepted and have friends in her first year of College." The Dean said as he walked over to me.

I laughed. "Have you taken a good look at me? I don't have to chase anyone. They call me 'Loner Girl' because I clean up at parties behind the popular kids that I don't even participate in. I never drink or party but I serve at the mission, campus events, and I help other students that are struggling at the counseling center. I am on call 24/7 by choice. I don't need friends or to be accepted because I know Who's I am and I'm not giving it up just so a boy would like me." I walked over to the health official. "Give a random test to your Head Cheerleader that dates the star basketball player and compare notes to see how many got it from having some form of sex with her." I sarcastically as I looked the Dean up and down. "I'm sure she's not cured yet because he just found out Friday, told me Saturday, and this weird rumor came out about me Monday. I hope I don't become an educated fool when I get as old as you two. Have a good day." I opened the door.

"Miss. Coleman we are going to test you by choice or force!" The Dean yelled as he closed the door I had just opened.

I angrily looked at him and said. "I guess it will be by force, because I didn't have sex with anyone be it oral or any other way. I will sue you! This is happening because some angry little girl was jealous of the time I spent with

her boyfriend and now she wants to…"
Suddenly the door swung open, which startled us.

The Dean franticly looked up at Kelvin. He heard the rumor about me and came to clear it up with Patricia's best friend Traci; who was not so willingly accompanying him. "Young man what is going on here, you can't just burst into my office while I'm in the middle of a meeting."
"Dean I had to let you know that Loner G…I mean Alisha Coleman is not the one spreading this disease. All of the calls you got were from the girl who spread it and her friends." He pulled Traci forward. "This is one of the girls that made the calls and spread the lies about Alisha." Kelvin made the confession while the door was still open, so the information spread around campus quickly. "Take a seat Kelvin Klutz and you too young lady." Once they sat down Kelvin told them everything, even who gave it to him and how. Traci confessed to the phone calls and spreading the rumor because Patricia told them that I was the one that spread the disease.

That event was the determining factor for big break-up of the most popular couple on campus, but it didn't last long. That day marked the beginning of Patricia's hatred for me and her plan for revenge. That was also the day that my disdain for a particular group of women started, the stuck up girlie females that had control issues and the females that blindly followed behind them. I received an apology before Patricia and her friends were put on disciplinary probation. That week Kelvin and I began a friendship was questionable and what we thought was the best kept secret on campus, but a tragic turn of events would change all of our lives forever.

For months Kelvin and I hung out off campus or at my house, but while on campus he ignored me because he and Patricia got back together again. He said he loved her and wanted her to feel comfortable. He thought that because he was her first she would always have a special place in her heart for him. Patricia hated me and wanted to bring me down a few pegs, so she thought she had come up with the perfect plan to do it. After that big mess I changed my mind about pledging but I did not stop cleaning up or assisting at parties. I gave rides to dorms, passed out condoms, and tried to stop all the drunk trains; when the girl was incoherent or passed out. My name also went from Loner Girl to Clean-Up Girl, because I cleaned up behind the popular students. Patricia thought it was demeaning. Patricia knew about the friendship Kelvin and I had and she did not like it. Did I forget to mention that she was a spoiled little rich girl? Our friendship caused her to expedite her plan and Kelvin's surprise birthday party would be the perfect time to unveil it.

A few weeks later Patricia saw me in the book store. She walked up to me with a few of her friends. "How's it going Alisha, haven't seen you around lately?"
I frowned "I am good," I knew she was up to something, so I was very cautious of my surroundings and what was said.
"I would like to apologize again for the mess I caused and wanted to be friends. We have a particular player we share concern for so I think that would make him happy." She leaned in as if to whisper the last part of her statement.
"What do you want?" I uttered unable to hide my disdain for her.
She smiled as if she was about to cheer. "I'm throwing Kelvin a surprise party next weekend and I am sure he would like for you to be there, but as a guest not the clean-up girl."
I rolled my eyes. "His birthday is the following week."
"I know but his parents usually come to town and we go to dinner. Since this is his last year I would like for him to have a party to remember."

"So, what time and where?" I leaned to one side as I asked. With a big smile she said, "Saturday, 9 o'clock at the Rush house. See you there clean...I mean Alisha." She walked off laughing with her friends. I did not care for or trust that girl, so I decided not to eat or drink anything at that party.

As I pushed the door open to walk out I almost dropped my bag and bumped into someone. With my head down I started apologizing "Excuse m..." I was saying until I heard a familiar voice. "That's ok I'm used to girls bumping into me on pur...I mean by mist..."
I cut him off with a push. "Oh please Mr. Full Of Himself, bring it back down."
"So are you coming to my surprise party?" he asked as he followed me out of the door. "How do you know, it's supposed to be a surprise?" I smiled. He tilted his head. "Come on, we are in college and everyone is talking about the party of the year. I know Patricia wants to regain her position with me." He walked closer and whispered, "are your grandparents staying this weekend?"
"No they are leaving tonight." I said adjusting my load.
"Can I come over and hang with you tonight or this weekend?" He said with pleading eyes.
"Yes but bring your church clothes." I smiled.

"Why?" he looked confused.

"We are going to church this Sunday." I said as I turned to walk off.

"Okay Mama," he replied with a laugh. "Pick me up in the usual spot around 7."

Kelvin spent most weekends with me playing video games and eating unless my grandparents were there. That's when he spent the weekend with Patricia or partying with friends.

The night of the big day came and Patricia's plan was ready and foolproof. I arrived an hour after the party started but just in time for the cake. I walked in singing the last line of happy birthday. When Kelvin saw me he smiled and winked at me. Everyone was crowed around him so I walked into the kitchen just to get out of the crowd. I was leaning on the kitchen island when he whispered in my ear. "Thank you for coming." I turned smiling ear to ear. "I would not have missed this for the world." For some strange reason I wanted to kiss Kelvin and he seemed to look at me differently, causing me to quickly avert my eyes. I was thinking to myself what is wrong with me and what is he doing his girlfriend is in the other room. I had never been attracted to a man like this before. I have noticed that they were cute or fine or even if they had a nice build but never this. I felt a tingle that I had only felt when Tommy hugged and kissed me on the cheek when he left for school. Why am I getting this extra feeling...and with him? Okay it is time to walk away. Patricia walked up so that was my chance to run. "What are you guys talking about?" She asked as she offered me a drink, but Kelvin declined for me. I saw a twitch in her face that told me how she really felt. I realized that Kelvin liked to dance and drink much at parties but I didn't know he smoke weed and he loved running trains on girls.

Over an hour after I had gotten to the party my water was gone and I started getting thirsty so that meant it was time for me to go. I looked for Kelvin to say good night, but he was dancing with Patricia to a slow jam, so I waved goodbye. He motioned for me to come over. When I walked over, he stopped dancing with her and grabbed my hand. "Don't leave I haven't danced with you yet," he said as he pulled me closer, That simple move caused me to smile.
"Ok I will give you one dance."
He pulled me even closer. "It's my birthday so I want it to be a slow one." Patricia told the DJ to play two fast songs and then slow it down. We danced for two songs and then it slowed down. Before the third song was over someone handed me a bottled soda. I

inspected the bottle and the top was still on so I drank it. Towards the end of our last dance I felt myself getting tired. When the song was over I hugged him and said good bye but he noticed that I slurred my words. "Are you okay Alisha?" Before I could answer Patricia ran over and said, "I'll see about her, you enjoy your party." Her roommate grabbed his hand and started dancing with him as Patricia rushed me towards the door.

Less than ten minutes later Kelvin realized I was missing, but my car was still outside. He started looking for me when one of his teammates ran up to him. "Man there is a girl up stairs all primed and ready. I heard she's a virgin." Kelvin heard him, but his focus was on me. He spotted Patricia and walked over to her. "Where is Alisha?"
"She left a few minutes ago" she said looking distracted.
"Her car is still outside are you sure?" he said scratching his head.
"Yes I saw her pull off after she got some cake," She frowned.
"Was she okay to drive?" he eagerly asked. Something did not seem right he thought and Patricia was being too nice to Alisha. Patricia put her hands on her hips and replied. "Yes she got in her car and pulled off." Angrily throwing her arms around she screamed, "I

did all this for you and all you can think about is clean-up girl. I'm leaving!" Patricia turned in a huff and walked out of the door.

Something in the pit of his stomach told him something was wrong because Alisha didn't drink and all she had was water, so why was...before he could finish the thought Reggie, his best friend, ran up to him again. "Man there's a virgin upstairs and since you're the birthday boy, you get to go first." Reggie and some other guys pulled Kelvin up the stairs as he walked into the dark room he started undressing. After he put on a condom and got into the bed. Kelvin whispered in the girls' ear as he always did "I'm going to tear that thang up."
"Kelvin," the girl whispered as she tried to reach out but her hand fell back down. Kelvin thought her voice sounded familiar and her words were slurred something was wrong. Kelvin had done this plenty of times but the girl never said his name and she was not that drunk. He was always overly cautious and didn't want to go down for rape. He always put his future first. Why did she call my name and is she passed out he though as he turned on the lamp. "Alisha," he said in horror as he jumped up. I was passed out on the bed naked. Without thinking he whirled around the room in a panic looking for something. After he regained his composure and was

trying to put his clothes on, he stumbled over mine. He step on my car keys in my pocket and picked up my clothes. He grabbed me up in the blanket and threw my clothes on top of me as he stumbled to the door. He covered my face before bolting out of the bedroom. The guys standing in line began yelling "Man come on, we want some too." Reggie realized what was going on, so he pushed through to clear a path yelling, "Get back!" A few of the other players helped Reggie. Kelvin put me in the car, pulled out my keys and drove off. Most of the girls had already left the party.

When Kelvin got to my house he put me in the tub and ran cold water over me. He thought I was drunk but when that didn't work he stuck his fingers down my throat until I threw up. He cleaned me up and put me in the bed. Kelvin lay next to me, holding me until he fell asleep.

I woke up that morning and felt the weight of another body causing me to immediately panic so I slowly shifted my weight. When I tried to moved Kelvin said, "Are you okay? You scared me last night."
"Yes, what happen?" I said with a sigh of relief. Looking around the room in a panic I asked, "Why are you in my bed?"
"You had too much to drink and the guys were about to run a train on you," he said as he sat up.

"I was what, and they did what?" I said as I bolted straight up in bed.

"Don't worry, I grabbed you and ran out of there. Then I drove you home, cleaned you up, and put you in bed." He said rubbing my back.

"But you know I don't drink, this makes no sense. The last thing I remember is drinking a soda as I danced with you, then you whispered something in my ear." I jumped out of my bed as I realized what had been done to me. "Why is my throat sore?" I yelled, as I turned toward him. "I stuck my finger down your throat."

I started pacing. "I was drugged? Y'all drugged me?" I begin to cry, "Oh my God, how many guys penetrated me? Did they use protection? Okay, okay," I said trying to calm down. I turned to Kelvin and said, "I have to go to the ER and get tested. Oh my God what if I'm pregnant, I won't know who the father is. What am I going to do?"

Kelvin got out of the bed and held me. "First you need to calm down. You were not penetrated I was the first man in the room." He looked into my eyes. "When I realized that it was you I covered you up and got out of there. I knew you didn't drink or do drugs, but I did notice that you slurred your words after we danced and I..." He stopped talking because he remembered who brought me the bottle and came to help me out. He pushed away his thoughts and continued, "Look I was the only one that saw you because I covered your face."

I sat on the bed as if I had been defeated. "I knew I should have left the party early, but I wanted to say bye to you." I looked up at Kelvin and realized I liked him. "If it had not been for that I would've been..." I couldn't talk anymore and Kelvin held me tighter when he looked into my eyes he said, "I am sorry, I should have kept a better eye on you."

"It's not your fault or your responsibility." I lay back on the bed. "Last night was your night and you were supposed to be having fun, not babysitting." I sat up in bed because what he said suddenly hit me. "Wait you were the first one in the room, why? Do you always do that to girls with other dudes?" I said with a look of disgust.

"Look I like to party, I drink a little, smoke a lot, and fuck even more. I love to have sex and if a girl is willing I won't disappoint her." After he expressed himself we sat in silence until Kelvin broke it by saying, "I need to go back to the school so I can find out what happened. Will you take me?"

"No, but I will let you drive my car." I said as I laid back.

"Okay, do you need anything?" he asked pulling up his pants

"Not now, but give me a call when you're on the way back. If you are gone more than two hours just give me a call, so I will know everything is okay." He kissed me on the forehead, mumbled something and walked out.

Kelvin went to Patricia's dorm. She spotted him first as he walked in so she rushed up to him, "Hey Kelvin, I heard about your little friend, I guess she's a clean-up woman now." She laughed. Kelvin had never hit or desired to hit a woman, but it took everything in him not to choke her. He looked at her and shook his head as he leaned in to whisper, "I know what you did. If I could prove it I would report your ass." As he turned to walk out he said, "This thing between us is over."
Patricia ran after him. "Kelvin what are you talking about?" She grabbed his arm. "What did I do?" He looked at her, causing her to let go of his arm. He turned around walked to the car and drove off. Patricia stood there trying to figure out what just happen, but she knew it was not worth losing him.

A few hours later the dorm was buzzing. A girl ran up to Patricia "Did you hear someone drugged the clean-up girl and the basketball team gang raped her? The police are at the frat house now but they can't find her or her car." Patricia remembered that Kelvin was

33

driving her car. "What did he do?" She said under her breath. She scanned the room and saw two of her accomplices. She walked over to them and whispered, "Keep your mouth shut."

"What are you talking about Patricia?" one girl said in fear.

"What are we going to do?" Traci asked.

"Keep our mouths shut and act just as surprised as everyone else," Patricia ordered.

Traci said, "What if someone saw us take her upstairs?"

"All we were doing is helping our intoxicated friend upstairs, so that she wouldn't drive home." Patricia barked through her teeth.

"But what if she's dead?" The girl said looking around. "It's our fault!" The fearful accomplice was nervous.

"She's not dead, I saw Kelvin in her car this morning." Patricia said turning to the frighten girl. "Look, just be cool and this will all blow over in no time."

Kelvin returned in less than an hour. I was getting ready to cook when he rushed in with some food. We were in the kitchen eating lunch when a loud knock on the door startled me. I told Kelvin to go in my bedroom with his food and hide. Thinking it was Papa, I got up and walked into the living room "Who is it?"

"The County Police," they said so I opened the

door. The officer asked, "Are you Alisha Coleman?"

"Yes," I said fearful something had happen to Papa and Grams on their way back.

"May I see your ID?" I walked into the bedroom. "Kelvin it's the police, but I don't know what's going on, so stay right here." I got my ID and walked back to the door.

"May I ask what this is about?"

"There were reports that you had been sexually assaulted by members of the College Basketball Team." The officer went into details ending with, "Are those accusations true ma'am?"

"No. I went to a birthday party last night stayed a couple of hours and came home."

"Is that your car?" I looked out the door.

"Yes!" I said so we talked until the officers were satisfied. "Thank you for your time and patience ma'am. This is one time I am glad this was a false alarm. Have a good day and lock up." Kelvin rushed out of my bedroom when he heard the door close. "Is everything okay?"

"Yes, but someone phoned in a report around 11 o'clock last night that I was being sexually assaulted by the basketball team. The message was left on security's answering machine." We walked into the kitchen as I talked and sat down. "The officer said that security got the message less than an hour ago and called the police. That's why they were just coming to see me."

"I wonder who called it in, because we were dancing after midnight."

"Me...wait how do you remember what time it was?"

He grabbed my hand. "I looked round for Patricia because I wanted to steal a kiss from you. When I didn't see her I leaned in to plant one on you. Then out of nowhere she appeared with the soda, so I faked like I was looking at my watch."

I sat back in my chair releasing his hand. "I remember now. That's who gave me the bottle of soda. When I started feeling dizzy she took me upstairs. Patricia drugged me, she set me up. I knew I couldn't trust that witch, I'm gonna tag that ass, where my keys at?" I got up and started looking around.

Smiling he said, "Calm down you little firecracker." He stood up and embraced me. "It's always the little ones that pack a big punch." He kissed me softly on the back of my neck. "Is she worth getting kicked out of school?" He kissed me again. "Remember what you taught me about actions and reactions." He turned me so I could face him. "Ask yourself, why I am upset right now?"

"I know why and I understand why she did it but I'm upset because I didn't do this..." I pulled Kelvin closer giving him a passionate

kiss. "Alisha I've been waiting for you to do that for months." He said through kisses. I looked up at him. "I didn't want to be the one that came between you two. I wanted you to see what you had in her."
He pulled me closer. "You did. The more time I spent with you, the more I realized I forced her into a position that she didn't deserve."

Kelvin and I dated for over two years. Because he was on the road a lot and all the groupie attention, he soon forgot about me so we went our separate ways. Five years later Kelvin finally settled down and got married. They have two beautiful little girls and a son was on the way the last time we talked. We kept in touch for a while because he said, "I reintroduced him to saving grace and was trusted friend that he could tell all of his secrets too."

2

My First Normal Relationship

Mikael Brats the comedian and trained dancer; what a combination, but he was the perfect man for me. I never understood nor could I comprehend how a thing that seems right or good may not be. I loved the idea of spending the rest of my life with Mikael without understanding I needed to heal before I could begin a life with my husband.

I met Mikael on a Thursday morning, while getting my hair done; he was getting a mani/pedi. We had been going to the same place for years. I noticed him about two years ago, but he never noticed me until today. He yelled out to me as I walked by, "Hey shoe string pants girl." My white capris laced up one leg. I kept walking, because I didn't realize he was talking to me. Ok I did, but I ignored him like he did me because I didn't know how to respond. "Excuse me young lady in the white capris that tie up with a shoestring." "Yes Mr. Funny Man," I said with a smile "I just wanted you to know you look nice. How could I get to know you better?" He said with a serious look so I knew he wasn't playing. "Well thank you." I held my hand and made direct eye contact. "My name is Alisha, how are you today?"

He grasped my hand while looking directly into my eyes. "I am great and seeing you has made my day. Hopefully this evening will be even better. My name is Mikael, Mikael Brats and it has been a joy and a pleasure to meet such a lovely woman as you Alisha."

"Well Mikael let me put on some hip boots and get a shovel so I can get through all this bull you're throwing out so I can respond." We laughed.

"I like you because you're down to earth and pretty, so is that a yes to my dinner offer?"

"Yes, where are you taking me?" I smiled as I rubbed my stomach.

"You're straight forward, another thing I like in my woman. One more question, do you have a job?" he asked rubbing his chin.

"Yes I do." I said tilting my head.

Okay, I know I said one more but..." Mikael got down on one knee as he pulled out a giant diamond ring "Will you marry me?"

"No because I don't wear prop rings, but I will allow you to buy me dinner." I said with a smile while everyone in the shop was laughing. "Ok 6:30 at...where would you like to eat?" he said sitting down.

"I'm not picky, your dime your choice." I said

walking toward the door.

"Okay I will surprise you. What's that address again?"

"We can meet near Customs Rd on 38." I walked back over to him and I gave him my card.

"Ok see you at 6:30." As I turned to leave he said, "I hope you wear a shoestring dress tonight 'cause one pull and baby it's on." I laughed as I walked out of the salon.

Mikael was a different type of guy, he was a comedian, but before that he danced in musicals and taught dance at his step mother's studio. He was raised by his father and step-mom. His mother, an actress, was very active in his life. Mikael's father, Bernard was a stage hand. He met Mikael's mother on a set and had a summer romance that produced Mikael, but they never married. A couple of years later Mikael's aunt, Cicely, introduced his father to Kimberly, his step-mother a trained dancer. Mikael spent most of his time with his step-mother at the studio that she operated with his aunt Cicely. During the summer and breaks he would spend time with his mom on sets or auditions. At fourteen, Mikael was cast in his first comedy play; which lasted for a year. Then at fifteen he had a small part in a comedic movie. Finally at sixteen he had a recurring role on a

TV comedy for four seasons, which opened the door for him. He was kind and easy going, but he had been in an on again off again relationship with Keira for the past four years. We were going out on an off moment. Keira was best friends with Mikael's agent Kerri; they ladies met in college.

Mikael called me a couple of hours later to change the time. He also told me a few things about himself. I think he was tipped off about my stylist calling me, but I could care less about what she said. I wanted to know him for myself. I hate when women do that, especially when it's unsolicited. My stylist had already told me about his girlfriend and how he flirts with other women, although she had never seen him get or give out a number before. "I just wanted to warn you," she said. That night when we met up, he drove. When he came over to open my car door I spoke as I exited my car, "Good evening."
"Good evening you look nice." He replied as he opened his car door and helped me into the car.
"Where did you decide we were going?" I asked as he entered the car.
He turned to me and said with a grin, "It's a surprise. I see you didn't wear that shoe string dress." He laughed and I smiled which broke the ice and started the conversation.

"What do you do for a living?"

"I work part time with my step mom and my aunt at their studio, but I'm a comedian full time."

"Well how often do you travel?" I asked.

"Six to eight months out of the year. I've been working on getting a radio show and I leave tomorrow morning. That's why I asked you out tonight." He said as he gave me a quick glance.

"Really, so how are the off issues of the relationship going; since it's only been a few days?"

"I am done because I'm tired that's how it's going. Staci said you were a pretty good catch and most of all single and drama free. I've known her for about ten years, so I trust her."

"I didn't even think about that. She's been doing my nails for a while too. The first day I walked in I noticed you and flirted but you never noticed me." I would try to get his attention subtly but once I found out he was semi famous and had a girlfriend I stopped. I knew he had women at his heels all of the time.

"I noticed you the first time you walked through the door but I was with Keira and I don't believe in cheating. I need a woman secure enough within herself to deal with my lifestyle and trust me."

"Are you trust worthy in front of her?"

"I don't understand the question."

"When a female fan comes up to you and disrespects Keira do you put her in her place?" I turned in my seat and leaned toward him.

"Yes. I introduce her as my lady, love of my life, and the only woman I see since the day we met."

"I don't understand then." I sat back with a puzzled look.

"She wants me to curse them out and say this is my woman right here, now get out of my face."

"Wait you can't do that, you would lose your fans."

"She wants me to quit both of my jobs and work full time on a regular one."

"I don't get it. Did you meet her before you had those jobs?"

"No, but she is extremely jealous and insecure."

"On that note, let's talk about where you're taking me."

"We are here." He said with a big smile.

With a questioning look on my face I said, "This is an apartment building."

"Don't worry about that. Staci told me you are the type of woman that deserved the best."

I helped Staci and her husband with their relationship a couple of years ago and they were married less than two weeks later; after dating for four years. Once we walked in and got on the elevator he blindfolded me. When the doors opened he led me by my hand and all I could hear was music being played gently in the background. Mikael pulled off the blindfold and there was a small band, candles and a waiter standing by a beautifully decorated table that was like romantic fairytale dream on the rooftop.

Mikael turned to me as he handed me pink and white roses. "For the past two years I've watched, asked about, even dreamed about you. I wanted our first night to be the beginning of this fairytale relationship that starts tonight."

I was speechless and for me that was a miracle. Mikael lead me to the table pulled out my chair, then kissed my hand. I realized that night that if a man thinks that you are special and wants to be with you he will do whatever it takes to get you.

"Mikael this is beautiful. I never expected this. You did your homework, because I don't like flowers, but pink and white roses amaze me. Now it's my turn to pull out a ring and get on one knee." We laughed and enjoyed our evening mixed with small talk and laughter. The ride back was silent except for the soft music playing and an occasional glance and smile as we held hands all the way back to my car. Mikael opened my door and held out his hand as I exited his car. He pulled me close as we entered into another first a kiss that was fulfilling, but respectful. We turned toward my car and Mikael said, "As I fall in love with you, I'm going to enjoy each and every moment. As I look into your eyes and see our future, and your smile, it gives me pleasure to think about the future memories we will have. One day you will remember this day as I look up at you and respond with a yes." He kissed my hand, opened the car door and we drove off into different directions.

At that moment our lives had been forever changed. That night we drove off with memories that would never be forgotten. I drove home and walked into my house smiling. When I got ready for bed I was still smiling. As my head hit the pillow the phone rang. On the other end I heard "I don't want to seem desperate but I had to talk to you again. I couldn't get you off my mind"
"I felt the same way but it's late and you have a plane to catch in the morning"
"You let me worry about that." We talked into the wee hours of the morning. He caught his flight that morning and I went to work; sleepy but happy. That whole day I was jumping awaiting his call. When I got off I rushed home to see if he had called. I had three messages

on my machine; Grams called to ask what
time my flight would be there; I almost forgot.
Tommy called to talk about his wife again and
how he messed up as usual. The final call
caused me to smile. Mikael was telling me he
had arrived safely and checked in. He left the
room number and name of the hotel. I was so
excited. I picked up the phone and called
Grams between the small talk and her fussing
at Papa I let her know my flight would arrive
at twelve in the afternoon. Next I called
Tommy. He was upset because Natasha was
going on a cruise with her mom, but without
him and he didn't know what to do. Natasha
was Tommy's first and he was whipped.
Everyone knew she was cheating on him, but
him. When Tommy called me about her I
would change the subject or just say yes. I
hated to talk with him when he was in a mood
about her, so I changed the subject. "Tommy I
finally met a guy worth bringing home."
"Really, who is he?"
"His name is Mikael Brats and he seems to be
perfect."
"Is he white and what kind of name is Brats?"
"What difference does it make and who are
you to talk about color."
"I was just asking, you know this is a small
town and people are closed-minded as if
slavery still exists."
"I know. We went on our first date last night

and it was amaz..."

"Wait you just met this guy and you already think he's the one?"

"Wasn't your wife the team's three point mascot and you wanted to marry her after one night?"

"That was a low blow and I told you that in confidence because, well you know because of the burn."

"Sorry about that but I...never mind." I could not stand his wife but he loved her and I loved him so I had to keep my feelings and thoughts to myself. "I first laid eyes on this man two years ago and he ignored me, but that was because he was in a relationship and now it's over."

"So how long has it been since they broke up? You know you could be the rebound." It was funny how our friendship worked. I would spare Tommy's feelings about his f'dup wife because from day one she had him hooked. On the other hand he would find every flaw in any guy I tell him about; Mikael was only the second one. "You are right Tommy, but guess what I am going to enjoy it while it lasts."

"Lisha I just don't want you to get hurt, so I try to protect you from men. I love you and I haven't met anyone good enough for my Lisha."

"I know Tommy. I'll be home this weekend." Tommy did not like to hear about me dating, he thought I should just come home and settle down with my grandparents.

"What time does your flight arrive so I can pick you up?"

"I get there at twelve, but Papa is going to pick me up."

"I'll go talk to him and let him know that I will pick you up, if that's alright with you?"

"I guess so, heck you already made up your mind." My phone clicked. "Hold on Tommy." I clicked over and felt like a little girl after I said hello because it was Mikael.

"Hey there sexy eyes, how are you?" After that I forgot all about Tommy being on the other line. I had a grin so big that I could barely talk but I uttered "I'm good."

"How was your day?"

"It was great and you how was your meeting?"

"I'll tell you when I get back this weekend."

"Oh, I forgot I'm leaving Saturday morning to go back home and visit my grandparents. I know this is last minute and a little forward, but would you like to come?"

He was bursting at the seams but contained himself enough to keep his cool. His voice broke after his answer. "Yes, I would love to come."

"I know you have to change your ticket at the last minute so do you need me to get the ticket for you?"

"No, but thanks for asking. You are really a

different kind of woman and falling in love with you is going to be easy." I gave him the flight information and we said our good-byes because he was getting ready to meet some people. After hanging up with Mikael I called Tommy back. "What happened?" He answered.

"That was Mikael on the phone and..."

"Now this guy is so important that you push me to the side?"

"Come on Tommy it's not like that." When Tommy first met Natasha he never returned my calls because she had forbidden him from talking to me more than twice a month until they were married. He does not know it, but I was not invited to the wedding, so I lie to him about not being able to come.

"He is coming with me," I said.

"What? So you are going to bring this strange man around us, your family?"

"Tommy stop, I can get Papa to pick us up."

"No, I'll do it. See you tomorrow at twelve."

We hung up and I called Grams to see if it would be alright for Mikael to stay. She was so overjoyed that I met a man and was willing to bring him home that she hung up before we could finish the conversation. The next morning as I was leaving a vase with an assortment of pink flowers was on my porch. I looked around and saw no one. I picked up the vase and took it into the house. When I opened the door to walk out Mikael was standing there with a pink rose and a smile. I threw my arms around him giving him a big kiss before I knew it. This man had gotten to a place that I did not know existed. "I guess that means you're just as happy to see me as I am to see you."

"I guess so." I replied with a smile.

"Are you ready to go?"

"Yes." He grabbed my bags and opened the rear passenger door for me, then put my luggage in the trunk.

"Alisha this is my agent Kerri, she's going to take us to the airport." We exchanged pleasantries and Mikael hopped in the back seat with me. "Hey I'm not a chauffeur," Kerri said.

"You are today. Now take me and my baby to the airport." She turned in a huff and started the car. Mikael and I were like teenagers whispering and kissing in the back of the car. Kerri did not like that at all.

Mikael and Keira broke-up twice a month because of her jealousy. She would accuse him of not standing up to his female fans and leave him. He would always call her to come back. The last time she left he called her she came over and he told her she would have to stop. This caused her to remove her things from his apartment and throw the key at him.

This was not the first time, but it would be the last time. This time he waited two extra days, but met me before he could call her back. Kerri introduced them over four years ago. After two years Keira would tell Kerri about Mikael's roaming eye and how she would find phone numbers and make-up on his clothes. She said she had even found panties in his pockets. Now these tales were tall and a figment of her imagination, but Kerri had no reason not to believe her since she was not around him 24/7. She knew how women would act around him. Mikael was about 6'2" with a slender build and hazel eyes. When he smiled his eyes seemed to dance and it was infectious, drawing people in. He was a love at first sight kind of guy that never met a stranger and made you feel like you belonged. Kerri thought that I was the woman that Mikael had been seeing behind Keira's back, but there was no other woman. Looking at our actions we seemed to have been together for a long time.

Kerri had to stop for gas so Mikael got out to pay and pump the gas. This was her opportunity to get information and plant seeds. "Alisha, how long have you been with Mikael?"
"He asked me out Thursday."
"No, I mean how long have you dated?"

"Since our first date this past Thursday." I knew what she was up to because he told me about her and Keira being friends.

"No, when did you meet Mikael?"

"Two years ago but he ignored me because he had a girlfriend."

"So you have been seeing Mikael for two years?"

"No, I saw him at the salon two years ago and Thursday he asked me out. I guess he broke up with his girlfriend."

"So you know he has a girlfriend?"

"No, he had a girlfriend and they broke up, so he asked me out."

"Did you know how long they had been together?"

"No, that's none of my business." Mikael opened the door and startled Kerri. "What were you ladies talking about?"

I said, "Unnecessary mess that's inappropriate."

"What?" He asked puzzled.

"We were talking about nothing baby." I gave him a kiss and got out of the car to watch him pump gas. We continued to the airport as he whispered in my ear and I giggling until we arrived.

Mikael held my hand and slept on my shoulder the entire flight. When we got off the plane and walked through the airport, a couple of women ran up asking for his autograph. I stepped back so he could take care of business, but he grabbed my hand and pulled me closer to him before asking their names and signing their book. As we headed toward the exit he turned towards me with a serious look and said, "Let me explain something to you, and hear this, because I will not repeat it. You are my lady and in the future I hope my wife so don't you ever stand behind me. You are my partner not my invisible mate."

"Okay." He kissed me on my forehead before we walked to the awaiting car hand in hand. Tommy was waving his hand erratically until I acknowledge him. "Hi Tommy, this is Mikael."

"Hello Mikael, it nice to meet you, I'm Thomas. How was your flight?"

"It was great." The guys made small talk while they loaded the car.

"Alisha, my wife is home but she's a little under the weather, so she couldn't make her trip. Maybe you can finally meet her."

"That sounds great Thomas." Both guys reached for the door but, Mikael turned and walked to the rear passenger door and got in. He laid back and closed his eyes. Tommy and I talked; well Tommy talked about Natasha all the way to my grandparent's house. When we pulled up Grams ran out the door, "Come on Tobias she's here, they're here." Papa looked around the hood of the car he was tinkering with and came running when he saw my face. They were hugging on me as Tommy and Mikael took the bags into the house. "I'm so glad to see you baby girl. I can't wait to have a little talk with that fellow, but he's starting out right."

"Tobias, leave him alone I know Alisha wouldn't bring him around you unless he was right."

"Papa you can have that talk with him," I said as I hugged my grandfather again. We walked towards the house as Papa talked. "Marie done made a fuss over you and she's cooking all your favorites."

"Well look at her she's skin and bones." Grams said looking me up and down as she squeezed my arms.

When we got in the house Tommy gave my Grams a kiss good-bye and shook Papa's hand. He gave me a big squeeze and kissed me on the forehead before he shot out of the door to see about his wife. Grams took me into the kitchen while Papa helped Mikael with the bags to our room, but not before Papa tested him. "Are you sleeping in separate rooms?"

Without hesitation Mikael answered "Yes sir, we are not married."

"Good answer son. So what do you do for a

living?"

"I'm a comedian and a dance instructor."

"A what," Papa yelled because he was not open minded and still believed the old fashioned about a man's responsibility. He wanted me to be with a man that could support me and our family.

Mikael quickly caught on. "I just signed a two year contract for my own radio show and I help my step mom and aunt on the side if needed."

"You believe in supporting the women of your family, son I think we are gonna get along just fine. Now what are your intentions with my Alisha?" Papa said as he put the bags down.

"Sir your granddaughter is the type of woman a man wants for a wife, so I hope that one day you will give me your blessing."

"Son my final question is, are you saved?" Papa put a hand on Mikael's shoulder.

"What do you mean?" Mikael looked confused.

"Do you believe in God or go to church?" Papa looked serious so Mikael was nervous.

"I've heard about God and Jesus but my parents never took me to church growing up."

"Son before you get my blessing you need to have a relationship with the Creator." Papa quickly walked to the rooms to put the luggage up.

"How do I do that? I'm willing to do whatever it takes to be a part of her life and this

family." Mikael said stepping behind Papa. "Son you know what? I was worried about what she was going to bring home 'cause she ain't never brought no one home to meet us. You seem like a good man, but I am going to show you how to be a righteous man before you leave here. Come on in my study so we can read. I'm not going to force you to be saved, so it has to be a choice whether my Alisha is in your life or not." They went down stairs and Mikael went into the study while Papa told Grams to fix them a plate. "Alisha did you know that boy wasn't saved?"
"No Papa."
"Well we gonna have a little talk."
"Tobias leave that boy alone he came to visit you gonna run him off."
"If I run him off at least it's now before she gets too far gone with him."
"Thank you Papa." I said hugging him. He turned and went into the study. After Grams brought them a plate Papa locked the door for the next four hours.

Tommy brought Ma Carrie over less than an hour later. She told Tommy she came to visit Grams but what she really wanted to do was get a look at Mikael. "Where is he Marie?" She whispered eagerly looking around.
"Tobias got him locked up in that study of his with the Bible, Carrie he gone run the boy off

before she can get him." Grams looked down the hall as if she could see in the study while she fumbled with her apron.

"You know he feels the same way about her as he did her mama, so just let him protect the girl." She said as she sat down with a sigh.

"That girl ain't had a relationship with nobody but that boy that played basketball and it didn't work out." Grams looked around nervously. "At this rate I won't ever get any great grandbabies."

"Marie you have some." Ma Carrie said looking at Grams as if she were seeing her for the first time.

"But not from her. I'm scared that...I'm scared what happened to her all those years ago messed her up. I'll never forgive myself for that day." Grams stood up.

"Marie that was not your fault it wasn't nobody's except those that did it." Ma Carrie walked over to Grams.

"I know who it was but we can't prove it," Grams said as they hugged.

"Well thank God you don't have to look at that thang's face. I just want to choke'em." Ma Carrie was still hugging Grams as they both wiped tears from their eyes. "What's going on in here?" Tommy said smiling as he walked into the room.

"We were just reminiscing over old times." Ma Carrie said as she wiped her face one last time. "Alisha, get over here and give me a hug." I darted over and gave her a big squeeze. "Girl, are you eating up there, Marie did you feed her anything?"

"Yes I eat and Grams fed me a bowl of mac and cheese."

"Tommy, why don't you go home and check on your wife because I'm staying for dinner. Alisha and her friend will take me home." I walked Tommy to the door. Once we were out of sight Ma Carrie started laughing. "Did you see my grandson's face? He does not like Miss. Lisha having somebody. I wonder if he thought about that before he married that thang."

"Now you know his father made them get married 'cause she was faking a...I mean she was pregnant."

"That does not mean he had to. I told them to wait and see because that girl is a jezebel; you can see it on her and her mama. The way she carries on I hope Tommy uses protection, cause she is sleeping with everybody. Making my baby marry that old nasty gal." she said pouting.

"Carrie put your lip in, Tommy was the one that fell for her and you know it. You can't tell that boy anything about her, his nose open too wide." They both gave a loud hearty laugh and continued to prepare dinner.

After Tommy left I sat on the front porch in the swing and looked in to the night sky. As I looked at the stars I thought about my future with Mikael. He was everything a woman could ask for. I knew I could like, respect, admire and even adore him as a person. But could I love him like a woman is supposed to love her husband? The bible tells me to submit and I could, but can I love him like a woman loves a man? Does it matter if I do everything because of the respect and admiration I have for him? I believe I could spend the rest of my life with him, so it is settled. I am going to work toward becoming Alisha Brats. After my mind was made up I heard a voice, "Lovely night isn't it?" He said as he walked towards me. "You look so beautiful tonight." I smiled and walked toward him. "Alisha I was not saved when you met me, but I am going to work on my relationship with God so that I can be the husband God would have me to be for you. I smiled as we hugged and kissed. His pager went off so he asked if he could use the phone and walked into the house. "Hello did someone page Mikael?"

"Hi baby, how are you doing this evening?"

"Keira?" he said motioning me looking puzzled and wondering why she was calling.

"Yes baby did you miss me?"

"Keira I've moved on. I'm with my lady right

now. I would appreciate it if you would not call me again."

"Mikael baby are you just going to throw away four years for nothing."

"I have made myself clear so don't page or contact me again." He hung up but she called back. I answered the phone, "Hello."

"Is this the stank bitch that's screwing my man?"

"This is my grandparent's phone and if you call again I will call the police." I hung up and told my grandparents everything. Mikael and I sat on the porch until dinner was ready. Twenty minutes later she called again, Ma Carrie answered the phone, "Hello."

"May I speak to Mikael?"

"He just left with his bride."

"No I mean Mikael Brats."

"Yes Mikael and his wife just left for their honeymoon." The next few sounds were incoherent and the phone was silent.

Papa walked on the porch "Come on in and wash up to eat." Mikael's pager started going off with 911 calls from his mother, Kerri, his sister, and aunt. "May I use the phone because something's happened?" Mikael said as we walked into the house.

"They probably want to know about your wife because that's what I told your stalker ex-girlfriend." Ma Carrie said. "If I caused any problems forgive me, but that little girl needed to stop calling."

"No forgive me for any problems I may have caused you, I am totally embarrassed." Mikael said looking nervous.

"Honey you can't control a person and you made it clear that it was over right, so all is well." Grams said.

"Use my phone in the study so you can talk in private," Papa said reassuring Mikael by patting him on the back. Mikael asked me to go with him while he made the calls. He called his mom first and told her about me before he talked about Keira. He asked her to straighten out the issue with the rest of the family. He called Kerri. Clearing his throat before he said, "Kerri did you paged me?"

"Yes I called to let you know about the meeting with the station so I can work on your schedule."

"I know, in three weeks so is there anything else?" He could hear Keira in the back ground.

"No please forgive me if I interrupted your vacation." She realized that she had mixed her personal and professional life so she had to regroup. After Mikael finished his calls he said, "I should have prayed first."

"Baby I was praying for you already."

"Can we pray now?" Mikael prayed and we went to eat dinner. As we ate dinner Ma Carrie asked Mikael questions that were uncomfortable at times. After dinner we took Ma Carrie home.

That Sunday Mikael attended church with us and officially gave his life to Christ. Mikael and I would spend the next two weeks reading the Bible by the lake during the day and in the evenings we were planning our future on the porch. Our two weeks seemed like moments because we were hugging as Grams cried and everyone showed up to see us off. Grams packed us a small suitcase of food and Papa took us to the airport.

We got home on a Friday afternoon and he would only be in town for two more days. After he ran some errands we hung out at my house watching movies for the rest of the day. Saturday night Mikael revealed that he couldn't hold out. "Alisha baby I really want to try this abstinence thing and wait until we get married, but it's getting harder and harder by the minute." He laughed. "Look let me taste it just once."
I popped his hand as he worked his way up my thigh, "No because I won't stop and you wouldn't be able to either." I stood up. "Mikael we just got tested Friday and the results will be in next week. Be patient so we will do it the right way on our honeymoon." It would be my first time so I wanted to wait, but I knew that's why I couldn't hold on to Kelvin. We

attended my Church together that Sunday so he joined and asked to be baptized. Our future was getting off to a great start. We were sad about him leaving but he promised to call every day.

Mikael had been gone for two months so my phone bill was outrageous. He came home Friday evening but told me he wouldn't be home until Saturday so he could surprise me. I went to the airport on Friday to pick Grams up but to my surprise it was Mikael. I was so excited that I had to let him drive. We had to stop by his apartment; which was a part of the setup, before going to my house. When I went to the airport and his house my yard was being decorated by his friends and Papa. When he came down, forty-five minutes later, he had changed clothes and put a dress on the backseat for me. Once we got to my house I changed into the dress. He asked me to go out back so we could look at the stars before we went out to eat. When he opened the sliding door and looked up tears flowed down my face. Mikael had recreated our first date and included the scenery of our two weeks spent at my grandparents' house. When I turned back around to hug him, he was on one knee. He had asked Papa for my hand two weeks ago. As my eyes shifted downward I covered my mouth as he proposed to me

through watery eyes. "Over two months ago when I asked you out I knew before our first date I wanted to create moments of firsts and memories. That night I said one day you will remember this as you look up at me to say yes." I was in shock as I stood there thinking this was not real. "Are you going to give me an answer?" Mikael exclaimed. As I looked down at my great grandmother's ring through tears I said "Yes Mikael, yes I will marry you."
He stood up after kissing my hand. We kissed as he embraced me tightly. Mikael picked me up carried me into my bedroom. For the first time he tasted the sweetness of me as I embraced the warmth of his passion. As I spread my legs wider I felt his insatiable thirst for me and I knew he was meant to be my husband. That night we made a commitment that would never be broken and spent the rest of the night exploring our love.

Grams, Papa, and Ma Carrie came in the day before and had Mrs. Steinberg picked them up from the airport. Papa, Grams and Ma Carrie helped him set me up for that night and the party. We awoke the next morning to the sound of ringing. When I came to my senses I realized it was my phone ringing and his pager going off. It was Grams asking me where we were. His Mom was paging him for the same reason. "What are they talking about?" I asked looking puzzled.

"We are having a surprise engagement party because I have to fly back out Sunday night."

"So everyone know knew I was getting engaged?" I said covering my chest with my hand.

"That's usually how it works." He kissed me on the cheek and jumped out of the bed smiling.

"That's not what I meant. You said we were going to wait until the end of your tour or the start of your show before we got engaged." I said standing up.

"Baby I couldn't wait because we fit together so well. Since I've been with you I have performed better than ever and my relationship with God is growing. After the party we need to sit down and talk about something very important. Now go get dressed."

We kissed and I smiled as I ran into the bathroom and got ready. We were out the door in fifteen minutes and arrived at the place twenty minutes later. When we walked in everyone yelled, "Congratulations Mikael and Alisha." We smiled as I squeezed his arm tighter. We begin to make our rounds and introduced each other to or families. My grandparents, Ma Carrie, and Mrs. Steinberg were the only people close to me there. Everyone else was my coworkers and church members. I averaged about 18 guests. Most of the fifty guests were family and friends of Mikael's. I realized Kerri was not there but I figured she didn't want to hurt her friend so she didn't come. People talked about how they met us and told funny stories. We had cake and danced in between meeting different people.

Today I would finally met Mikael's family face to face. He is the middle child, the only boy, and the only child his parents had together. When he lived with his mom, Olivia, his great uncle Floyd helped raise him. Mikael was primarily raised by Bernard his father, Kimberly his step mother, and Cicely his father's sister. Bernard had two younger daughters with Kimberly and Mikael had two older sisters from his mother's first marriage. His sisters Barbra, Olivia, Michelle, and Connie came over and asked me several questions. Connie and Keira were friends, but she treated me with respect. His mother came over with Uncle Floyd. I was tested and questioned by Uncle Floyd. The last set of question and approval came from Bernard, Kimberly, and Cicely. I met his extended family members, friends, and coworkers.
"Mikael where is Kerri?" I asked.
"We'll talk later." He said rushing off towards Papa. We stayed for about twenty more

minutes before we let his parents and my
grandparents know we were leaving. When we
got in the car he told me he fired Kerri
because she could not separate her personal
and professional life. I was in shock so it seem
like we were pulling into the driveway. Mikael
revealed something that would alter our
relationship forever, but the how was still
unknown. He said it again. "Please forgive me
but about two weeks ago I slept with Keira." I
looked up at him and as my eyes shifted I
said, "Let's go in the house and talk." He
followed me towards the house like a hurt
puppy. "That's why you fired Kerri." I said as
he opened the door.
"Let me tell you how it happened." He said as
he led me to the sofa to sit down.
"I know how, just tell me what happened." I
said as I sat back.
"I had been drinking with Kerri because we
were celebrating the success of the show." He
slowly took a deep breath.
I went to my room alone but Kerri always has
my room key." He looked to gauge my
response before he continued. "I was asleep,
but was awakened to a familiar pleasure." He
stopped and grabbed my hands. "Baby I'm
sorry but I love oral sex."
I pulled my hands back as I moved farther
away from him. "Look, don't apologize to me
anymore because you haven't done anything

yet, so just tell the story." I sat back folded my arms as I waited for him to continue.

"I tried to stop her but it felt so good." He looked at me to gauge my anger, because he was used to Keira's rage. "I have not had a woman in over three months." He said with pleading eyes.

"I told you to tell me the story but you keep stopping to give irrelevant details so the only things getting on my nerves are the nonfactors or excuses you keep elaborating on. So far the details you've given me proves you're human." I said as I got up and started pacing.

"I grabbed her head and I was saying stop but I wanted her so..." He stopped and looked at me because he slipped up and told the truth. "She climbed on top of me and started riding but before I could pull her off I came. I threw her out of my room while she was still naked and found two room keys in her pocket. I walked to Kerri's room and found her in the room crying, so I fired Kerri." He sat back full of himself because he thought he had done the right thing and I would be proud of him.

"Did you get retested?" I said as I walked toward him.

"What?" he sat up puzzled.

"Retested for STD's?" I said putting my hands on my hips because I was so upset with him I could burst. I understood why he had done this, but I had to find something to be angry about.

"No," he whispered as if all the air was let out of him.

"So you came home and put my life in danger?" I sat next to him and tears rolled down my cheeks.

"No." He looked concern but then he thought about the fact that he knew her. "I know she hasn't slept with anyone else." He clasped my hands as he kneeled on the floor in front of me.

"Really, how do you know?" I knew in my heart he was right but I needed reassurance because I was angry.

"I just know." He said as he pulled my hands to his chest.

I shook it off and regained my thoughts. "Well I know this was a set-up to either get you back by breaking us up or to get pregnant. She never called me or sent pictures about it so this was not done to get you back. We just have to be patience and wait it out. I'll get retested next week I advise you to do the same." I said as I stood up looking out the window.

"Baby why are you upset with me I was set up." Mikael walked toward me wrapped his arms around me.

Tears rolled down my face as I turned around and said, "Because you put my life in danger, so you showed me that you were selfish."

"Baby I'm sorry." Mikael led me to the sofa to sit down.

"I know you are sorry, most men are so wait until I get the test results before I stop being upset with you." I leaned over and kissed him on the forehead and went to my room to change clothes. He sat on the sofa and put his head in his hands.

Less than an hour later my grandparents and Ma Carrie came in, "Hey there Mikael, where's Alisha?" Grams asked.

"She went to go change her clothes." He said as if he lost his best friend.

"Is everything alright, son you look like you lost...?" Papa was asking him when I walked in and interrupted, "Hey y'all."

"Girl, where's a room Ma Carrie needs a nap before we head to the airport." She said yawning.

"Come on its back here." Ma Carrie and Grams followed me to the bed rooms. "Alisha I know Mrs. Steinberg would love if you would stop in and thank her for helping us set up this surprise." Grams said.

"Son is there something you want to talk about?" Papa said as he sat down next to Mikael.

Mikael sat back in shame. "No sir, I just want to be perfect for Alisha, but I keep making mistakes."

Papa sat back and placed his hands in his lap. "Son you can't be perfect for her or any woman, only God sees your perfection through the blood." Papa turned his head toward Mikael. "Your job is to seek God's face, pray, repent, spread the good news, and to do the will of God; not man daily."

"Yes sir." Mikael closed his eyes.

"Now I just say don't hurt my baby on purpose because she will forgive you, just give her time. But I will hurt you," Papa patted Mikael on the leg and smiled.

"Yes sir." Mikael said nervously as he cut his eyes toward Papa to see if he was serious.

"Papa, you're not going to take a nap?" I asked walking into the living room.

"No, I'm going to get my rest on the plane," Papa said getting up. "That reminds me, I have to call Thomas and remind him to pick us up." Papa rushed off towards the kitchen.

I walked into the room and sat down next to Mikael putting my arm around him. I held his hand and whispered in his ear, "Baby I love you so I'm going to be your wife. Let go of your past mistakes, learn from them, and move on."

"I feel bad because I wanted to have sex with you and all the things I allowed her to do as I closed my eyes I thought about you. When she gave me oral pleasure, I pretended it was you

71

because I had been masturbating to the thoughts of having you." he said with pleading eyes.

"It doesn't matter what happened unless you called her up and told her to come over, or you've been talking to her behind my back all this time. It's not easy to go without sex once you've had it. That's why I believe when a man is married his wife should never deny him that pleasure."

"Last night was so good that I didn't want to tell you what happen. All I know is that I won't touch another woman." Mikael slid closer, "Baby do you want to leave?"

"No, I'm not leaving you," I said.

"No Alisha I have to pack and your grandparent's flight is not for another couple of hours." He squeezed my hand.

Without a thought I jumped at the opportunity for some alone time with him.

"Papa I'm going to Mikael's house while he packs but we'll be back before it's time for you to leave."

"Okay baby," he smiled. He gave Mikael a stern look, "Remember what I said Mikael." Papa said walking into the room. He gave me a hug and shook Mikael's hand while patting him on the shoulder.

When we got to his house he took a shower so as he stepped out I was standing in the bathroom. He quickly wrapped the towel around himself. I walked over and snatched his towel off, and dropped down with my legs open so I could pull him closer. While he stood there I gently kissed his rising nature until he was fully extended. I allowed him to feel the back of my throat and swallowed causing his knees to buckle as he grabbed my head. I swirled my tongue around the thickness of his manhood and he softly called my name. I gave him the fullness of my experienced mouth and he relinquished his strength falling back onto the tub screaming. "Baby what are you doing, oh my god I love you so much..." He had given a part of himself to me and with pure pleasure I received it all. Mikael rolled onto the bathroom floor. "What the fuck was that?" Searching for his next breath he said, "What did you just do to me? I can't move without...oh my god," his body continued to jerked involuntarily as he sat on the floor.

"I just gave you a sample of what your future wife has to offer." I smiled as I stood up wiping my mouth.

"You paralyzed me, shit." He said trying to stand up. "Can you do it again."

"No." I put my hands on my hips. "You told me when she gave you head you wished it was me. I don't give head; I give experiences that you'll never forget." I was extremely competitive so I tried to be the best at everything I did. I had practiced for years on the art of the oral pleasure by using a chocolate coated vanilla ice cream and peanut butter cups. I would try to suck some of the vanilla out of the top without breaking the chocolate coating and lick perfect holes in the peanut butter cups without breaking the cup. I didn't know that strengthen my ability to control my tongue and vacuum pressure of my suck. I did know I would love pleasing my husband more than anything.

"You just created a memory I will never forget." Mikael said as he stood up. "So I guess that means you're not upset with me anymore?"
"Yes I am, but I also understand you've never tasted nor had the pleasure of enjoying my skills, so that was just food for thought." I laughed and walked into the bed room.
"After last night and today I feel like I was getting my first piece. Baby, you can believe I won't be a minute man on our honeymoon," he laughed.
"Yes you will until you learn how to control yourself while enjoying me." I smiled as I lay across his bed.
"I learned how to do that as a young man." He said sticking out his chest.
"Baby I'm a different kind of pleasure," I

winked.

"You ain't lied about that." He said licking his lips as he walked toward me. "Baby I need a nap so..."

I cut him off, "No! You are going to pack and we are going back to my house." I got up and opened his suitcase.

"If you had not just whipped me, I would..." He quickly turned. "Who's knocking on my door?" He walked into the living room toward the door. He continued to fuss until he opened the door. I had a funny feeling in the pit of my stomach, so made my way toward the living room. I heard Mikael saying, "You need to leave." As I entered the living room, I saw Keira standing there with her coat open and her eyes closed. I walked up behind Mikael and put my arms around him. "Baby I didn't do anything." He said with his arms in the air and eyes slightly closed. Keira opened her eyes as she was saying, "That's not what you said the other..." Once she realized I was in the room holding Mikael she whispered the last word of her sentence as if she was in shock "...night." Thinking she had the upper hand, she became bold. "Mikael what is she doing here?" She said pointing at me with one hand on her hip.

"Please leave." Mikael said calmly.

"No, you tell this bitch to leave! We had fun on your tour making sweet love and now you're going to try and play me?" As she talked she made her way further into the apartment. I whispered into Mikael's ear, "bathroom." So he walked over to the door. "Keira leave or I will call the police," he said angrily.

"Did you tell your girlfriend about us?" Keira said smiling coyly.

I walked up to her with no expression and boldly said, "Yes he did and now it's time for you to leave my fiancé's house, before I put you out." She looked kind of strange because she had Mikael whipped but I enter the picture and he asked me to marry him after only a few months. "But I thought y'all were not having sex," she said confused as her eyes pleaded with Mikael.

"I heard about what you and your friend did but even that crap between your legs is not enough to break our bond." I said as I turned to walk out. "Oh yeah you can leave now." I disappeared toward the bedroom and Mikael opened the door as she stormed out.

Mikael came over to me laughing, "Baby I love you. Oh my god you are amazing." He embraced me and kissed me on my forehead before looking into my eyes. "That is why you're going to be my wife."

"She's not done yet and she's planning something else." I said as I pulled away from Mikael.

"After that she's not going to try anything

else." Mikael said pulling me back.

I held his face in my hands. "Listen to me Mikael the next time you slip I'm leaving you."

"But baby you see how she just walked up in here?" He said pointing towards the door.

"If I had not been here, what would you have done?" I stepped back waiting for an answer.

"I would have called the police on her."

"While this naked girl stood in your living room willing to do anything to get you back." I turned up my mouth.

I will take out a restraining order." He said pointing one finger towards the ceiling as if he had a brilliant idea.

"Why, she hasn't broken any laws." I said turning up my mouth.

"She raped me in my sleep," he exclaimed.

"And you woke up and assisted her in the crime." I said as I chuckled.

"Baby, that's not funny," he said shaking his head.

"Yes it is. Now call Kerri and rehire her as your agent because she's good regardless of her actions and believe me she won't do it again." I said handing him the phone.

"Baby the way you're talking I need to hire you," he said pushing the phone away smiling.

"That's not my niche, so call her and hire her back. Tell her Keira can't know your whereabouts if she comes back." I said dialing her number.

"Okay, but I don't like it." He said putting the phone to his ear.

He walked over to the side of the bed and talked to Kerri. Just like that she was back on the team. "She's coming to your house tomorrow so we can discuss the details and later you can take us to the airport."

"Cool you know I love you right and I'm your partner in this? Just keep it business with her no personal details or time." I patted his strong chest and sat on the bed.

He pushed me back and lay on top of me. "I'm so blessed to have a woman like you. Can we get married now?"

"I would love to but we have to get some stuff together and tie up loose ends." I said thinking about Papa having a fit if I don't get married in a church.

Mikael packed and we were out of the door in twenty minutes. When we got back Papa had fallen asleep on the sofa so we walked into the back yard and sat on the swing. "I have never had so much peace and joy in my life. Papa T introduced me to the word and showed me how to have a relationship with God. I don't understand how I keep messing up. I had a talk with him this afternoon and he explained some things to me. After everything that happened at the apartment today I realized a life with you is my destiny and the will of God. When I'm with you I see, hear, and feel tranquility. Alisha I've only experienced that when I'm dancing. I never told you that my desire is to dance this radio show, stand up, and acting just pays the bills. I love to dance but Keira said I looked gay and should stop so I did." He said sadly but suddenly he got a revelation. "Alisha dance with me?" We danced to music only he could hear ending with a leap. He embraced me for a kiss final kiss.

"Time flies when you're getting some good sleep," Ma Carrie said as she stumbled out of the bedroom. "Alisha your bed sleeps real good child. I need to take it home with me." Grams came out of the kitchen. "Tobias, are you ready? I fixed us a bite to eat before we head out." She was bringing him a plate while Mikael and I went into the kitchen with Ma Carrie to eat. "Son, get your plate and come in here with me," Papa bellowed from the living room. Mikael got up and walked into the living room with Papa and watched TV. Papa and Mikael talked about what was on TV and life. Mikael told Papa he wanted to marry me today but he never got a response. Papa just kept talking as if he never heard him. In the kitchen we talked about marriage and I told them that Mikael wanted to get married now.

Ma Carrie got excited, but Grams said, "It ain't right, you got to do it in a church with family; plus Tobias ain't ready for you to leave him like that."

Ma Carrie said, "That boy's bones is itching to get in the bed with you. I can tell the way he always wants to touch; y'all ain't doing nothing is ya?" Ma Carrie looked at me as if she knew so she changed the subject. "Now baby be careful cause times ain't like when me and Marie were young. These women will do anything to get a man and you have a keeper. I'm not telling you to have sex but I am saying get married as soon as possible or keep your man."

"Carrie, don't tell her that because Tobias will have a fit if he can't walk her down the aisle."

"I know Grams and I won't elope but I will keep my man." Ma Carrie and I laugh as Grams folded her arms and shook her head at us before a smile appeared. The time seemed to fly by and they were out the door and on their way back home.

Mikael straightened up while I finished up in the kitchen. After he finished he took a shower and got in the bed. I finished cleaning the kitchen and called Tommy about our grandparents. He was getting ready to go out the door. Mikael's pager started going off so I responded to the call and it was Kerri confirming the meeting and flight times. Grams called to let me they were home. After we hung up I took a shower and got into bed this caused Mikael to immediately pull me closer and wrap his arms around me. I slept for about ten minutes before Mikael slid under the covers and awoke me with moans of pleasure. Mikael said he enjoyed pleasing me because it tasted so sweet to him. After a few minutes I gave him his reward for pleasing me just right. I turned him onto his back and reminded him of the skillful works of my tongue. Within minutes he gave in to me, but I continued until he awakened with full vigor. I mounted my husband to be as he cried out my name in pleasure. Within minutes I called out his name. He convulsed squeezing me tighter and tighter. As he pulled me closer he ended with a kiss on my forehead. Mikael turned me over and held me as tight as he could without hurting me and fell asleep. I was not far behind him. We slept peacefully all night.

Kerri was there on time so we sat down went over the clauses in the new contract I wrote and shook hands. Kerri apologized for being unprofessional and Mikael apologized for firing her without a thought or talking to her about her involvement in the incident. Kerri and Mikael's profession relationship never ended after that day and we became friends. During the meeting we found out that Kerri had nothing to do with giving Keira the key to his room but she wanted to help get them back together. She knew Keira loved him and Kerri felt obligated because she set them up. After the incident, she knew Keira was using their friendship to set him up. Now their friendship is a little shaky, at least until she can prove she's a trust worthy friend. After the meeting Mikael loaded the car and I took them to the airport. He would be gone for two months. I was to plan the wedding so when he got back that following weekend we would get married.

When I was a child I would always plan out everything. Every time Papa would see me planning he would say "Man plans, but God guides." The first time he said it to me I asked, "Papa what does that mean?"
"Baby girl, it means all those ideas you have down on that paper will only happen when God says so, in His time not yours. Don't stop writing or planning just pray before, during, and after so you will continue to do God's will by delighting yourself in Him. Don't be stubborn and let the light of God guide you." From that day and every time I planned I did so in writing because I remembered what Papa told me as a child so some things I

would plan in my head. Papa explained in a way I would never forget, but I tried to get around it by not writing it down, which would lead to many devastating, results in my life. During my planning process for the wedding I recalled Papa's words and prayed often. When Mikael left we talked every day at the same time. A few weeks into his tour he was an hour late calling. He would call late so I would take a nap when I got home from work. That day was no different except, I had a dream. I dreamed that he had broken off our engagement because he had eloped with Keira. In the dream they had kids. I was awakened from the dream by the phone, it was Mikael. "Baby I am so sorry I met this director that wants me to play a role in his movie. We had drinks after my show. You know since they postponed my radio show until next year I need the exposure."

"Oh Mikael I'm so happy for you. Wait, did you get the part.?"

"I have to read for him next week. Baby this is a major movie, with a lot of big names." He paused. "Okay let me calm down and thank my lovely wife, because of you I rehired Kerri and she is making things happen. Girl you are going to be a great counselor and business woman because you know your stuff."

"Thanks, that's why we are such a good team." We talked well into the night about the opportunities and offers he had before hanging up.

Mikael's youngest sister Connie and Keira were friends and they would hang out a lot. The last month on his tour Keira called Connie and asked her to come over. Connie, like Kerri, did not know the other side of Keira. Connie was upset with her brother for not doing his part at the studio. Her mom was always defending what Connie thought was his selfishness. When Connie got there, Keira told her a distorted version of the events over the past few months. She talked about what happened between her and Mikael at the hotel, his house, and now how he has been ignoring her. Keira was in tears and Connie comforted her. "He's out of your life now and he can't hurt you anymore." She said as she comforted her. Unbeknown to Connie Keira wanted him back.

"But you don't understand we are connected for life now." Keira said looking pitiful.

"Was he your first?" Connie said looking into her eyes. "Oh my god that dog." Keira never told the truth.

"I'm pregnant." She said and burst into another round of tears.

"Oh no Keira, I'll help you and my family will support the baby." Connie comforted her and asked, "Does he know?"

"Yes, he said it was not his fault so get rid of it." She said as she cried into her hands. "I will not mess up his future with his new wife." She peeked through her fingers to see if Connie took the bait and she did. "Okay Keira, I will take care of it." Helping her up Connie led her to the bedroom. "Let's get you in bed." When Connie got home she paged Mikael with a 911. Mikael was on the phone with me. "Hey baby let me call you back, my sister is calling me with a 911 and she never calls." He sounded worried.

"Okay," I hesitated as we hung up the phone. Mikael quickly called his sister.

"Hello," Connie answered the phone in an angry tone.

"Hey Connie is everything okay?" Mikael asked in a slow steady tone.

"No, you selfish dog you. How could you?" She yelled.

"Is this about the studio again, I've talked with mom." Kimberly knew that Mikael had to leave the studio because of Keira, but he didn't want her to tell anyone. Recently they talked about him coming back full time once things settled down in his career.

"No, it's about your unborn child," she barked.

"Alisha is pregnant, how did you find out before I did?" He began to smile but that smile soon faded.

"No you pig it's the one you been cheating on her with!" She screamed.

"I'm not cheating on Alisha!" He yelled.

"So you're not playing with another woman's emotions to get your selfish fulfillment?" She quickly said.

"No I'm not even having sex, well twice with...wait what am I saying, you're my baby sister. Please tell me what you're talking about and who." He sounded lost and confused.

"Keira is pregnant with your child. About a month ago you guys were together on your tour." When those words flowed out Mikael's heart sank, because he remembered what I said, "She's setting you up and she's not done yet, next time I'm leaving you." He was so confused that he mixed up the conversations and the time frame. His only thought was hurting me and losing me forever because of that one slip.

"Connie it's not true. It can't be because I only made that one mistake. I love Alisha and she's the only woman I'll ever love." He pleaded for his sister's sympathy, which was not shown.

"Well selfish man it only takes one time and if you really loved Alisha you would've kept your pants on." She laughed, "Your best bet is to leave her alone before you destroy her life too." Connie hung up the phone on him.

Mikael sat on the edge of his bed and cried as

the thoughts of my smile, Papa T's words, and the pain that would destroy all we were building. He lay back on the bed and thought about praying but instead picked up the phone and called me back. I was sitting on pins and needles awaiting his call. "Hey babe," he said as if he had just suffered a great lost. "Is everything alright because you sound sad? Is your family alright or is there something I need to do?" I said panicking as I stood up. "No everybody's good," he said calmly. "What's wrong with you? Mikael you sound like you've been defeated." My voice had mellowed out.

"My sister just told me about her friend and asked what I would do." He wiped his face.

"What did she tell you?" I said giving him my full attention but trying to figure out the unknown.

"Her friend is pregnant by a man that's engaged to someone else, but the man loves his fiancé and is scared to tell her because he may lose her. She has already warned him about making mistakes and now a baby is involved." Mikael's breaths were short and strained.

"Well if she warned him he deserves what he gets for not taking the proper precautions." I jumped on the bandwagon so missed what he was saying. "When will men learn if you're going to cheat use a condom? This does not

just protect you but protects your woman."
"That's why I love you and could never give
my heart to another woman again." I could
hear his painful smile. "I'm getting tired and I
have to get an early start tomorrow.
Remember what I told you at the airport that
day. You are my partner and we are doing this
thing together because some day you will be
my wife." He took a pause and took a breath.
"I also want you to know that no other woman
has had or will have the part of me that you
do right now, I will love you forever goodbye."
When he hung up the phone I knew he was
breaking up with me because Keira was
pregnant. I called Grams and cried.

A few days later I got a pink rose with a
note. ONE DAY YOU WILL BE MY WIFE! On the back
of the note he wrote: *The day I send you two
know that I'm standing beside you.*

I knew I could never love a man the way the
world says and I didn't. I was ready to love my
husband the way God told me to and that's
how I loved Mikael. I thought to myself from
that day on, I would never be with a man
longer than three months unless I could
control the situation. I would never admire,
respect, or adore another man like I did
Mikael Brats. I would also learn that Papa was

right, never is a long time and impossible to do. Love is natural so you can't control it but you must love yourself and have forgiveness so it can flourish.

3

My Man Of Distinction

__Charles Richmond__ my seasoned man of distinction. Charles was in the line of men I dated without sexual contact because they were special projects. He taught me class, while giving me a glimpse into old school thinking and he was extremely smooth. I met Charles when I had my car serviced. He was a part time mechanic. The moment I saw that tall, bald, milk chocolate, golden brown-eyed man I was hooked. I wore my favorite mini skirt because it showed off one of my best assets. I flashed him a smile and he got the message without hesitation. With caution he grabbed the card I was slipping him. I love older men because they have lived long enough to appreciate the true assets of a woman and not just the obvious big butt, pretty face, and tiny waist. I love when men see there is more to me than my looks; it causes me to desire them more. I also know my looks are how I get their initial attention.

That evening Charles called me and informed me we would be going out Friday night, but because this was our first date we could meet at the restaurant. I love a man that knows how to take charge and Charles established that from day one. This man was mmm mmm good and I enjoyed every moment we spent together. Friday night we met for dinner and since we were both early that gave us a chance to talk before dinner. He was 24 years older than me, but didn't look it, so he had no problem keeping up. Charles liked exotic foods, dancing, hiking, and traveling. He probed me with basic questions. I responded like a gitty little girl, "Well I love to dance and eat so we will see how far this will go."

"You don't look like you eat a lot so I guess the dancing works." He laughed. The hostess took us to our table. "I've never been here before." I said looking around.

"Great, so I get the opportunity to assist you ordering, beautiful." He smiled.

This dude was lip smacking good and I couldn't wait to get to know him better. "What should I try first?" I squeaked.

"The lamb is great. Have you ever had lamb before?" Charles asked as he leaned over to point it out on the menu.

"No, but I'm willing to try anything at least once." I said winking.

"I can see now that I could fall in love with you," he said caressing my face.

The waiter walked up so Charles ordered appetizers and drinks.

"So you don't drink alcohol, may I ask why?" he asked sitting back in his chair.

"I just don't like the taste or how it makes me feel." I never told people the real reason but most people accepted that answer until tonight.

"Don't start lying to me now beautiful." He said as he held my hand. "What happened to you?" he asked gently caressing my hand with his thumb.

"I really don't want to talk about it," I said as I shamefully held my head down.

"Well maybe you will tell me once we get to know each other better." He kissed my hand. "Alisha I will never hurt you but I'll love on you causing you to expect more from every man you meet after me." He smiled as he winked and sat back in his chair.

I thought this man has a good mouth piece so I need to stay on guard. After dinner we drove, in separate cars, to a nearby park and walked arm in arm. He told me things about himself and on the way back I had to tell him about me as I asked questions. Charles later explained that this technique caused a person to relax and unknowingly be honest about whom they really are. It has to be done correctly to work. Charles told me about his childhood. He moved here with his first wife and their children, which were almost my age and one older than me. He never said if he had remarried but I figured he had and did not want to talk about it.

During our time together he taught me how to be smooth and tell men things they wanted to hear, without sounding like I'm blowing smoke up their butts. He also taught me to listen and hear what a person is not saying. My time with Charles was always an adventure. I was working full time and I attended class at night. Charles admired that about me. I was ready to establish a clientele, but I was not yet licensed. He was pleasant and a gentleman so he would always opened doors for me, put me on the inside as we walked, pulled out my chair, and everything else a southern belle would expect from her mate. He was a quick thinker and a shrewd business man. He owned several businesses but worked at the dealership part time to get free training on the newest equipment to support his hobby. He loved working with his hands, as did I, so we spent plenty of time under the hood of cars and building projects. He taught me how to play golf as we worked out business deals. He taught me what to look for when buying a home, where to buy, and options I should look for that would provide future growth. I loved and respected this man.

Six months after meeting Charles invited me to a cook-out. I didn't realize it was his family until I got there. That following weekend he picked me up and I was a little nervous to meet some of his friends. As we walked in everyone greeted him and the women stared as they rolled their eyes at me and whispered. The men looked on and shook their head in agreement with Charles. I looked younger than my years but I was a catch and knew it. I gripped Charles's hand tighter to reassure the male onlookers I was with him, so don't even think about it.

A woman ran up to us, "Daddy who is this gold digging little girl you done brought in here." I would find out later that was his youngest daughter, Elaine. What most people don't understand is that an older man's wisdom is worth more than the money; which will fade, but the lessons learned will increase your livelihood. Charles and I had already started a business together.

"This is my friend Alisha. Alisha this is my daughter Elaine," he smiled.
She turned up her nose and said, "Does she know how old you are and is she legal?"

Charles gave a hearty laughed "Yes and yes, Alisha this is my youngest daughter and she's very outspoken." Charles was so cool that it seemed as if we were having a conversation about the weather instead of the awkward interaction we were actually having. He complimented her on her disrespectful behavior, and because his laugh was contagious it ease the tension.

"Hello Elaine, it's a pleasure to meet you." She rolled her eyes when I stuck out my hand. "Now I know why my daddy is with you. You may look young but you act like an old person." She threw up her hand and walked off. Elaine was twenty and aware of her youth and looks. We walked over to a table with some other people. Charles introduced me to everybody before we sat down.

I looked up to see a very handsome young man walking up, as he got closer, I thought this has to be his son. "What's up Pop? I just got here and big mouth told me you were going to jail..." He turned and saw me, "but as I see this vision of beauty before me, I would gladly go in your place." I could see the apple didn't fall too far from the tree.

"Alisha this is Charles Jr. but everyone calls him Deuces."

"Hello Charles Jr." I smiled and stuck out my hand.

He kissed my hand, "Hello Alisha, the pleasure is all mine"

"Charles, is he called Deuces because he's junior or for some other reason?"

"Yes baby girl." He laughed "I liked it better than junior."

"Excuse me, Dad may I speak to you for a moment in private." His son pulled him aside to let him know his second wife, Gladys who's five years younger than Charles, was there. They had been separated for a few months because Charles caught her with another man and had not decided if he would divorce her. He didn't tell anyone he just packed his bags and moved into a hotel until he could find a house. They walked back over to the table talking with Mark, his younger son. Charles introduced us and his tongue was just as silver as his fathers. "So where did you meet my dad, elegantly beautiful young lady?" He said as he reached for my hand to gently kiss it. I looked at Charles to see if it was ok to respond, some people are really private, I always give that respect when being questioned by friends and family. "While he was working," I answered.

His son blurted out in surprise. "Daddy you got a woman like this while you were at work looking all broke and dirty, you must be putting it down." He saw the look on his father's face and changed his demeanor. He turned to me and said, "Please forgive me for my behavior. I didn't mean to disrespect you, but you're a lovely young woman and most women your age can't appreciate a man like my father." I could see the red in Charles' eyes, but I couldn't help blushing. Before Mark could say another word a voice behind him said, "Hello Charles I see you bought a toy, I mean a guest."

Charles spoke, "Hello Gladys, how are you?" He turned his back so she smirked and said, "I'm good." Gladys made a snide remark under her breath. "Well it seems as if you've gotten better." She said and gave a slick smile as she walked away. I was the first woman he had dated since the split.

In the distance you could hear "Daddy, Daddy". Mark threw his hands up and said, "Oh lord here she comes, Daddy's Girl." Mark and Deuces looked at each other as if they got a revelation. They smiled and gave each other high-five because they knew she was not going to like me. Andrea was the second of four, but she has always had her daddy's heart and he was wrapped around her finger.

Charles stood up and she ran into his arms and he squeezed her with a joyful bear hug. She still lived at home with his wife. "Daddy I've missed you, so when are you coming back home?" she pouted.

"I don't know if that will happen, Baby Girl."

He said lovingly.

"What do you mean?" she said stumping her foot. "I just don't understand." She said folding her arms and pouting.

He whispered in her ear, "Baby we will talk later in private."

"Alright Daddy," she smiled. By that time the table had cleared and it was just Charles, his sons, Andrea and I. She turned to speak to her brothers and noticed me, "Hello I'm Andrea, how are you?" she stuck out her hand.

"Hello I'm Alisha" I stood up and we shook hands.

"So which of my knuckle head brothers are you here with?" They both started giggling.

"What's so funny?" Andrea said as she put her hands on her hips and stomped as if she were chastising children.

Charles said nervously, "Baby, she's here with me." Looking between her brothers she said, "Oh, so which one of these knuckle heads are you fixing her up with?" She said turning toward her father. "You guys need to stop giggling because you're making a bad impression." She looked at me and said, "They are really great guys, just silly sometimes." She said nudging them as tears began to form in their eyes.

"No baby, she's here with me." Charles said as he held my hand and pulled me closer to him.

By now her brothers were laughing uncontrollably. They were slapping high-fives with each other and holding their chest or belly. Andrea looked around in a panic as if she was searching for someone to rescue or awaken her from a horrific dream. "Stop laughing! Nothing's funny!" She screamed at the top of her voice. She calmly turned to her father and said, "What do you mean she's with you?" She stepped closer toward him. "You are a married man," she whispered looking around as if it were a secret to just the two of them. "She's young enough to be your daughter or granddaughter. My God Father what has happen to you? Are you going through a midlife crises or something?" She looked him up and down as if she would see the problem. "No baby, calm down." He said as he gently rubbed her shoulder.

"I will not." She turned toward me. "Excuse me young lady, but did you know he was married?"

"Andrea this is not the place or the time to talk about this." He calmly said, but with noticeable irritation.

"When is it?" She turned to face him. "Your wife is a few feet away and you are playing Sugar Daddy," she said with her hands on her hips and a matter of fact look on her face. Charles turned toward me "Please forgive me. My wife and daughter were not supposed to be here and if I had known they were coming, I would not have brought you." He looked up and scanned the crowd. "Is there anything else you would like to do?" I asked Mark to fix me a to-go plate during the conversation between Charles and Andrea because I knew where it was going. "Whatever you want to do Charles," he grabbed my hand and we departed the same we came in. Charles received the same looks from the women I had gotten earlier; which were angry glances, but approval from the men and Charles got a few handshakes. Gladys walked by me and bumped into me so I said, "Oh I'm sorry ma'am, I didn't hurt you did I?" She ran into the house crying. Charles rushed me to the car as quick as he could. We rode to my house in silence. As soon as he pulled into my driveway, the silence was broken. "Forgive me for hiding the fact that I was married." Charles was embarrassed. I raised his head by his chin with my index finger. "Charles, when we walked in I knew why you brought me." I took off my seat belt. "You had something to prove to your wife. I know you didn't know she would be there, but you thought she would hear it through the grapevine." I turned his face toward me, so we could be eye to eye. "Charles, I only have two questions. Do you want your wife back and do you want to forgive her?" I knew Charles was impotent, but I kept that to myself.

"You're smarter than I gave you credit for," he smiled.

"Did you forget I have a degree in psychology and I'm working on my masters in Marriage and Family Therapy?" I said as a matter of fact more than a question before smiling.

He chuckled, "Yes I did."

"Would you like to come in and talk, Charles?" I said turning to open the door.

"Yes I would." As Charles walked around and opened my door we walked to my house.

There was a box sitting on the porch. I knew it was my rose from Mikael, so I picked up the box and walked into the house.

   Charles and I had a long talk about why his wife cheated on him. Charles started to have issues with impotence because of the medication he started taking less than a year ago.

"Now tell me the truth what did you catch your wife doing?" I said holding his hand.

"She was embracing another man." He said as if he were defeated. I made him realize that he may have over stated the actual events and his insecurities were hurting his marriage.

"How did you know I exaggerated the events I saw?" He said smiling at me. "I still believe if I had not walked in they would have gone all the way." He boldly stated.

"I've only known you for a short period of time

but I think you felt like your wife embarrassed you." I sat closer to him and put my head on his chest. "You felt like you were less than a man and had something to prove." Rubbing his chest I said, "I know that's a hard thing for your generation to deal with because that's stuff that you're supposed to keep private and now it's out." I raised my head and looked in his eyes. "Go back home Charles."

Before I could finish his wife was calling and wanted to work it out. "Charles you know we will forever be friends, but put everything that has happened before this moment behind you." I walked him to the door and said. "To go back to her you must forgive her first." He hugged me, "You know where to come for therapy and counseling." When Charles left I ran into the house and opened the box, but again, only a single pink rose. My heart sank as I cried myself to sleep on the sofa.

That was the last time Charles and I had personal contact. But I did get a thank you card in the mail from his wife. "Thanks to you we are doing great. I will send an invitation for our vow renewal in a few weeks." I never told Charles I knew his wife and he was a special project. This was a part of my life that no one knew about unless they were a client.

Charles taught me how important it was to love in spite of what the world says and what peace looked like in the natural.

4

My First Experience

Terrance Powell was a man I met a few months later and a taste of something I had never experience before. We met at a charity dinner while he was working security. Terrance or Tee was a police officer and he owned a security company. He had a way with words, but not like a player; more like he was concerned about you and he felt bad for anything he did. I felt as if I were obligated to stay after he finished talking to me. I remembered what Charles always told me, "Listen to hear what's not being said." With Terrance it was a challenge because I could never put my finger on what it was about him that made me uncomfortable.

He had three children with two different women, but the mothers and children were close. I guess the baby mama hatred for Terrance brought Renee and Tonya together. Tee and I had been dating for two weeks when I met his three boys, Terrence 14, Tyler 10, and Timothy 8. Tee was moving a little too fast for me, but I was going with the flow because I knew in three months I would move on. My life couldn't stop because of Mikael and I had to try if I was going to have a serious relationship. The reality was I was waiting, I just didn't know it. One night we attended a football game and had box seats courtesy of my friend. We had so much fun and the boys got along as if they were raised in the same house. Tee loved his boys and they were close. After the game we had ice cream and took the boys home.

The following weekend was Tee's scheduled weekend with the boys. On Friday's they would order pizza, eat junk food, and watch movies. As we were watching movies Tee stepped out to use the phone. Timothy walked over and sat next to me. "Is Teddy alright?" he said. I leaned over so I could hear him, "What baby?"
He said "Is he coming back, because we miss him?" I thought he was talking about a toy until Terrance Jr. jumped up and came over. "Get back over here and watch the movie," he yelled and snatched Timothy by the arm. Tee walked back into the room looking upset and said loudly. "Is everybody enjoying the movie?" The boys cried out "yes" as if they were singing a tune. He sat down next to me and asked, "What about you, or are you too good to enjoy the movie." His demeanor had changed from joyful to angry. I blew it off

because the call seemed to upset him; he was happy earlier before he walked out. With a big smile I replied "I love it and the boys are keeping me informed on who's who." Tee rolled his eyes and slid on the floor with the boys and never said another word. After the movie, the boys jumped up to take their showers and get ready for bed. Terrance Jr. looked at me, "Hey aren't you gonna get to work?"

I was getting my things together and thought I misunderstood him. "What?" I said looking confused.

He walked towards me, "Aren't you gonna get this living room cleaned before we go to bed." I learned a long time ago you don't mess with folks kids and still think you were going to be cool. Tee and I didn't have that type of relationship and that wasn't the first time it happened. Tee wouldn't say a word unless it was to back up his son. I politely smiled, turned and walked away. I began to realize his sons were well mannered, but they were little male chauvinist pigs. That older boy was always stepping on the line. I thought I might have to dump this dude sooner than I thought...and who was or is Teddy?

Tee walked in and kissed me on the cheek. "Baby will you help me clean up this mess?" As I started helping him I remembered my graduation. "Tee I almost forgot I graduate next weekend, so I will be spending that week with my grandparents."

"Okay, I will finally get the opportunity to meet your grandparents." He smiled.

"We'll see." I said with a frown.

Tee looked up at me with full rage, "What the hell you mean? What I ain't good enough to meet the royal country bumpkins? What I got to be like the punk that keeps sending you a rose begging to be with you? Hell I can't even hit it."

I took a short pause and picked up my stuff as I said, "No, my grandfather is in the hospital, so I'm not sure if they will make it. I believe it's time for me to go." I said as I walked toward the door. Tee ran over to me and grabbed my hand. "Baby, please don't leave, I'm sorry, it's just that my..." Tears began to flow. I thought, no this MF didn't. "Sit down and just let me finish before you say anything." He led me to the sofa. "I was in a committed relationship that had gotten to the point where I was about to propose, but she ran off with another man." He held my hand. "She won't let me see my son Teddy, he turned four today." He fell back on the sofa. "That's who I was on the phone with earlier." He sat back up and held me by my shoulders. "I want to file charges, but I don't want to lose my son or send his mom to jail. My relationship with Tamika has been over for months." He grabbed my hand again.

I was thinking of ways to dump him because I knew he was full of crap and I didn't have time for him or his mini drama. "So you have four kids and you were going to get engaged less than a month ago...well you seem to be handling that well."

"What about us, will you give me a chance to work it out?" he pleaded.

All I could think about was I'm good and I will dump you in a week because it's something about you I don't like. "We're good, but I'm still leaving because it's getting late." I got up to leave.

"Come on stay with me tonight," he begged.

"I can't because your boys are here and I refuse to do that while they are here, it's inappropriate," I said shaking my head.

"All we're going to do is sleep." He said pulling me by the hand.

"I know that, but I don't want your boys to think we are, you know." I whispered.

"Alisha you really need to grow up," he sneered. "I probably wouldn't be so uptight if you gave me some." He pleaded. He was giving me puppy dog eyes as we walked to my car. On my way home I started praying. I thought this dude is foul. I'll dump him in a couple of days. I remember Grams telling my mother, "A man can get any woman he wants at the right time even when she doesn't want him. Because she allows her tragedies to overrule her reality." I didn't understand that until I met Terrance Powell.

I turned my last paper in on Friday and couldn't wait to get my final grade. I was overwhelmed with excitement when my phone rang. "Hello."
"Is this you Lisha baby?" I could barely hear her.
"Ma Carrie," once I said her name my heart sank and my eyes filled with tears.
"Baby, I need you to come home." She paused as if she was getting her words right. "Thomas said he got you a ticket and you need to take your time and pack a bag." The phone call dropped and I pulled over and cried. After five minutes my phone rang again. "Hello" I tried to sound as if I was okay, but Tee could hear it in my voice "Is everything alright baby?" he sounded concerned.
"I don't know," I managed to utter in a raspy whisper.
"Where are you, what happened?" He said as he panicked.
"I think it's my grandparents." I cried.
"What happened?" The concern had come back.
"I don't know, she didn't tell me."
"Who didn't baby? Alisha; damn baby, are you okay? Do you need me to pick you up?" He

was getting upset. When my pager beeped and I looked at the number.

"No I'll call you back, it's Thomas." I said.

"Who the hell is Thomas?" He barked.

I never called him Thomas. Ma Carrie and I were the only people that called him Tommy. Why did I say Thomas?

"Thomas is he dead?"

"No, Papa T wants to see you Lisha, he's been asking for you." His voice cracked. "I got you a ticket and your flight leaves in two hours. Can you make that?" I knew he was hiding something.

"Yes, I'll call you when I get there, thanks Tommy." I said with relief.

"You know I'll do anything for you Lisha," the phone went silent. When I got home there was a huge vase of pink flowers sitting on the porch. The card said "Congratulations." I put them on the kitchen table, packed and headed to the airport.

The plane landed and I picked up my luggage and called Tommy to let him know I was there. The thought of why Ma Carrie and Tommy call me instead of Grams didn't hit me until I landed. Tommy was at the airport in no time. He jumped out of the car and grabbed my bag as he opened the passenger door. As soon as he got in the car I asked, "Where is Grams Tommy?" I fearfully asked.

"She's at the hospital with Papa T," he sighed.
"Why did Ma Carrie call me instead of her?" I
knew something wasn't right.
"We thought it was best because she needed
to stay with Papa T.
"Tommy I'm not stupid, what's going on?" I
yelled.
"Okay Grams is with Papa T, but she's in the
hospital too." He grimaced.
"What?" Trying to calm down I took a deep
breath. "Well is she okay?" Before he could
answer I asked, "What's wrong with her?"
"They believe she passed out from exhaustion,
she's been at his bed side for three days."
"Why?" I looked at Tommy before saying,
"Grams told me Papa was doing well and he
would be out on Saturday."
"I don't know, but Papa T is extremely ill." He
looked worried.
"I know why, I'm graduating Friday and she
didn't want me to worry." I sighed and sat
back.
"That's right, I almost forgot." He smiled.
"I was supposed to come home that evening
and stay with them for a few weeks if they
couldn't make the graduation." Tommy
reached over and held my hand. The car was
silent until we reached the hospital. Before
Tommy could stopped the car I jumped out
and ran towards the entrance. He yelled, "208
is the room number." He watched me until I

faded into the distance before he parked the car.

I ran to the elevators and it seemed like the lomgest ride I had ever experienced. Before the doors opened up good, I was out and on my way to their room. When I walked in the first person I saw was Ma Carrie, she spoke to me, but all I could hear were the beeping and dings from the monitors attached to my grandparents and I froze. Ma Carrie walked over to me and led me by the hand to the beds, which held the strongest people I knew. "Hey precious, what are you doing here?" Grams uttered as she reached for my hand. Tears began to form in my eyes and Papa said, "Don't start that fuss. Now get over here and give me a hug." I smiled and ran over to my grandfather. Tommy walked into the room smiling. "That's what I like to see, my favorite family members doing what we do best, loving on each other." Before I could walk back over to Grams Tommy grabbed my hand and pulled me toward him for a hug. "I was waiting until you felt better, but I had to steal it."
"That's what I'm talking about boy," Papa shouted.
"Y'all look good together." Grams smiled, "You were meant to be." Before she closed her eyes and went to sleep. "Ma Carrie, are you ready to go home?" Tommy asked his grandmother.

"Yes baby, I guess I am." She eased back up and walked over to me. "You take care now Alisha and come by to see me before you leave."

"Yes ma'am." I said smiling as I gave Ma Carrie a hug she whispered in my ear, "Did you see all the flowers and cards?" I hadn't even noticed them, because all I saw were the two people that supported and loved me.

"Alisha I'll be back once I drop Ma Carrie off," he walked over to me gently placing his hand on the back of my head and kissed my forehead gently.

"Lee baby when you gonna marry that boy?" Papa T proudly proclaimed.

"Papa you know he's married." I smiled. "Tommy and I are just friends and we like it that way." I said sitting on his bed.

"I wasn't talking about him." I looked up at Papa puzzled. "But somebody needs to tell his heart that because it shows every time he looks at you." He said rubbing my back. "I was talking about Mikael, he came to see me and sent Grams those flowers." When he pointed them out I realized what Ma Carrie was talking about.

"Papa once he gets stable we'll talk again, but he wants a relationship with God first." I lied about Mikael because he had moved on and had a son.

"I'm glad he's putting God first." Papa looked

up as he reminisced about him. "Now Thomas is in love with you too and I've known him all his life." Papa stopped talking and smiled. "Papa not you too, Ma Carrie and Grams have been saying that since we were kids and ain't nothing changed in our relationship. We love each other as friends." I argued.

"Okay, but I've been living a lot longer than you and I know when a man loves a woman. I still look at my Marie like that to this day. She's my soul mate and God saw fit to bring us together for life. I can't wait for the right man to find you; whether its Mikael or Thomas only God knows, but you need to settle down and give me some great grandbabies."

"Papa you got some," I said knowing I didn't want kids.

"Yeah, but from everybody but you," he laughed. It was hard to tell Papa I didn't think I would ever have kids. He kept talking as I kept my thoughts to myself. "When we lost your mother you became more than a granddaughter to us. She was your mother but you comforted us instead of the other way around." As he reminisced he looked as though he had to remind me of something. "Alisha, remember what I've always told you, secrets are held within the eyes of man. Our eyes can't lie because they give us a glimpse into a person's soul the good, evil, and truth.

When I look into Thomas's eyes I see an innocent love for you, which stems from your childhood. When I looked into Mikael's eyes I saw a genuine love for you, but it was mixed with a fear of disappointing you; which I believe came from his lack of faith in God. These are good men, but Alisha remember to seek God first in all you do whether writing or thinking."

"I will Papa," I said as I snuggled under him. "Alisha I never told you this before, but I think it's time you know. The day you were born I looked into your eyes and I saw the hand of God on your life. I knew then that you would not only face greater trials and tribulations, but strange attacks to try and pull you away from God." He laughed. "Grams, Ma Carrie, and I covered you in prayer day and night. We anointed your head with oil, so that your heart will never harden to God's word." He paused and took a deep breath. "My only regret is that I couldn't always protect you and I'm sorry for that." Tears flowed from his eyes as he remembered that summer day.

"Hey Papa T, I see you're doing better." Tommy bellowed as he walked into the room causing us to refocus.

"Yes, I have my baby girl here so I am good." He smiled patting me on the back.

"Are your other kids coming to town?" Tommy asked.

"That boy of mine is driving down with his family Wednesday night. I guess the rest will come in soon. He's the only one Marie talked to. He was supposed to call the rest since she wasn't feeling well." He said shifting in the bed.

"Okay. Alisha, how long are you going to staying?" Tommy asked.

"Until they leave the hospital and go home." I said sitting up.

"Well Lisha, I guess I'll be here with you." He sat on the little sofa next to Grams bed.

"Would you like for me to get you something to eat or is there anything I can do?" He said looking excited.

"No thank you," I said standing up.

Papa coughed, "The eyes, it's in the eyes" I smiled, but Tommy jumped up and ran to his side, "Is everything okay Papa T?"

"Yes Thomas, just had a little cough." He smiled, winked at me, and closed his eyes.

Grams opened her eyes, "It makes my heart proud to see the two of you together. I just hate that it took an old woman passing out for it to happen." She smiled.

"What are you talking about Grams?" I said walking to her bedside.

"You and Thomas, Baby finally getting together and settling down," She said closing her eyes and going back to sleep. I sat down on the sofa and Tommy sat next to me. My pager went off just as Tommy was about to say something. I called the number back, "Hello." I frowned. "Hey Tee." I said rolling my eyes. "It was my grandparents, they are in the hospital, but I'll call you later." I hung up and Tommy started as usual. "Was that your boyfriend?" Tommy asked in a slow broken tone.

"No, just a friend. I was talking to him when Ma Carrie called." I blew the thought of him off. "You know Mikael's been here to visit Papa T and he sent Grams those flowers." They were her favorite color. I missed Mikael so much I had to change the subject before it showed that we had broken-up. "How's your wife and when am I going to meet her?"

"She's packing to go on a Cruise with her mom, she leaves tonight."

"That sounds nice." I could tell by Tommy's expression he didn't want to talk about it. We sat quietly as my grandparents slept. I laid my head on Tommy's shoulder and hour later Tommy's pager went off. It was his wife. He turned to me and said, "I have to take her to the airport, but I will stop and pick you up something to eat on my way back." He rushed out of the door.

"Thanks Tommy." I said laying back.

I picked up the phone to call Mikael but it rung before I could dial, it was Tee. We

talked until I heard Tommy come in with the food so I quickly rushed off. "Oh my god you remembered." I exclaimed grabbing the Styrofoam plate. "Let me see if you got it right. Oxtails, mac & cheese, cucumber salad, and a slice of red velvet cake," I looked around. "What did you get me to drink?"
"Lemonade and tea with an extra cup of ice so you can mix it." He smiled. "Thank you Tommy, I guess Papa was right about you."
"What did he say?" Tommy always thought Papa was mad at him because of that summer day.
"That you were a good man and have always been sweet to me." I smiled and nudged him. Tommy was smiling ear to ear because he was wrong all these years. "Of course, you're my best friend and I remember the butt whippings you gave me when we were little."

We laugh and talked about old times as we ate. "After that meal I need a nap." I got up and cleaned up our mess as Tommy stretched out on the sofa. "Where am I supposed to sit I'm sleepy too." Tommy sat up and leaned back so I could sit down and lay on his chest. While Tommy and I slept, Grams sat up and smiled at us. "Look at them Tobias, aren't they picture perfect?" Tears came to her eyes. "Yes they are Marie, yes they are." He smiled. Grams and Papa talked about their younger years, their love, raising kids and ended with me and Tommy. Grams thought we were a couple and Papa didn't say anything to change that thought. "I love you Tobias." She said smiling. "Thank you for loving me and sharing my life." Grams closed her eyes for the last time. I jumped up dazed and confused as the bells and whistle started going off. Before I could make sense of what was going on nurses were running into the room and ushered us out. They pushed Papas bed over and pulled the curtain. When it hit me what was going on. I cried into Tommy's chest as he prayed. Ten minutes later the doctor came out, "We have done all..." my hearing stopped and everything went black. When I opened my eyes Tommy was holding me, "Alisha, are you okay?" he said.

"Yes, where is Papa?" I looked around. Tommy took me to him. I could see the remnants of tears on his cheeks, but he was strong for me. "Alisha, get a pen and piece of paper," he ordered.

"Yes sir," when Papa called me Alisha he was serious. I didn't ask questions, I just did what he said. Papa gave me instructions on the preparations of Grams funeral and the location of everything. "But Papa, you're still here, I don't need to know all that." I said painfully.

Papa sat up and said, "Alisha go home take a

shower, get some proper rest in a bed, and come back to see me in the morning." I didn't want to leave, but Papa wanted to be alone so he could mourn his wife and protect me. I kissed him on the forehead and we talked for another ten minutes before saying our goodbyes. Tommy and I walked towards the elevators. After the doors closed I heard the code and knew it was Papa. I turned to Tommy and cried again this time he just held me tight and kissed me on the top of my head. He pressed the button for us to go back to the second floor. When I got to the room I heard the words again from the same doctor. I didn't faint this time, but it was as if I were outside my body watching from a distance. Tommy and I turned to go home.

When I got home I did as Papa said I took a shower and got in the bed. Tommy called Ma Carrie and told her what happen. They began to make phone calls to family and friends. Tommy came into my room and lay on the bed and held me.

My mother's four sisters didn't like me, but they didn't like my mother either. She was ten years younger than the youngest girl and eight years younger than the youngest boy, which made her the baby. My two uncles loved me and always invited me to their homes, but not my aunts. That was my only concern about the funeral, all of us being under one roof. The family started arriving on Wednesday evening and the drama began. They brought stickers and started claiming their items. When my oldest Uncle, Junior, came in Thursday morning he got things under control. By Friday morning, Auntie the original baby girl (that's how she introduced herself), arrived and that's when I had to leave. Tommy came over that afternoon and my hungry cousins started throwing themselves at him. Tommy was always polite. Once he found me, he told me to get my bags and took me to his house. I found Uncle Junior before I left. "I'm going to Tommy's house. The reading of the will is after the funeral on Saturday. If you need anything give me a call."

"I understand baby, go get some peace and rest. I'll take care of things here." After a big hug, he kissed me on the forehead. I ran and jumped into Tommy's car.

When I got to his house I slept until it was time for the wake. The wake was drama filled and out of control. My Aunts complained about everything they thought I did and couldn't understand why a little girl had so much control, yet they only called home to get money. We arrived late and left early to go back to Tommy's house. I lay across the bed and cried. Tommy came in and put a blanket over me and he held me until we fell asleep.

I kept hearing a banging noise and I shook Tommy, "What's that?" Tommy jumped up and ran out. I slowly walked out behind him. It was Ma Carrie, "It doesn't look right, you over here a married man with this single woman. There's no telling what y'all doing." She let out a laugh, "That's how your Aunts were carrying on at the wake about the two of y'all to your daddy, Tommy"
"I didn't care for them as kids and I can't stand them now. I can't believe sweet Marie had those hateful heifers. Your mama and that third girl, Maggie, are the only ones I could tolerate as kids." We all laughed and Tommy went to get her bags out of the car. I went into the kitchen to make the tea she handed me. We sat around the kitchen table and reminisced. Ma Carrie said, "Now I know y'all been sleeping in the same bed since you were kids. Tommy used to sneak out of the house and come to your bedroom when things were bad for either of you. I know y'all doing it now and Tommy, if I didn't despise that cheating thang you married, I would make Alisha leave. I am going to stay to keep the rumor mill from stirring."
"Thanks Ma Carrie," we said in unison and kissed her on the head. "Don't thank me yet. Tommy your daddy is on the way over."

I walked away thinking how bad Tommy must feel about his wife because of the look on his face at the hospital. Fifteen minutes later Christian II, Tommy's dad, knocked on the door. They walked into his study and twenty minutes later they walked out. Tommy's father gave him a hug and departed. "What did your father say?" I asked running up to him.

"My dad wanted me to remember my image because people look up to me." Tommy wasn't telling the truth.

"I can go to a hotel." I said looking concerned.

"No, as long as Ma Carrie is here everything is fine." He walked off.

I went upstairs and got ready for bed. Tommy was in the kitchen with Ma Carrie.

That morning I rode to the church with Tommy and Ma Carrie. I refused to ride in the family car. As we were driving I thought I saw Mikael standing in line but my attention was drawn to the confusion, Aunt "I'm the Original Baby" was causing. Before we got into the church, they had a scene. I dreaded the reading of the will at the house later. I told Tommy I was leaving on the first flight out of here. Uncle Junior quickly restored order and the funeral was calm. At the reading of the will the surviving kids split the businesses and got some money. All the grand kids got money. I got the two houses, one business, and the cars. I was the only grandchild that received more than money. The girls didn't know about the second house that they bought for me when I went to college. They used the money from my Mama's insurance policy and the cars were ten years old. As soon as Aunt "I'm the original baby girl" stood up. I walked out and headed for the airport. I have no idea what happened after that, I didn't go back home for over a year after that. I knew Ma Carrie and Tommy would take care of the house.

My Grams would always say, "If you had to hit a woman, then she's too much woman for you and you need to find a more compatible mate." That same saying applied to women as well. She added some wisdom to the saying, "If you hit a man be prepared to stand in a man shoes if he wants to hit you back."

When I got home that Sunday Tee called and he dropped everything and rushed over. For the first four days I didn't get out of bed. Tee made me eat and held me as I slept. Before I left I was going to dump Tee, but he showed me a different side of him and I change my mind. In the state I was in I figured I might as well stay with him. That following weekend I would meet the real Terrance Powell. He came over unannounced and just walked into my house. I found out later he made himself a key. I was on the phone with Tommy when he walked in. As we ended our conversation, I turned around to see Tee standing in my kitchen. I dropped the phone and bowl that I was holding. "Where did you come from," I asked breathing heavily. "Who was that on the phone?" He stood over me as I picked up the contents of the bowl. "It was Tommy, my friend from back home." I said looking up.

"It sounds like y'all are more than just friends to me." He said folding his arms.

"He's my best friend," I said standing up.

"I don't believe that a man and woman can be friends and not be fucking." He walked closer to me. "So did you fuck Tommy while you were gone?"

"No and we've been friends since we were kids." I was appalled.

"Well you ain't kids anymore and you ain't giving me none." He stood face to face to me.

"You are talking crazy and you need to leave." As I stepped back to turn Tee slapped me so hard I spun around before hitting the floor. "Bitch, you don't tell me what to do, I'm the man in this relationship, so I tell you."

I looked up confused. "What, you want to call the police. Bitch I am the police, so call'em and we'll all have a party in that ass. Bitch you been playing me. I take off for a week and here you are laid up on the phone with some punk ass pussy. Get yo ass up and get in the bedroom. I'm finding roses on your door step saying we'll be together. Bitch who you fucking, 'cause it sure aint me!" He leaned over yelling at me.

I felt like a little girl again and I knew I was powerless. He dragged me into the bedroom while I pleaded with him and ripped off my clothes. "Please Tee stop, what are you doing?" After he punched me in the face a few times I stop pleading. He snatched my legs open and did what he wanted while slapping and cursing me until I passed out.

I awoke the next morning tied to the bed, I struggled until I freed my hand as I tried to get my other hand loose, Tee walked in. He started pulling off his clothes. "If you don't behave, I'm going to let my partner have a go at it. Now shut the fuck up." He climbed on top of me and with his face buried in the crease of my neck he grunted, "Damn this pussy is good bitch. Yeah you have been holding out on me." He slapped me as I shed silent tears and did as he pleased. With each pump he uttered, "Bitch give me a baby." I had only been with one man and that was Mikael and he was doing this unprotected, so I felt like I was dying in more ways than one. Tee's partner ran to the door, "We got a call."

He jumped up and ran out the door. I untied my arm and packed as much stuff as I could. After throwing it in my car I went to a hotel.

Two hours later Tee called, but I didn't answer. I was too ashamed to tell anyone and he was a police officer, so who would I tell. I thought this was déjà vu, it can't be real, it can't be happening again. I begin to pray asking God for revelation and a way out, but not just for me. He called and texted my phone repeatedly, leaving voice and text messages. Later that night I was startled by a knock at the door. I jumped up and put on some clothes, then I heard his voice. "Alisha baby please forgive me. I've never done that before and I'll never do it again baby, please I'm sorry."
I opened the door and let him in. I spent the night in Tee's arms and the next morning we went back to my house.

Tee and I had a long talk about his actions, why he was so angry, and how he would control those feelings. Now I know what I saw in him that I couldn't figure out before because I had never experienced something like that.

Grams said, "Watch how he treats his mama, what he says about his exes, the way he feels about his daughter or his overall opinion of women. That will tell you what kind of man you got and how he'll treat you." She was right. After her and Papa's death and with all the drama behind it, I couldn't think straight. I was going to dump Tee as soon as I came home, but I was in a state of depression and now I'm trapped. The first time I try to date a man after Mikael and this is what I get. During those next few days Tee was the perfect mate. I made it a point to get to know Tonya, Renee, and Tamika better. We had talks and became a support system for each other. If I were dating Tee then Tamika could come out of hiding and the brothers could be together. I have always been a person willing to take the blow to protect and help others or the underdog. I knew through Christ I could handle anything. Papa said the hand of God was on me, as I looked back over my life I could see it. Tee did personal security downtown sometimes as a part time bouncer for the Secret Lounge. He blackmailed the owner and some of the dancers to maintain the lifestyle he wanted.

Three weeks into our refreshed relationship, I was at Tees's house on a Friday night with him and the boys. Tee's head bouncer called him because they needed extra security and couldn't reach anyone. I watched Tee's boys until he got back from the job.

When Tee got back the boys had cleaned up and were in the bed. Tee walked in drunk and loud, "Bitch where you at?" I stood up and walked towards the door. With a slap Tee said, "Where are you going?" He stumbled over to me. "Get your ass in the bedroom and give me a son." He slurred.

"Terrance your boys are here, so lower your voice and let me help you to the bedroom." I wrapped my arm around his waist and we walked towards his room. Bam, I hit the floor, Tee had hit me in the head with his fist. "I'm the man and this is my house, you don't tell me what to do." He stumbled to the bed room. "Now get your stanking ass up and get naked," he yelled.

"Okay Tee," I stumbled up to see his older son standing there smiling. I made my way into the bedroom. Tee made me undress him before falling out into a drunken sleep. I shook him to see if he would wake up. When he didn't I bolted out the door.

That morning, like clockwork, Tee was standing in my room with flowers. I never noticed that the flowers were pink and not from him. "Good morning beautiful." He smiled.

"Good morning Mr. Terrance Powell officer of the law." I greeted him with a big smile. He sat the flowers down and kissed me on my neck as he pulled my panties off. My phone rang and I didn't answer but the person kept calling. Tee started getting frustrated he rolled over to unzip his pants when the phone rang again. Tee jumped up "Answer the muthafuckin phone and if it's that pussy Tommy I'ma whoop your ass."

"Hello," I said with a shaky voice.

"Hey Tom...." Bam, Tee punched me in the head and started stomping and kicking me. He never noticed his surroundings when he was in a rage. He pulled me up off the floor and forced himself in me. I screamed.

"Terrence Powell get off me, I don't want to have sex with you I don't want to be with you anymore, please stop you're hurting me."

"Bitch you belong to me now and you are going to give me a son, just like those other bitches. Now be still and open your legs before I tie your ass up again. I bet you open your legs for that punk sending you them pink flowers." He grunted.

"Terrence stop or I'll call the police." I cried.

"Bitch I told you I am the police and if you call them we'll gang fuck you in every hole you got." He said slapping me.

"But Terrance I can't get pregnant." I lied because I didn't use any form of birth control since I was not sexually active but I had an old pack in my bathroom.

With a punch to the head he said, "Yes you

can bitch, I changed out your birth control just like I always do, now give me that pussy." He choked me until I passed out. He continued to have sex with me until he got tired. I opened my eyes and he rolled over next to me when he was done. "Terrance, how did you get a key to my house?" I asked.

"I made my own because you wouldn't give me one." He sat up. "If you try to run and hide again I will kill you." He kissed me and rubbed my face. "I found you the last time and I will find you again. Now open up so we can make a boy and if you give me a girl I will kill you."

"No. Terrence Powell you are going to have to kill me because I refuse to have sex with you." He pulled out his gun and put it to my head. When I saw the gun I took a deep breath, repented and started praying. He pulled the trigger after saying, "Then die bitch." The gun was not loaded. He slapped me and raped me again and again until my screams were silent. The next day he got up to go to work. I called Tracy so she could take me to the emergency room. I told them I had been raped and I needed help because he's still after me. I was cleaned up and admitted. Within an hour I fell asleep. When I awakened Tee was standing over me. He whispered, "Bitch, what did you do?"

I smiled, "Terrance I just altered the rest of

your life."

"I'm going to kill you." He raised his hand and paused when I said, "Did you hear that?"

"Hear what bitch?" he said looking around.

"I wasn't talking to you Tee." Two detectives walked in and handcuffed Tee and read him his rights. I said, "Detectives here are tapes of him beating me with his kids in the house and a tape of him beating and raping me. I also have his confession to several crimes. Don't worry, at the beginning of each tape I warned him that he was being recorded." Tonya, Renee, and Tamika walked out of the bathroom and waved good bye. "You dirty bitches, y'all set me up. My boys will always love me more." He yelled as they dragged him out the door.

Terrance Powell beat the mothers of his children and threatened them if they tried to leave. Tonya was in high school when they met. She moved in with him and he manipulated her slowly pulling her away from her family. Once she gave birth to her son it got worse. He told her he would shoot her up with drugs and make it look like she had overdosed if she left. After the second child she gave in to his demands and the beatings lessened. He dumped Tonya and made her move out the week he met Renee. Renee was educated, independent and a successful business owner. She received the same punishment until she got pregnant a month later. She came from a strong family. Tee would tell her that he would plant dope on different family members or in her place of business to keep her in check while she carried his third son. A few years later he met a daddy's girl, Tamika. She was raised with both parents, except for the five years her father spent in jail for a crime he didn't commit. Tee was dating her and Renee at the same time until Tamika gave him an ultimatum; he chose Tamika and the abuse started. His threat to her was easy because they had already gone through a wrongful conviction. That's what he promised her, but four years later she got the nerve to leave him and then came me. This man dated women from different back grounds. Each one had been held captive because of the life they refused to give up and the fear of losing not only their livelihood, but their loved ones. Tee was a psychotic sociopath that preyed on the lives of those who loved life. He is serving time for his actions in general population. We won't see him until his first life sentence without the possibility of parole and the three he got behind those are over.

The women moved into the same neighborhood, got family and individual counseling and now they are living in peace. The biggest adjustment was Terrance Jr., but he finally came through with counseling. The ladies and I became lifelong friends because I put my life in danger to save their lives and their boy's. We set up voice and video recording devices around my house and just like clockwork, Tee came over and did what he does best. This time I would be the one going to the police, so they would be free and clear of any retaliation. I didn't want them anywhere in sight, but he came in before they could leave. After he was arrested they felt freedom and wanted him to know they had a hand in that freedom. Terrance showed me how dangerous fleshly or worldly controlling love could be.

That day I swore off available men. I didn't want a committed relationship anyway because I knew who my husband was. I bought a new house in an upper middle class neighborhood on the east side of town.

5

My First Husband

Rodney Mitchell was in McKay's shopping, he was a tall, chocolate, handsome, strong, just right kind of man. Dang he has a ring on so I can't approach him or let him know I'm interested. What's a girl to do? Suddenly he walked over; looking perfect as usual with a low haircut, dimple in his right cheek and showing that beautiful smile. His glasses always made him look professional and ready for business. I had seen him in here a few times, but I never noticed the ring until now. With his deep voice he politely asked," May I help you?" My mind, flesh, and mouth gave him a different answer. I was so distracted by him that I forgot I was dropping my fruit. I learned few years ago that I had to be sure my eyes were blank. I gave a quick, "No thank you," but to no avail because he began to help me anyway. I saw no reason to put up a fight; after all this was innocent. I had been shopping there for about two months and had seen him at least four times, but we had only given pleasantries; until a week ago. We talked about thirty minutes on a spiritual matter, but why didn't I see the ring then. I started thinking was he wearing a ring then or is he a player?" I knew I had to use caution around this one because I don't know his plan.

After Rodney helped me pick-up my mess he formally introduced himself, "Good evening, I'm Rodney Mitchell and you are?" With great restraint I said, "Thank you, I'm Alisha, Alisha Coleman." And I shook his hand with a firm grip and after making eye contact I placed my glance in my basket. I wanted to say more, but his ring silenced my thoughts, eyes, and voice. My distracted act didn't deter him at all. "I enjoyed our discussion the last time I saw you and wanted to know what church you attend or if you had a church home. My wife and I have been considering checking things out closer to home."
"Well I've attended Little Rock and Missionary First, but my home Church is Mount Zion American Methodical Evangelist Church North in my home town."
"My wife is out of town as usual, but when she gets back we will check them out. Have a good day, hope to see you soon."
"You too," I said rushing away.

Yes, that went right over my head. I wanted unavailable men not married men because they were off limits. If I caused the breakup of a marriage I could never forgive myself. Now a boyfriend/girlfriend relationship, engaged for over a year or shacking; I could do and did, but a covenant with God, I could not do. I continued shopping as my thoughts drifted to my last visit back home and how I missed my best friend Tommy. After my grandparents died I would only go home once a year and the visits was short and bitter sweet. Everyone was married and building a family so that was sad to me. All I wanted to do was work and keep short ties, but the when are you going to settle down question came; which caused my visits to be short. No relationship, marriage, or babies for me because that was not in my future. Well not since Mikael. I missed him and every time I got a box I would pray for two roses, but a single rose every time. I knew Mikael was keeping up with me because the day I moved into my new house I received a vase full of pink flowers. The card said, I will be with you soon. Congratulations!!! Love Mikael. I quickly dismissed the thoughts and feelings.

Rodney was a husband that lacked security not only within himself, but his wife and their relationship. His wife constantly threw out demeaning and emasculating remarks toward him; which created these feelings so they became his reality. Rodney had moved into the area three months ago with his wife Nichole. Nichole was a beautiful, 5'7", well-educated woman that was not afraid to let you know it. Nichole lacked one thing; she didn't admire or respect her husband anymore. Rodney loved her from the time they met in high school and his love never changed, but he begun to dislike her. In high school Nichole was different.

She was raised from the age of 12 by her well advised, God-fearing grandmother until her death in Nichole's junior year of College. That's when Diane, her mom, came back into her life. Diane was little taller, but just as if not more breathe taking than her daughter. She traveled extensively with her rich boyfriend at that time. Diane never had time for Nichole, nor did the grandmother want her in that sort of unstable environment. Rodney was a 6'3" 200 pound loving, devoted, physically active, and well educated man. According to Nichole that was not enough. At age 10, Rodney's parents died in an accident, so he was raised by his grandparents. Rodney's grandfather was the Pastor of Greater Eastern Star Baptist Church and his grandmother was a Missionary. Rodney traveled around the world during the summer doing missionary work at eleven. When he became a young adult he would help his grandfather prepare sermons and bible study topics that catered to the youth and young adults in the Church. Rodney discussed his desire to marry Nichole with his grandparents after undergrad, but his grandmother cautioned him and directed him to pray. She instructed him to focus on what the Bible says about a wife. Rodney didn't want to face the truth, so his thoughts forced him to believe Nichole fit that scripture. Five years into their ten year marriage, Nichole started to climb the corporate ladder. She would take a lot of unexpected and unplanned business trips. After she started making more money she started making plans without Rodney's advance knowledge or input. Rodney was not ruthless or as coldblooded when climbing the ladder as Nichole, but to her that made him weak. Rodney was the best asset his company had and they knew it. Everyone called on him for projects or when a higher management position was temporarily vacant. As Nichole moved up she expected her husband to move as well, but Rodney wanted to be available to help his grandparents, serve others, and have time for his future family. When he didn't move up the ladder, Nichole berated and belittled him. The issues started with meaningless arguments between the two of them. As time went on she would argue in front of family and finally in front of their friends or in public. This was putting a strain on their relationship and future. Rodney thought about the words of his grandmother before he asked Nichole to marry him, but was it too late. "What does God's word say about a wife?" He would repeat in his head during one of her outburst.

After our first conversation, but before I knew he was married, I hoped to see him again and now I try to avoid him. Two months later I saw Rodney sitting in his car with his head down. I pretended not to see him, but he looked up when I closed my car door. With that familiar smile that was now forbidden. "Good afternoon hard working lady, how are you?"
"I'm well," I said as I focused on the store.
"Is work good or slow right now?" he asked feeling the tension.
"It's good." I smiled by mistake. "How is your wife?"
"I am so glad you asked, because that reminds me we need your help." He smiled. This was good because my initial thoughts were wrong, so I could relax he was not flirting with me. "My wife wants me to get some work around the house done and I told her about you, so would you be interested?"

He asked as he pulled out a buggy.

I thought about the possible revenue of future clients. "Yes Mr. Mitchell I'll do it".

"When did we become so formal?" He laughed.

"When you asked about my services, because business is business and that is my focus now." The only problem with that is I turned off my radar and my defense mechanisms. I know I should be on guard even if he's not interested anymore, so that was a big flaw on my part.

"Well how about this weekend at 9 a.m. You can look at the project with us and give an estimate or see what needs to be done or what we may have over looked".

I gave him my business card and told him to let his wife call if she had any questions, so he texted their address to my business phone.

That Saturday at 8:45 Rodney called, "Are you close?" I was pulling into the subdivision. "Is there a problem?"

"No," he assured me everything was fine. He said he was just making sure I could find my way. The truth was his wife did not come home, but left a message that she had to take a last minute flight to California to handle some issue at a new facility. As I pulled into the driveway a strange feeling came over me when Rodney opened the garage` door. We said our pleasantries and started downstairs when I realized his wife was not present. I asked, "Rodney where is your wife before we go any further?"

He replied, "She went to Cali last night" I was a little annoyed, but this was business. "Why didn't you call and cancel?" "You were almost here and I didn't get the message until 8:30 this morning, it was a last minute thing." I could tell he wanted to cry, so I turned and asked, "What do you want done?" I pulled out my notebook and started writing.

He replied, "Tell me what to do about my marriage?" He stared off into space and I became uncomfortable.

"Well I can't help you with that, but I'm sure your Pastor would. Can we get back to business?" Rodney invited me upstairs to show me the design scheme Nichole had come up with and her own cost estimate. At first I was uncomfortable, but his wife knew I was a female coming to do the job and didn't call to cancel so I was cool. After I considered all the facts I began to feel at home.

Rodney was a southern gentleman that believed in chivalry. Before it was over we were laughing and talking like old friends. We talked about our childhood and life experiences but we became a little too comfortable. At four o'clock the doorbell rang.

It was a man coming to drop off a Gang Box for the work that was to be done on the basement. Before Rodney could speak the man said, "Mrs. Mitchell called us to come over on Wednesday to give her an estimate, so we can get started on Monday. I just need you to sign this form saying that I did drop off the box, you're not responsible for any damage, and we start at eight Monday morning." Rodney signed the paper with a worried grin. He closed the door and turned to me. I could see the look of apology on his face before the words came out. I said, "It's ok Rodney, your wife knew what she wanted and there was no hand shaking, promises, or signed documents." But he was upset, so he offered me a check because I completed the estimate and gave a list of future issues to prepare for. That evening he called to apologize again, I reassured him it was behind us.

Two weeks later I saw Rodney at the store. I was coming out and he was going in. He asked if he could help carry some of my bags and I allowed him to do so. The connection was made and I didn't even notice. I had let my guard down because I felt sorry for him. Once the bags were in the car he said, "I have tickets to a blues concert, but my wife won't be able to make, so would you like to come? That is if it's okay with your boyfriend?" I still

didn't pick up the fact that he was fishing.
"I don't have one, but how would your wife feel about you taking me?" I said closing my trunk.
"I don't know, but I will ask her if that would make you feel better," he said with a chuckle.
"Well when you get an answer, give me a call and we can meet at the arena" I said getting in my car.
Rodney pulled out his phone and made a call before he turned around and said, "I'll pick you up at six." He ran into the store before I could respond.

Two days later Rodney called and asked for my address. I didn't want to give it to him because I wanted to meet him there and keep it casual without any confusion. After a brief conversation I gave him the address so the limo could pick me up. I had not paid attention to how attractive Rodney was anymore because he was off limits to me. When I walked out the door I saw the familiar box and again I said a prayer before I opened it. The box contained a single pink rose. This was not a date, so I walked outside trying to erase the memory of Mikael out of my mind while waiting on the Limo. When the limo pulled up, I could throw my feelings away and enjoy my new found moment of freedom. The chauffeur didn't have time to get out before

Rodney swung open the door and told me to jump in; which I did without hesitation. I thought this was not a date for either of us and I breathed a sigh of relief. We had a quick bite to eat and off to the concert we went. I had gotten so comfortable with him I threw the entire lady like stuff to the curb and I was relaxed just being myself. The concert was great we took pictures, he drank like crazy, and we bought CD's.

The ride home was a little different. Rodney was drunk so everything came out about his marriage; eventually there were tears. I felt sorry for him because he never complained about his wife or the marriage before, but I always saw the pain and disappointment in his eyes. That night Rodney told me he wanted kids. He told me how they planned it out in the beginning of their marriage. They had agreed to wait at least two years, but Nichole couldn't get pregnant, or so he thought. He later found out that Nichole never wanted children and was secretly on the pill. Rodney turned to me and said, "My quiver is empty; therefore I will have no descendants to leave an inheritance to."
At that moment Rodney put his arms around my waist and held me tight as he cried and fell asleep. I had instructed the driver earlier to take him home first and at that moment I

was glad I did. We helped him into the house. I placed a blanket over him and locked up. On my way home I pondered what his wife may be going through, but I quickly brushed it out of my head because it was not my business.

The next day Rodney called and asked, "What happened last night?" Taking a deep breath he said, "I know I didn't get lucky because I had all my clothes on." He had a nervous laugh so I knew he was unsure about his actions. I replied while grinning from ear to ear, "Nothing you didn't want to happen." I realized I had gotten too familiar with him and I reeled it back in. "What's up, has your wife gotten home?"
"No but I have a friend that wants to use your services." I will call you later.
 Rodney wanted to meet with his friend Richard to discuss a project.

The three of us met for lunch that day. When Richard got up to take a phone call Rodney asked, "What happened last night?" He looked around nervously. "I don't really drink but I had a lot on my mind." He whispered, "Did I cross the line or say anything out of the way?"
Richard came back to the table "My son is sick so I need to leave, but can I get your card?" He ran out of the door. Rodney turned to me with a puzzled look on his face and

whispered with nervous excitement, "Well?"

"Well what?" I said because I forgot his question.

"What did I do or say," he asked eagerly.

"Man, you said nothing. Nothing at all," I said as I shook my head.

With a slight wipe to his forehead he said, "Whew" and the conversation went on. "So did you enjoy yourself?" he smiled leaning back in his chair.

"Yes," I said trying not to look at this sexy man.

"Have you ever been to a concert before?" he smiled.

"Yes," I glanced at him because he had a beautiful smile and I knew he was trying to make small talk.

"Would you go to a concert with me again?" he said licking his lips as if he saw something good to eat. "I don't know," I said looking down.

"Okay, what happened?" He asked after we paid for our food.

As we were leaving I said, "Nothing" with each glance I could feel the release of my desire in my panties and it grew stronger and stronger. I had not been with a man for a while so I knew where this passion was coming from.

When we got to the door he grabbed my hand which caused me to shiver. When we got to my car Rodney grabbed me and started kissing me. I pulled away but it felt so good and I didn't want him to stop. "I'm sorry. I just couldn't hide my desire for you." He stepped back. "Every time I look into your eyes I feel that you see into my soul. It is as though you know me and love me already."

"Rodney what about your wife," I said looking around, "This would hurt her."

"I know, but I want you so bad." He pulled me closer. "Alisha I need you, please just once, I beg of you and then it's over."

Thinking to myself, I've heard that before, but I agreed. He confessed his feelings for me and the fact that he bought the tickets and was drinking that night to get up the nerve to tell me how he felt.

We talked all the way to the store to get protection and to the hotel. Once we entered the room we were like teenagers and this was our first time meeting. That feeling quickly passed for him as he embraced with kisses that lead us to the bed. I don't know when or how our clothes fell to the floor. Once he entered the release of my warm desire was my only concern and the pleasure I enjoyed and longed to be fulfilled. We tied our bodies into the pleasure we both desired. I cried out in fulfillment as he cried out his love for the seduction of my essence. He held me tightly as if he were to loosen his grip I might flee. I knew then he was hooked. This was the beginning of a forbidden romance that would only satisfy our own selfish desires in which we were content with at that moment.

For the next two months Rodney and I lived a secret life with passion and a lust for the aroma of love. Rodney could never get enough of me. I made him feel like he was the first, last, and only partner in my life. That ability came from studying the needs and desires of men. I knew exactly what to do so that men would put me first in their life. Before it was over my needs and desires came first. He gave me things I didn't ask for or need.

This man was such a catch that I didn't want to give him up. Rodney and I met every day at the same place and the passion only grew stronger. By the middle of the first month if Nichole was out of town Rodney would stay at my house until she came back. Once a day was not enough for Rodney, the more he fed off my passionate essence, the more he desired. He would work from my home and I would savor his essence as he sat at the computer. Rodney loved the way I would allow him to flow into me, devouring the evidence of his uncontrollable love for me. Rodney would explore areas never touched by any man and mark his territory with the flow of his essence; causing me to give in to his every desire. I had to break away from this man; but his gentle touch, pleading eyes, and awaiting passion consumed me over time and I couldn't stop.

Rodney had lost his desire for Nichole. The routine she had created was forgotten and gave way to stolen nights of brisk pleasures. Rodney would couple the incomplete essence of my passion by sharing the final moment embracing my thighs as his tongue massaged the source of my pleasing aroma. The center of my body rose toward the ceiling as I cried out, "Rodney, give me all of you!" He responded by twirling his tongue around mine as he slowly turned me onto my stomach, penetrating the sweet flower he caused to bloom. Rodney grabbed my hair and with each pull he slid deeper and deeper until he caused a flow of pleasure. The deeper he slid, the more he lost control. To his surprise he erupted into full passion, causing him to exchange his essence for a deep sleep. With each moment he would hold me tighter to keep me close. Day after day we spent our moments together and with each day we spent I prepared for the end, but I couldn't stop.

During the first two months of our affair Rodney was not as available to his wife, but by the third month he totally ignored her and she started to feel unsure about their relationship. Nichole would ask him to drop her off and pick her up from the airport, but most times he would be too busy with me for the task. Rodney and I stayed together the nights she was out of town and some nights he would lie just to be with me. Rodney and I would take short romantic trips. Nichole was starting to worry because the calls from her to Rodney increased in frequency. He would ignore her calls when we were together. I became his Queen, so he wanted to leave his wife and marry me. This was my first time being with a married man and I fell hard for him. However, this was a 10 year marriage and a relationship they shared for over 16 years. I can't destroy that, it's time to put me aside and go to work. I started asking him more about his wife, why he loved or what he disliked about her. The third month was when things had to get rocky, but we were into our sixth month. My plan was to get Rodney to see what he was missing at home, but I wanted to keep our relationship going forever. The goal was for him to like her and her to respect and admire him again. I wanted this to cause them to seek counseling and mend their marriage, but my selfish desire was getting in the way.

Half way through our sixth month I would encouraged him to look at what they had, so I started annoying him. It was a struggle, but I had to get him to a point that would cause him to never cheat with me again. I not only studied what pleased men, but what causes them to flee and become skeptical of women. I would slowly torment Rodney. This caused me anguish and pain, because he was a good man, but lonely. I cared about him more than I wanted to admit. I wanted to be with him because I loved the way he catered to his wife, which I now had the opportunity to enjoy. I knew that if I tried to be with him the question in the back of my mind would always be would cheat on me. Within the third week of that sixth month Rodney started picking up and dropping Nichole off at the airport. The nights we spent together were short we would only have sex once a day and by week four I stopped having sexual contact with him completely. Because his sex drive increased with me, I had to cause him to desire sex with his wife by going cold turkey. Our time was limited to short phone calls until he finally said, "its over."

Nichole changed her mindset once she thought she was losing Rodney and took a less demanding position in her company. Nichole realized success was not enjoyable alone and money was not the answer. This revelation caused her to stop listening to Diane, her mother. Rodney and Nichole sought a spiritual relationship with God together; which caused them to prioritize their marriage, outside relationships, and career goals. Next was to find a God fearing marriage counselor. Counseling caused them to renew their marriage vows. This caused them to create a 2, 4, and 10 year flexible plan that included seeking God and knowing their future would be by God's will. Within that first year of renewal, they had their first child. They promised that every five years they would renew their vows or covenant with God. Nichole and Rodney now have two children, attend church on a regular basis, and take time off as a family for missionary work.

Rodney called me to thank me for pushing him away. He said, "It took me a few months to forgive you because the hurt was so deep. But as I look at my sleeping wife I realize the hurt, pain, and rejection catapulted me back into the arms of the woman I fell in love with as a teen. I never wanted to lose that special love again. What we had was special, but it was a forbidden love that was drenched in lust and full of sexual desire." I still see Rodney from time to time when he's shopping and if he's alone we talk.

Nichole never found out that Rodney cheated on her. In a session she said she didn't need to know what caused him to change, but to focus on what she could do to never cause that change again.

My motto is "respect the wife by knowing your place..."

6

My Mocha Dream

Julian was my 6'2," mocha colored, muscular man that loves to sing and dance. That night he danced the night away with me. Now this is the perfect, unavailable man, because he has a girlfriend and she was not living with him. Julian had issues with commitment and was a little selfish, well extremely selfish. His girl Rasheda gave him everything he wanted. Rasheda was from the hood, but did everything to overcome her upbringing and what she thought was her ignorant family. She was a very successful accountant and Julian, a privilege rich kid, was the CFO in his father's company; by title only. Julian played hard but was somewhat faithful to Rasheda. She was successful, beautiful, could cook, and looked good on a man's arm. However, she was insecure and ashamed of her past, because she grew up poor. Julian was an open flirt, but respected his girl and never gave a girl a second look or had sex with them. Julian loved to dance at clubs that Rasheda thought were beneath him and would never go dancing with him. That allowed me to walk right in.

Rasheda and Julian had been dating for two years, but she decided never to come to his house. She thought his mom didn't like her and her family wasn't good enough. Well the truth is her family wasn't rich but that was her hang up not Donna's. Julian's house was on his parent's property, a half mile away from the main house. Mike and Donna, Julian's parents, grew up poor but his father had an idea that he didn't give up on and a wife willing to support his dream; now they are millionaires.

I liked me some Julian, he was just okay in bed, but could dance and we had fun. Again I did the things his girl wouldn't like have fun, be real, or just hang out. Rasheda gave Julian everything but that. Now my time line is three months and I had to move on before the guy became attached, wait a few months and do it all over again. Julian was different because the sex was not really good, but with most selfish men it's not. Because I loved to dance and be taken care of, Julian was a keeper. Even though he was selfish, he was a gentleman and down to earth. His attributes were worth the lousy sex. "An even swap ain't no swindle," Gram's would always say. I made him feel needed. He took me on shopping sprees, bought me a car, and paid off my house. Most men want to feel necessary and needed in their woman's life or some other woman will. Julian had no idea what I did for a living, but he thought I couldn't have a life without him. All men are not the same, but the core of a male is constant. Wait to see his reactions or thoughts to your action and watch for his actions or thoughts with other's before you reveal your thoughts. Once you figure it out you will know and will soon have that man. If he's shallow and superficial this may not work, but who wants a man like that anyway? This is what makes a man feel like you are just what he needs and this is how women bring down powerful men. We know and have possession of all his deepest and darkest secrets.

The night I met Julian, we danced the night away and then walked around his lake laughing and talking about life. At that time I didn't know he had a girlfriend. We fell asleep as I lay in his arms under the stars, only to be awakened that morning by the sprinklers. We rushed inside and he had his maid prepare breakfast for us. We disappeared upstairs to clean the nights dancing and wetness of the sprinklers off. Julian took me to his room and laid out a pair of shorts and tee shirt for me. He took me into his bathroom and gave me what I needed to get cleaned up before he walked out. He went into the guestroom to shower and change. After we showered and changed, he escorted me to the kitchen for breakfast.

Julian started the morning conversation. "Well I must say you just popped my cherry last night and this morning as well. I believe we will become great acquaintances."
I was thinking was he too drunk to remember what I looked like and what actually happened, but I had to play it cool because he was loaded. With a coy smile I said, "What do you mean?" looking at him.
"I've never slept with a woman when all we accomplished was sleep," he replied with a hearty laugh. "You are also the first woman to use my shower, eat at my table, and wear my clothes that didn't give up the goodies first."
"So you're telling me you're a man that believes in hit'em and quit'em, or should I say a man of opportunity?" I said with a slick smile and sexy look. I knew then I had him.

"No I have a regular friend, but she never comes over," he said picking up his glass for a sip. "So she eats a lot of fiber or she can't come over because she's regular." I smiled. Telling a corny joke always gives confirmation of where you stand with a man. Once he laughs, I know without a doubt I'm in there.

So I said, "Why didn't you just say you have a girlfriend or a lady friend that you're really into. You don't owe me anything. I'm just a one night dance that popped your cherry." I smiled. The second corny joke was to ease his fears or concerns. Okay the truth is I am kind of corny anyway I'm told, but guys want the same thing from me that I want from them so they laugh.

Julian said, "I've only known you for less than a day and I've known Rasheda for over two years, but I feel more comfortable with you." He scratched his head as if he were trying to figure something out. "I have talked to you more than I've ever talked with her. Hell I told you more secrets about me last night than I have ever told her." He stood up. "Alisha, I don't know what it is about you, but I don't want you to leave. Will you at least spend this weekend with me?" He asked holding my hand. With a smile I said, "So now you want me to pay for last night, breakfast, the shower, and your cherry?"
He quickly replied, "I know you are joking, but you have affected me in a way I cannot put into words. Your eyes are so beautiful and mesmerizing and your smile is so sweet that you've already captured my heart" He got down on one knee and pleaded for me to spend the weekend with him, no strings

attached. I knew I was going to seal the deal before the weekend was over, but I had to time it just right.

Oh yes I plot, scheme, and allow men to spend money on me, but I never ask for anything. I give my all to make sure their wants and needs are completely satisfied during my short time with them. This weekend both of us will get what we want. Again as my Gram's use to say, "An even swap ain't no swindle." After breakfast Julian told me he had several engagements that weekend so he had to make some calls to get out of them.

This will be the weekend I find out why he didn't marry Rasheda a year ago, flirted with other women, and didn't really want to leave his girl in that order. One thing I did notice was how he called her his girl, but never his woman or lady. I was thinking, what's up with that? Before I could finish my thought, I heard a females' voice and she was coming my way. I picked up my dishes and ran into the laundry room. I didn't want to cause a scene just in case Rasheda had changed her mind about coming over. It was his mother asking him about his whereabouts last night and this morning. She was fussing about him hanging out in those clubs, but not letting her know when he was home safe and sound. I smiled because he apologized and said yes ma'am after each nag or fussy mama question and statement. I knew then he loved and respected his mama. I smiled because I made the right choice. Yes I'm a love'em and leave'em better kind of girl, but I want a man that will always treat me right. He let her know he was sick and that's why he hadn't called. "Mama I tried to eat a little something this morning, but I forgot my phone was still dead from last night," he said.

She was silent for a moment and said, "Okay where is she?"

"What do you mean?" he said nervously.

"Julian I raised you and I am no fool." She smacked his arm. "Where is the little fast tail you met last night?"

"Mother I have no idea what you're talking about nor would I do such a..." Julian was stumbling over his words. Before he could get the lie out she cut him off. "Look honey I am glad you still try to respect me and I kind of like her for staying out of sight respecting me too. I know you and that is not your car outside." She kissed him goodbye. "Call me later," she said as she walked towards the door. Before she exited she shouted, "make sure you use protection." We laughed and finished breakfast before cleaning up.

Ten minutes later the home phone rang. "Hello," he mouthed it was his mother. After he got off the phone he said, "She reminded me to charge my phone and turn it on or she would be back." He smiled. That reminded me of his girl, "Julian, have you called Rasheda?" Julian exclaimed, "Oh my god, she is going to kill me, we were meeting for brunch!" He ran from the kitchen to the bedroom and plugged in his phone to call her. Julian explained that he was under the weather and just woke up. He let her know that Aralia, the housekeeper/maid was taking care of things. He told her that he would be turning off his phone until he felt better, but would keep her updated. After he made his call he came back down and told me we would have to go get his car. We would pick me up a few things and meet somewhere so we could to go to Manantial Spa and Resort.

Manantial, which means spring in English, is a secluded member only resort for the wealthy. The owner is said to be unknown and each bungalow has a different theme and it's extremely private. Potential employees are required to sign a confidentiality clause before an interview and a second if they are hired. The hotel got its name because the first owner's family sprung from a natural spring. No it doesn't make any sense and they say the

owner is unknown. People with a lot of money, time on their hands, or smoke weed come up with crap that make most people stop, stare, and shake their heads as they keep it moving. "Have you ever been there?" he said as he walked with me upstairs to pack.
"No, I've heard of it, but I'm not in that circle yet." I laughed.
"What do you mean?" he looked puzzled as he stopped on the stairs.
"I'm not considered wealthy." I quickly replied.
"Well young lady we are about to have a weekend to remember." He said as he ran up the stairs.
"I will hold you to that." I said as I ran behind him.
"I am a man of my word or I will die trying." He grabbed me and quickly let me go.
"Let's go get my car and I will follow you home so you can pack," he said. "Sounds good to me," I quickly replied. After about twenty minutes we were on our way.

We talked about favorite songs and how we love to dance even as kids. Suddenly there was a shift and his question changed to a more serious tone. I just met this man, but I've known of him for months so a relationship was the last thing I expected to hear from him. His first question caught me off guard. "Have you ever been married?"

"No," I said as I sat up. "Have you?" I retorted.
"No," he cut on the blinker. "Do you have a
man now or are you seeing someone on the
regular?" He kept his focus on the road.
"No and no." I said looking directly at him to
see if I could tell where he was going with this.
"Oh really, what about being engaged?" he
smiled with that question.
"Again, I must say no," but I was lying
because I wanted to keep Mikael a secret.
"Why?" he asked with a frown.
"I guess I've never met the one or I wasn't the
one for him." I sat back thinking of Mikael
and his silent departure.
"I wanted to marry Rasheda, but the night I
was going to propose she revealed a side of
herself I had never seen." He hesitated as if he
were hiding something. "I put the ring in my
wallet and it has been there since that night."
"What did she do that was so bad?" I asked
trying to forget Mikael.
"She has an issue with poor people." He said
turning the radio down.
"I don't understand why some people with
money see us as a project, someone to work
for them, or act like we have a make you
broke disease." I smiled.
With a laugh he replied, "No we don't." We
pulled up next to his car. "My parents grew up
in the hood and they are the most down to
earth people in the world. I have poor relatives

and friends, but I accept them and we are not ashamed of them." He turned the car off and sat back. "Rasheda is ashamed of her own parents and siblings, that's why we have problems." He looked at me, "but this is what pissed me off. Her sister was working at the restaurant the night I was going to propose. When I looked up I realized the waitress looked just like her, the only difference is that she was a younger and relaxed looking version."

"Okay, I hope you didn't say that and that is not a reason to change your mind about proposing."

"That was not the problem. The woman was her sister Monica, but Rasheda was rude and condescending. I had never seen her act like that. After Monica took our order, Rasheda excused herself. I thought it was to use the restroom, but she went to complain to the manager and have her removed from our table. If the manager had not come to the table to apologize, I would have never known. Rasheda was not at the table, so I couldn't question her about it. What Rasheda didn't know is that the owner, Richard, and my father were best friends growing up. My father gave him the money to start the restaurant; which is now an exclusive chain of upscale restaurants, two locally and six others in different states. I asked if I could speak with her in private. He went to look for her and took her back to his office so I could apologize. That's when I found out she was Rasheda's older sister. She had worked two jobs along with her parents to put her through college. Rasheda was ashamed of them because they were poor. I thought she was an ungrateful snob." He opened my door and walked me to the driver's side of my car. "Can I follow you home?"

"Yes if you promise to behave." I smiled. I drove off and he followed me home.

Julian talked while I packed. He told me that he had only met Rasheda's parents and didn't know she had siblings. The two older brothers were truck drivers and her sister Monica. This caused him to see her as a fraud, but he couldn't stop loving her. Julian Casanova, the player and heart shredder (as his friends called him) had never been in love or had a serious relationship until Rasheda. His friends were shocked that after six months he shut the parties down and spent all of his time with her. In their seventh month of dating he met her parents. That night was the eighth month and her actions caused him great doubt about a future with her. He did get Richard to give her sister a nice raise and the night off with pay.

On our way to the spa we listened to music, talked, and laughed until I got sleepy. The next twenty minutes of the ride were quiet. I laid back and closed my eyes, until we arrived at our destination. I was awakened to the soothing voice of Julian saying, "wake up sleepy head we are here."

"Okay, so do we need to check in?" I asked looking around.

"That's right, you've never been here before. I called earlier and gave them instructions, so they texted me the bungalow number and voila' your room madam." That's why you have to be a member. You text or email them what you want and they charge your account after verifying the information provided and reply with the keypad code. It is reset after each guest checks out.

I have been in some nice places, but this room was breath taking. It was as if we had stepped out of the real world into a movie or a fantasy. There were flowing water falls that gave way to still waters on a tropical island, surrounded by flowers and clear blue skies.

"Oh my, this is nice." I said looking around.

"I am glad you are pleased." He put our bags down. "What would you like to do first?"

"I don't know." I felt uncultured and unexposed at the moment. "Will you take the lead on this one because I'm still trying to take it all in." I said while looking around the room.

Julian walked over to the computer and typed in something before escorting me to the bathroom. "I want you to take a nice hot shower and put on this robe." I followed instructions and walked toward the bathroom. Julian snatched me back and embraced me while he kissed my neck, causing me to giggle. I walked into the bathroom and my eyes were filled with fairytale beauty. "I thought you would like that," Julian announced from the other room. After his true confessions on the way here, I knew I couldn't have sex with him this weekend. My plans were quickly changing. I had to think of a way to get them back together.

I was sitting on the bed when a large man, that looked as if he were on steroids, walked into the room along with a beautiful woman. They were both dressed in black. Personally I don't like men that look like body builders, but I knew he would give me an excellent massage. Julian walked out of the bathroom the moment she asked for him. Julian, in his robe, escorted me to a back room and helped me up on a table. He whispered in my ear, "I decided to give you a weekend of relaxation. Today you will get a head to toe massage and then dinner." He hopped up on the other table. "I haven't planned tomorrow, but let's play it by ear." He said as he lay down.

Two hours later all I wanted to do was sleep, but the dinner Julian ordered arrived. The appetizers consisted of bread, salad, and a seafood sampler. Served with a dry white wine, but I had sweet tea. We had cold avocado soup before the main course, Arugula-Stuffed Leg of Lamb with Roasted Spring Vegetables. Julian swapped his drink to sweet tea. My favorite course was next, dessert. Julian allowed me to choose. They had amazing choices, so I ordered the Chocolate Ganache cake and Bananas foster crepes; which we shared. With full bellies, we retired for the night.

The next morning, I awoke to a beautiful breakfast. Julian had Apple Cinnamon Ricotta Pancakes and I had Almond Crusted French Toast with Strawberries. After breakfast we lounged around, snuggling and talking. Julian felt compelled to confess again. Out of the blue he said. "I haven't cheated on Rasheda since I realized she was the one. I've just flirted with other women, but never cheated." "Where did that come from?" I said looking up, swallowing air.
"I was just thinking out loud because I'm here with you and this is nice. I feel kind of guilty." He said with an uneasy smile.

"What do you mean Julian?" I said as I caressed his face to ease his mind.

"You are in a position that I've never put a woman in, not even Rasheda, and I haven't even tried to have sex with you." He stood up and walked onto the terrace, but he quickly turned saying. "Don't get me wrong I want to, but I'm enjoying just being with you." I walked toward him and he held my hand. "Most women push a man for information or a commitment whether its sex, dating, or going out." He kissed me on the forehead. "I know behind each question there is a motive, but you...you're different Alisha. You just wait for my lead without manipulation. Unlike most of the women I meet, you listen."

I kissed the palm of his hand and said, "I believe it's my duty to please you while I'm with you and allow you to lead." I looked into his eyes.

"They don't make women like you anymore." Squeezing me tighter he asked, "Are you willing to submit and support me if I were your husband?"

I wrapped my arms around his neck. "Yes. As your wife that is my duty, but as your lady I want to discover all of your wants, needs, and desires. Then I'll be capable of supporting you as a submissive wife."

He laughed, "You know you just pissed off a bunch of women." He picked me up and carried me into the bedroom. "They think women like you set them back a hundred years." He laid me on the bed.

"Yes and that is why a clean-up woman has their man." I said with a chuckle.

"See that's why I like you." He rolled over and kissed me. "I've never met a woman like you. The women I usually flirt with are rich, but trashy. They see me with Rasheda and will still pass me their number or a room key." He said flopping onto his back.

"Well, what are you if you flirt back and accept their number or key." I lay on his chest. "You accept the invitations of trashy women, so what does that make you?"

He rolled his eyes back as if he were thinking. "That's what I'm talking about. You are real and not afraid to say it, but in a way that makes me think." He pulled me on top of him. "Well I guess I do it as a slap in her face behind her back kind of thing. You know like she did me." Julian started kissing me.

I rose up and said, "You know you're acting like a witch with a capital B. Julian have you talked with her about that night?" I rolled over on the bed.

He sat up. "No, I don't know how to approach her. This is har...wait did you just call me a bitch?" I smiled as I hunched my shoulders and he just shook his head. He leaned back as if he were pondering the last question. "I

171

got it now. You remind me of my mother. My mother said the exact same thing, damn." He smiled as he rolled on top of me.

I smiled saying, "well usually mothers know best and the wisdom of a mother rarely falters."

He rolled his hips and stood up. "I guess I'll think about it because I love that woman. The ring is still in my wallet, see." He said as he pulled out the ring. "I guess I keep it in here just in case I look at her and all the hurt of betrayal is gone. I don't want to miss the chance of her being my wife." He said looking up into nothing, but smiling with thoughts of her.

"Well said, so what's next?" I was getting tired of the conversation because I was getting hungry.

"Lunch and we head back, or we can head back now and stop somewhere for lunch. We can do this again next weekend at my family's cabin?" He said while juggling his hands up and down like scales.

"I'm game for that." I jumped up off the bed and wrapped my arms around him. "Two weekends in row with Mr. Casanova the player and heart shredder, as his friends call him." I had to laugh because it was lame; rich folk. "I wish they could see you now, but I guess I need to watch out next weekend, you might shred my heart" I exclaimed with laughter and he joined in.

"Go pack Alisha and let's get ready to hit the road." He said kissing my forehead.

"Damn," he said when his phone came on. "Is everything ok?" I turned and said.

"No, I forgot to call Rasheda and worst of all I forgot to call my mother." He said rubbing his head.

"I told you to do that when we got here." I said as I zipped my bag.

"I know, but I was trying to think of a way to fuck you." He picked up my bag.

"Oh really, well I guess that was a wasted thought and now you're in double trouble." I grabbed my bag and picked up his. "I will get the car ready, call your mom first and then Rasheda."

"Why in that order?" he looked puzzled.

"Because your mom won't talk long and then you will know if Rasheda talked to anybody close to you, so you can get your lie straight." I said walking toward the door.

"I know for a fact that Rasheda would never call my mother." He quickly replied grabbing the bags and walking to the car.

I opened the trunk and he closed it. He opened my door and I said, "Just listen to me this one time and I will owe you."

He kissed me on the forehead and ran into the room dialing.

Twenty minutes later he walked out to the car with a big smile on his face. "You are good Miss. Casanova. I hope you don't break my heart." He said laughing, "You were right, she called my mom because she couldn't reach me less than twenty minutes before I called my Mother. My mom had gone to my house and was about to call her back when I called. I called Rasheda and apologized for not calling sooner but my mom just woke me up and told me to call you. Hell that worked better than I thought. I get to spend next weekend with you and without interruption because she is spending the weekend with my mom for a mother and daughter weekend spa get away." He got in the car. "I need to take you on a shopping spree, because my good luck charm needs to be compensated." He kissed my hand and drove off.

"Thank you Master Julian." I replied and we both laughed as we headed toward home with a shopping spree pit stop.

Julian took me to several high end boutiques. He introduced me as his cousin, because most of the ladies knew him and his family. After shopping and getting a bite to eat, he took me home. Julian couldn't wait ten minutes after dropping me off before he called me. He said he wanted to thank me for giving up my weekend for him and all he did was

talk about Rasheda. We talked for an hour. I
didn't hear from Julian again until Thursday
night to give me details for the weekend. I had
to play catch-up and get some order forms
filled out, give some final estimates, and make
some deposits to the payroll account. That
kept me busy for the rest of the week and I
was hoping my weekend would be free.

My phone rang and I ran upstairs to
answer it. I had left it in the upstairs office
and I was in the kitchen. Out of breath I said.
"Hello"
"So I guess you are a heart breaker" he
laughed.
"Julian?" I smiled.
"Yes Miss Heartbreaker," he tried to sound
serious.
"What are you talking about?" I asked
confused.
"I haven't heard from you all week," he
replied.
"I was working and I thought you might be
spending the week with Rasheda. Julian I
didn't get any instruction on when to call, but
you could have always called me." I tried to
sound apologetic.
He tried to sound sad. "I just can't believe..."
and before he could get it out he burst out in
laughter.

"You make me sick, I felt bad." I lied because he was a bad actor.

"You are right, I didn't." He got serious. "That sexiness in your voice is causing me to drive faster to get to you. Are you packed and ready to go, I'm headed your way."

"Now," I said in a panic.

"Yes now, I miss you and I wanted to get an early start." He said eagerly.

"Okay, but I have to bring some work with me if we leave today." I was annoyed.

"Can't you get someone else to do it?" he pleaded.

"Hey rich kid, I own a small business and I do all the paper work myself. I'll be ready and I'm bringing some work to do in the car."

"Okay," he said sulking.

Julian arrived at my house ten minutes later. He walked in. "Hey this box was on your doorstep."

I looked up from my living room floor. "How did you get here so fast?" I asked as he handed me the well-known box. I put it to the side.

"I dropped my mom and girl at the airport and headed straight for you. Then I thought I don't want to just pop up on her, so I called and it was that sexy voice." He said groping me as I pushed his hands away.

"You are funny," I said with a smile. He put

my bags in the car and hours we drove for two. I was working and except for the radio and a few jokes at my expense we didn't do a lot of talking on this trip. We made two stops and one for groceries and the other was for gas.

When we got to the cabin he unloaded the car while I held the door. He decided we should have a picnic at the lake. After we ate we sat there for hours holding hands, while enjoying the view and each other's company. We walked back to the cabin before it started to get dark and washed up. I started dinner and he looked for a movie to watch. While the chicken was baking, I curled under him and fell asleep allowing the movie to watch me. He got up and turned the food off after it was done and put it up while I slept. I felt soft kisses on my neck and turned over. Before I could respond I felt his warm kisses between my legs causing me to moan as my dress slid further up. I felt the release of my passion and was ready for him. I tried to keep my cool, but he pulled my panties to the side. While enjoying his perfect pleasure, I let him know how much I enjoyed it with scream of pleasure that came from a place within me I didn't know was there. What this man lacked in waist motion he would more than make up for in perfect pleasure. He picked me up and laid me on the bed. "Forgive me for being so forward, but is it alright if I continue what I started?" He said pulling off my panties. I tried to keep my composure because after that I was drenched within my secret place with anticipation and lust. As he entered me he held me tighter and tighter until he grunted in pleasure. He rolled over and kissed my hand. I lay there thinking am I dreaming, did I just wake up, or is this brother only good for less than two and a half minutes? I lay there thinking, with all that he can't give me more than two minutes? How is he carrying around all that and can't use it but two minutes, I kept thinking. Is that all I get? Is it over? I rose up in bed to get a better view of him and expressed a thought I wanted to fulfill, "I'm on top next time." I rolled over a little annoyed, but without bringing it to his attention and went to sleep. He cuddled up next to me and whispered, "I could fall in love with you baby, you're something else." He kissed the back of my head. "I didn't expect it to be that good, but I'll be ready next time." We both drifted off to sleep. I fell asleep thinking this was a one-time thing and he was thinking he just struck gold. I could sleep a little easier now because he knew that the quick draw and release experience was not acceptable and was going to do better next time.

I awoke first that morning, took a shower, got dressed and started breakfast. By the time he woke up and got dressed breakfast was ready and on the table. He walked into the kitchen kissing me on the back of my neck, with his arms around me. I let him know that breakfast was ready and unlike last night, we are going to eat first.

He replied, "I did eat and I was well nourished and completely satisfied, if I must say so myself." He said squeezing me tighter.

"Well I didn't, so we will eat first and play later." I tried to look serious.

"But I would like to play now," He said as he placed his hands on my thighs while standing behind me.

I bumped him with my butt and walked to the table. "Well I need something that will give me nourishment," I was thinking about satisfaction, but I knew I couldn't go there. It might hurt his quick draw ego.

"Okay, I will be good for twenty minutes and then it's on," he said sitting down.

I was hoping he would last at least half that long in the bed.

Before I could get the dishes in the dishwasher, he was standing in front of me at full attention. "Breakfast is over my dear, now it's time to play." He said rubbing his attention with a big grin.

I looked up and laughed. I started the dishwasher and followed him into the room. I was thinking, okay he was tired last night, but now he's rested and ready to go. I was in for a surprise. We started off like last night. I swirled my tongue around his throbbing manhood until I could feel the throbbing in the back of my throat. Julian pulled me up until he was face to face with my sweet aroma. He enjoyed the sweetness of my juices until I gave in with the arch of my back. Losing control, I called out his name and the moment of the sweetest pleasure was temporarily over. I slowly kissed his forehead and mounted that sexy stallion and with the swirl of my hips, I glided down and back up several times. He screamed giving up his essence as his eyes rolled into the back of his head. He couldn't speak, only inhale as if he was having an asthma attack. I was like, what the... this dude is tripping, so I asked the question. "Are you and your girl having sex and if so how long has it been since you hit it?"

"Yes we have a very healthy relationship." He pulled me closer. "I have never had the pleasure of being with a woman like you." He turned me over and was face first into my burning desire, as if he was starving. Within moments I gave up the last of my essence for the night. He kissed me on the nose and we fell asleep in each other's arms. He slept until morning. I got up and finished my paperwork and made some calls. I ate a sandwich and went back to bed after I finished.

In the wee hours of the morning I awakened to Julian saying, "I didn't want to ruin the moment last night, well yesterday. I am a little embarrassed about both events. Damn you got some cum-quick and I am going to keep coming back for more." He pulled me closer. "Girl I don't know what Kung Fu sex master you been studying with, but ain't no man just leaving that cold turkey." He stuck his finger into my sweet passion and licked my essence off his fingers. Putting on a condom he said, "I'm glad I waited. I would've been messed up waiting for you to call. I would be driving by your house and telling my girl she needs to do it like you." He laughed as he spread my legs. I looked at him and laughed because he was right. I did study and I perfected every skill. My reply was as if I was innocent and didn't know what he was talking about. "What do you mean? There are no schools or training on a natural act." I moaned as he slid inside of me.
"Well I don't know about that. Before my girl I was out there and women flocked to me because of the rumors in our circles. Shit," he grunted with pleasure. "What I want to know

is what did you do to take me from an hour long, break yo' back dude, to a minute man?" He said as he began to pump faster.

"I don't know what you mean Julian." I moaned.

"Yes you do." His thrust became faster. "What did you put in there to make it so warm, moist and sweet?" He gave his last grunt and lay on my chest before he said, "I've never heard of a sweet one before." He said as he maneuvered between my legs. "I have to ask my boys about that." He said as he gently licked my warm sweetness causing me to pull his head further in to the rhythmic movement of my hips. Exploding, I wrapped my legs around him and rose off the bed with silent screams.

Once I caught my breath and he lay next to me I said, "That's natural and my main goal is to please my partner." I looked at him. "Next time use two condoms."

He looked worried, "Do you have a partner at this time?"

"Yes. You just asked me this last week and it's you."

"No I mean are you in any type of relationship that does not include me?" He sat up rubbing his face.

I sat up kissing his back. "No I am not. I've been single for a while by choice."

"Why me," he asked nervously. "I mean, why did I have the pleasure of you last night?" He asked with a puzzled look.

I looked into his eyes. "If memory serves me right, you didn't give me much of a choice." I replied with a smile as I gently caressed his face and kissed his hand. I knew he was wondering if he had been set up, so I quickly changed the subject. "So you love your mama I see, well technically heard" I laughed.

"What do you mean?" he said confused.

I scooted closer to him. "I heard you and your mom in the kitchen last weekend and you were so sweet to her. I can respect a man like that," I said. I started kissing his neck and saw all concern fade. As the concerns faded away, he was putty in my hands again. I remembered he had to call his mother. "Have you called your mother yet?" He jumped up grabbed his phone and called his mother. He was supposed to call her when she landed. Checking in to make sure Rasheda had her approval. The conversation was short and funny because she knew his plan was to get with that respectful girl from last weekend that she might like. Julian turned to me. "Mother told me to tell you good morning," he smiled.

"What?" I was taken aback.

"Mother knew I was with a woman." He laughed. "She said it was unusual because since I've been with Rasheda, I haven't spent quality time with anyone else but her." He pulled me closer. "Now you know you're special, Alisha. Rasheda didn't even get this kind of treatment for six months." He kissed my hand and put on a condom. "I guess she's right. I haven't cheated on her in over a year and a half. When I did sleep with other women it was at a hotel or their house." He pushed me back on the bed. "Pretty lady I don't know what kind of spell you put on me, but I like it and I'm ready for more." Julian eased his wide throbbing love into the depths of my desire. I moaned as the tightness of my love received him. My overflowing passion guided the way as he slowly succumbed to the overflowing love. He increased his drive as he snatched me to the edge of the bed. He searched harder for the sweet essence he craved. Julian eased me on my stomach and pulled me to my knees as he regained control of the search. He squeezed me tighter until he gave up his power and released his essences of pleasure to me. He hid his face between my legs caressing the sweetness of my desire for him until I exploded with passion and giving him the sweet love I had for his experience. Once I gave him the scream, releasing my essence and moan he entered me again and told me not to move. The feeling was so incredible, so I couldn't control myself and with the slight move of my hips the last bit of passion within him was out and he fell into a deep sleep. I knew Julian was mine for as long as I wanted him. This time he lasted almost ten minutes in all and the man had something to work with, but it had a hair trigger.

For the next six months Julian and I would take trips, go on shopping sprees, and sometimes I would secretly accompany him on family trips. The more we explored our passions, his time increased. He got up to fifteen minutes. He was spending less time with Rasheda. He would have completely stopped having sex with her but I wouldn't let him. Seven months into their relationship, Julian wanted to marry Rasheda but her attitude about poor people annoyed him. His grandparents were those people and he had family that was poor. Julian only met her parents once and that was during a dinner at her home and he never saw them again.

About eight months into our relationship while on the family cruise I asked Julian, "When are you going to marry Rasheda." All I received was a stunned look and finally he said, "Baby I love you."
I couldn't look him in his eyes because he would know how hard this was. I had fallen in love with him and wanted to get married, but he belonged to her. "Julian I know you love

me and I know why you're in love with me, but Rasheda is your girl." I looked at him through tears as he raised my head. "She's the one that hangs on your arm and eats with the family and that will grow old with you." I said looking away.

"I don't understand. Are you dumping me or have you found someone else?" He said as he stood up.

"No baby I'm with you and that's all I will ever need or want." I held him to assure him. "I just think it's time for you to see the woman you have and not the girl."

"But baby I see you as my woman and I want to spend the rest of my life with you," he embraced me.

'No not me, Rasheda" I said snatching away.

"But if I marry her, I can't have you." He said pulling me back into his arms.

"She deserves more than what she's getting and I know she has an idea that you are with someone else." I said in his chest as he held me close.

He looked at me. "Alisha you deserve better." Sitting on the bed he said, "Why are you concerned about her needs rather than yours, ours?" Tears rolled down his cheeks.

I ran over to comfort him and pleaded. "Because she was your girl first and you guys look good together." He pulled me close again. "She will give you more fulfillment over time than I ever could." Julian knew I was right, but he didn't want to hear it. Rasheda had changed and his mother loved her.

He stood up and said, "I can't talk to you anymore I have to go to dinner." He raised me up from the floor by my hand. "Do you need anything?"

"No." I said as I unzipped his pants, "but you do." Falling to my knees, I gave Julian a touch of his favorite pleasure as I swirled my tongue over his manhood until it touched the back of my throat. Causing him to want my sweet pleasure I he spread my legs and buried his head until my essence was released. He continued to enjoy the sweetness until I tried to run. He roughly forced his enormous love into my flowing essence like never before. I called out and lost control of my breathing, as did he. Julian moaned out apologies several times while we explored our forbidden pleasure. He reached the peak of his pleasure twenty minutes later. We were out of breath and tired. For the first time I received multiple releases from my new found love. He took a shower and stuffed an object from his pocket into his wallet and ran off to dinner late. That night he asked Rasheda to marry him. He had taken the ring out of his wallet and replaced it with a bigger ring for his true love. We continued our forbidden romance and betrayal for another year or so as I slowly weaned Julian off of me so I could end our forbidden relationship.

It was hard for Julian, but he kept the ring he bought for her in his wallet, so I knew she would always have his heart. I just had his pleasures. That woman worked hard to please a man that couldn't see what he had. Rasheda did have her issue with poor people; which stemmed from growing up without certain wants being obtainable. She didn't realize how much her family sacrificed to give her more. The moral values and standards in their lives came from their unconditional love for her. After I broke Julian's heart, as he had done countless women he began to value her presence. Because of Julian's absence at family functions, Rasheda had intimate conversations with his mother and their relationship blossomed, causing her to value her parents. She learned the purpose of sacrifice in any type of relationship.

Rasheda and Julian married three months after they were engaged and became the proud parents of two beautiful children, Julian and Monica. They started their own finance company and Julian's calls decreased. He had a wife, friend, and partner that would always be by his side. Her supporting him and he was supporting her. I never contacted Julian after he was married, but on Julian and Rasheda's first anniversary I got flowers and an unsigned "Thank You" card.

Julian was fun; he taught me how to play golf, and how to enjoy the moment. I hated to give him up, but Rasheda was a better fit. Julian allowed me to see what fun times, forgiveness, and satisfaction with my mate looked like. This caused me to look at and reevaluate my life; once again in my thoughts I saw pink roses and Tommy. I prayed a prayer that night that would slowly change the rest of my life but not before I bumped my head.

7

My Teacher

Blair, Blair, Blair Earl Macintyre the teacher that taught me I deserved to be pleased. My 6'0" tall math lesson had a beaming smile, the patience of Job, knowledge of ultimate pleasure, and a sex drive lasting for hours. He was the only man I had met whose sex drive was compatible to mine and could hold his own. This man caused a release of my desire every time I heard his voice. In the bed he was everything a married woman secretly wished her man could be and single women dreamed about.

The first time I saw Blair we were ordering curb side at Cooking Cajun. I looked at him and thought "I hope this sexy man who's causing the release of my desire asks for my number." He turned and said, "Hello." That was the opening I needed and I was in there; boy was I wrong for the first time. His phone rang; he grabbed his food and was gone. Something in the pit of my stomach dropped because I knew he was a good lay. I messed up a perfect opportunity ant that caused me to go over my technique in my head. Knowing this would haunt me every time I came here. I thought, man that sucks, well I can't win'em all. I got in my car drove off.

Before I met Blair I was struggling with my walk. I began to ask God to take the desire to be with unavailable men out of my mouth, but not the sex. I was not ready to make a commitment to not have sex until I was married. Blair was going to be that man to cause me to desire more than just sex, but a commitment. At the time I met this man God had started doing a new thing within me. Because of my own desires this relationship was the perfect set-up.

A month later I went back to Cooking Cajun. I looked around before I ordered my food and sat in my car until my order was ready. I sat in my car pondering where I went wrong when suddenly there was a knock, which startled me, on my car window. I looked up and it was Mr. Cause of the Release of my Desire Sexy Man giving me his number. Trying to contain my excitement I replied, "I'm old fashion, so I believe the man should make this first call." I believed a man should call the woman first, thus showing his ability to lead in a situation and seeing where I stand with our first meeting. I don't play games but a call within 24 hours is a good sign and it will cause me to make him a priority, because I was. After I gave him my number he told me he had been there almost every day hoping to see me again. He was about to give up when he looked up and saw my car. He said, "Look I have to go to a meeting so I'll call you later." I coyly smiled and responded. "Okay, that will be fine hope to hear from you soon." Before he left my food was ready, so he picked up my food, paid for it, and handed it to me with that beaming smile. I said, "Thank you." and we drove off.

Within five minutes my phone rang, it was him. I tried to keep it together until I found out where he was, but with panties full of desire it's hard to keep control. He started the interview, which I preferred. "So beautiful lady, how has your day been so far?" he sounded sexy.

"It has been wonderful and yours?" I said smiling.

"I can't complain. I'm going to a meeting for the little league team I coach." He paused as if he wanted a response. "So what do you like to do with your free time?"

"Watch movies and eat," I replied. "What about you?" I thought this conversation was boring.

"I love to eat as well, but for such a small

woman I would have never thought you would love eating. Do you have any kids?"

"No just me. No responsibilities except for my house. What about you?"

He replied with a laugh, "What responsibilities or kids, just kidding. I have about 20 kids during the day, 12-14 during the season, and two adults that I see about."

"Okay we can discuss that topic face to face." I said in a dry tone.

"How about tonight, I don't really know you, but you made an impression on me and I would love to meet for drinks around seven. Wait, do you live close to our meeting spot?"

"No I don't, but we can meet for drinks. Let's meet at Mike's, near Crossroads. I hope you know where that is."

"Yes. I have to go, I just pulled up so I will see you around seven o'clock at Mikes Sports & Wings."

Now I really started to ponder my next move because this man was a teacher, who took care of his parents or college bound kids, and coached kids. That means he has no money and he might live at home with his parents. Or he may have just gone through a divorce and loves kids. "This man seems like a good lay. How should I approach this thing," I thought as I drove home. When I arrived I could see the familiar box on my doorstep. I jumped out of the car, grabbed the box, and walked into the house. I opened the box it was a single pink rose with a card. "You did the right thing. I LOVE YOU!!!" I threw the box. Through tears I screamed "Mikael where are my two roses!" I walked up stairs to change.

I arrived at Mike's early. I was always early, therefore I'm considered reliable and dependable. It's sad that my best qualities resemble a dogs. I grabbed a table in the far corner near the restroom, but far enough to avoid a smell or traffic. I texted him instructions to get to the table and I realized I didn't know his name. He was going to be a few minutes late, but once he arrived he found me. He apologized and properly introduced himself.
"Hello young lady. My name is Blair Earl Macintyre." He shook my hand. "I am a recently divorced teacher that takes care of his parents and I love kids."
"Hi Blair, I'm Alisha a contractor that's never been married and I have no desire to be a mother."
"Okay, you are a very blunt and feisty little woman. Have you ordered yet?"
"No. There's the waitress, excuse me Miss..."

We had a nice four hour conversation, but I was ready to get to the juicy stuff and I hope you are too (readers). That conversation didn't stay at the bar, but ended at his house. He caused the release of my desire remember? And yes, I am going to be whatever you're thinking about me tonight. He led me to the living room while he went to check on his parents. I turned on the TV and watched it until he came back. I made myself comfortable and found a good spot on the sofa. He walked in with two glasses and a bottle of wine. I had to turn him down on the drink and asked for a bottle of water instead. I didn't drink in the company of men so I could keep a sound mind. Do you drink at work, well this was my job. That sounded good, but I don't drink because of that summer day. Blair brought me the water and before I could blink he had attached his tongue between my legs. Now ladies I don't know what you like, but this is my favorite sport as long as he can play the game...and he could. He licked me as if he were starving for my sweet juices. He moaned with each motion as if it gave him as much pleasure to give as I was receiving. After I let out the final moan he rose with a glaze on his face of pure satisfaction and gratefulness. He began to enter me, but I stopped him and made him sit in the chair. I was not about to let this man get the best of me without giving him the best ride of his life. Once seated in the chair I placed the condom on with no hands and rose to straddle his throbbing manhood. With the release of the desire he created. As soon as I slid over the tip, I retreated from it. He grabbed the chair and moaned for me to give him more as I slid over his massive manhood. We both cried out in pleasure. He grabbed me tightly around my waist and placed me on the floor forcing every inch of himself in me, causing me to release my essence. As tears rolled from my eyes the pleasure engulfed my body. I had never felt this type of pleasure in my life. I was whipped for the first time in my life. He had me instead of the other way around. Two hours later he gave me the last of his essence and we fell asleep. Satisfied and exhausted I was content. I awoke an hour later and went home. Ten minutes later he called. "Why did you leave? I wanted to eat some more of that warm and juicy sweet potato pie," he groaned.

"I have an appointment in the morning and I had to get ready." I smiled.

"When can I see you again, because I'm already up just thinking about you." I could hear him moving around.

"What about tonight, but it has to be early. I have church in the morning." I replied.

"I do too. Would you like to go with me? You can be my Sunday breakfast, lunch, dinner, and in between snacks. Girl what the hell you got between your legs, I'm already whipped." He exclaimed.

"Ha-ha dude I'm not falling for that, but I will see you tonight." I continued to laugh.

"As soon as you're free, pack a bag until Monday. I'll order in for today and we can go to church and come back to my house and not leave until Monday." He said.

"What about your parents?" I quickly replied.

"They left yesterday to go on vacation with my sister and won't be back for two weeks."

"Okay, my meeting should be over by noon. I followed you in, so send me your address and I'll call when I'm on my way." I said in a rush.

"Okay, see you later." He slowly replied.

"Wait, I want to know one thing, why Earl?" I blurted out.

"What do you mean?" he asked with a puzzled look.

"With a first name like Blair how did you get Earl for a middle name?" I shamelessly asked.

"My mother's father and my father's grandfather were named Earl. I was the second son so I got the maiden name and namesake." He begrudgingly said.

"Oh, I was just wondering; well I'm at home, see you in a few." I quickly hung up. I knew sex drove me and that was not a desire from God. I was still in a selfish state of rebellion because of my desire for temporary feel good and what it brought.

When I walked in I saw the box I had thrown earlier. I walked over, picked it up, and put the flower and card in the book with the others. I took a shower, set my alarm, and fell asleep. Once my alarm went off I packed a bag and got ready for my meeting. My meeting ended successfully and surprisingly early, so I called Blair. I asked if he needed anything and told him I was on my way. I had to stop by the drug store to pick up some protection. Safe sex is important to me so I got some more plastic wrap as well.

When I pulled into his driveway my phone rang. Blair was calling to tell me to walk in. I walked in to scented candles, a picnic set-up, and a naked Blair holding sparkling apple cider and two glasses. I gave off a laugh and started undressing. I pulled my shirt off to reveal my supple breast. As I removed my bra my nipples perked and were ready for him. As I slid my pants down revealing my thick thighs, I could see in his eyes that they would be his weakness. Before I could remove my panties he had already pulled me down by my tight waist over his awaiting tongue. I struggled to pull my panties down to reveal his warm and juicy sweet potato pie. He caused me to cry out in pleasure instantly and my juices flowed over his face. He whispered, "I can't get enough of you. I don't know why but you do something to me."

"I feel the same way, so stop talking and get to work."

He pulled my legs back over my head and entered me. It was as if he had lunged into a never before felt pleasure. He grabbed my legs and spread them further apart as he thrust himself deeper. Blair caused me to release my essence several times within seconds. With my last release to his surprise he also gave himself up and screamed out from his inner most parts and falling to the floor in exhaustion. I lay across his chest and asked, "Are you okay?" breathing heavy.

"Yes." He paused to breathe. "You just surprised me, so were you tired last night?"

"No I was just holding back so I could give you the full package and I'm not done yet." I said rolling onto the floor.

"You are gonna have to give me a minute. I can't...move. Hell, I'm still cumin." He said jerking.

"Well would you like to eat something?" I asked ready to sit on his face.

"Yes, but I can't move. Damn lil' mama, you need a nickname." He said sitting up to think.

"Oh really, well you can give me one." I smiled closing my eyes.

"Believe me after that I will. Come here and give me a kiss." He rolled over on top of me, but I avoided his kiss. I smiled and got up to put on some clothes.

I washed my hands and went into the kitchen to prepare the food. I warmed up our food, fixed the drinks and set the food up in the kitchen at his little table. When I walked back into the living room he was on the phone. He got up and walked out for a few minutes. When he walked in I asked, "What would you like to watch on TV?"
"The game I was watching before you came in here distracting me." He exclaimed playfully. He put a movie on instead and sat down. Five minutes into the movie his phone rang. He put the phone on vibrate and after two more ignored calls the doorbell rang. I just sat there and pretended as if nothing was happening. I curled up in my spot on the sofa and pretended to fall asleep.

Blair got up to clean up the picnic setup. He blew out the scented candles and gently picked me up and carried me into the bedroom. As soon as he placed me on the bed I said, "Thank you. I didn't feel like getting up."
"Oh you were not asleep. You just wanted this strong man to carry you!" he smiled.
"Are you calling me fat?" I exclaimed with a smile.
"No your lil' sexy ass is perfect. That's your

new name TNT because you come with a big bang in that little package!" he said sitting next to me.

"I like that. I think I might just let you do that." I said smiling at him.

"Girl you got my attention." With that he pulled my legs open and entered me again. For the next two hours and with each cry of passion, we changed positions and created a different moment until there was nothing left to give but rest. I awoke to a ringing phone. As I jumped up to retrieve it I heard voices in the distance. It sounded like it was coming from outside. There was a woman outside yelling at the neighbors. I heard screeching tires as she abruptly sped off by the time I reached the living room. The vibration of Blair's phone startled me. I sat down and realized I am at the house of a man I know nothing about because he made my head spin in circles. I always do recon on a man before I enter his home, car, or make shift dwelling (friend's house or hotel). I looked around, everything was nice and neat, but this was a basement apartment. He lived with his parents. That's why he went upstairs last night to check to see if they were gone, so he would have privacy. I have failed to plan shoot what kind of car does he drive. It doesn't make a difference he's a teacher. Okay Alisha calm down, this dude was worth it because your

legs are still wobbly. I was so addicted to sex I couldn't see the truth. I started pacing the floor and he walked in, "Is everything okay?" "Yes." I stopped pacing. "Why do you ask?" I said looking at my phone.
"I could hear you talking and you sounded like you were panicking. Did someone call and upset you?" He asked walking toward me.
"No. I was trying to work out some figures in my head." I lied with a smile.
"You look worried, are you sure?" He said with concern in his eyes.
I asked, "Would it be ok if I were to leave and come back?"
"Before you do let's sit down and talk." He grabbed my hand and led me to the sofa.

I thought, here comes the lie or the okay I've been caught and I will tell her what she wants to hear so I can get out of this mess. Blair had me sit down and started talking and talking and talking. Man was I wrong; this guy was honest and asked for my forgiveness. Blair let me know he and his wife, Nikkei, separated four months ago because their sex life was almost nonexistent. He was beginning to desire other women, but he refused to cheat on her. They have one daughter and he helped raise Nikkei's nephew; both are in college. He moved in with his parents two months ago when his mom became ill, per his father's request, who still works. Before that he was rooming with a good friend that decided two weeks ago to move back home. Blair said, "I don't want any more kids, but I love to teach and coach little league." Standing up he said, "I almost had an affair with a player's mother. I filed for divorce six months ago, but my wife wanted to work it out, but only going to one counseling session won't work. Nikkei got mad at the counselor because she wanted to be right about everything and not face her faults. The person on the phone, ringing the doorbell, and auguring with the neighbors was Nikkei. She did that because my parents are not home. I just want to apologize for bringing you into this mess."

"I'm not shocked because that's life, but I'm shocked you told me the truth." The conversation lasted until the next day through breakfast and without lunch. I thought how I am supposed to tell my truth. I'm a semi-kept clean-up woman that's addicted to sex. No I was not about to tell him that. I just needed to know if he wanted his wife back. I knew I would have to wean myself off this sexually aware man that pays close attention to detail. My teacher was well educated in the studies of pleasing a woman, which was a characteristic I loved in a man. Over the years I have learned that most men are inept when it comes to pleasing a woman.

"That still doesn't tell me what you think about me," he asked sitting next to me.

"Okay, call me a blonde right now because I don't get it." I said looking puzzled.

"Would you still want to date me?" he questioned with a hopeful smile.

"What about your wife?" I sat back with a questioning look.

"I filed the papers Monday." He said holding my hand.

"Well, how do you feel about cheating on your wife with me?" I said, smiling.

"I'm not cheating. We are separated and in my mind divorced." He said with annoyance.

"Are you sure you want to leave her?" I asked.

"Yes, if there was any confusion you made my decision clear last night." He kissed me on my forehead and traveled to the place that stays moist and ready for him. Before I could take hold of his head, he wrapped his arms around my thighs. As he pulled his favorite delicate dessert closer and begun to caress the sweetness of it with the tip of his tongue. As his desire to taste more grew, his face disappeared into the sweetness of his sweet potato pie. His moaning increased as he devoured the sweetness. The more he indulged, the sweeter it became and his muffled cries grew louder and more intense. I gave in to his demand by allowing my essence to be released. He would not stop. The pleasure was so tremendous that the arch of my back rose up from the oversized chair with my legs wrapped around his head. He turned me over on my knees in the chair as he licked me as he put on a condom. He slowly entered the warm essence of my desire, gripping me tighter. The tighter his grip the faster his hips moved until my head was buried into the cushions of the chair. I began to swivel my hips so as I received I gave. He gripped me tighter and tighter until he called out my name. Falling to his back he said, "Damn TNT you have got to stop doing this to me. I won't have any fluids left if I keep messing with you."

I smiled saying, "Flattery will get you everywhere so stop." I sat up, "What did you have planned today?"

"All I wanted to do was chill at the house, because my money's not looking too good right now." he said it with a pitiful look.

This was the statement that would make me dislike this man forever. The messed up part was he kept saying it throughout the sexlationship. I thought. I know you don't have any money you're a teacher and that was the most underappreciated job in America. My thoughts continued aloud. "But that's not what I asked," I said with an annoyance in my voice.

"I don't know. All I wanted to do was have you today." He said smiling, which annoyed me. "Well what would you like to do?" I asked getting irritated by the moment. "I just told you." He said pulling me closer.

"Okay funny man. What do you like to eat?" I said and sighed after the words fell from my lips.

"I just told you." He said as he kissed my thigh.

He was stepping on that last nerve. I already have an issue with men that make that statement and now he wants to play.

"Okay let's talk and find out more about each other and past relationships." I said pushing him away.

"Do you have a man and if not, am I the only guy you're doing?" he asked pulling me back.

"No and yes," I said standing up. "What's up with your wife and sex and when was the last time you had sex?"

He stood up and wrapped his arms around me. "I don't know, but we only have sex when she wants to and its missionary and it's been a minute." He kissed the back of my neck and squeezed me a little tighter. "What about you?"

"What is a minute?" I turned my head with a frown as I continued. "Are you sure Nikkei wasn't cheating on you?" I tried to move. "It's been a few months."

He loosened his grip as he thought. "I don't think so, but about two days ago I slept with Nikkei." Getting the message he sat down. "Why has it been so long?" He said as I walked toward the window thinking about Julian. I said, "I was waiting for the right one."

He gave a big smile and asked, "So was I the right one?"

I wanted to say dude you're just a rebound for the lost I suffered giving up Julian but I said, "I guess so for the moment because I'm here."

"What do you mean for the moment?" he looked shocked.

I wanted to say because you're broke and married. The broke thing didn't bother me until he said, well I don't have it right now.

"Well you are still married," I said trying to hold back my annoyance for him.

"Have you ever been married?" he asked sitting back.

"No and no I don't want to do that." I said fervently. "Why did you get married and has your wife always had a hang up about sex?" I asked with a frown because I couldn't understand why women got married and stop satisfying their husband.

"I fell in love with the sex first and then Nikkei." He said sitting up thinking. "What do you do for a living and who do you live with?"

"I have a contracting business and own two

houses without a mortgage." I looked at him and thought maybe there's hope. "Do you guys own a home?"

He shook his head. "No we rented a house because she couldn't keep a job. She was always starting something or in the middle of it." He felt self-conscious so he asked, "Did you go to college?

I smiled before I answered, "Yes, I have my masters and I'm working on my PhD now." He looked impressed so I asked, "How far did you go?"

He looked at the floor before he replied, "Just my BS. I got married and started a family right out of school."

I changed the subject, "what do you like to eat?"

"Food," he said with a laugh. I was glad he broke the ice because I was getting bored. I smiled, "so where would you like to eat or have never been, but would like to go?" I asked. "Aerials Delicacy, I've seen the way they change food around its almost acrobatic." I shook my head, but he laughed saying, "I did a play on the name."

I stood up to get dressed. "Okay, go get dressed I know the owner." While he was getting ready I called my friend and got us a table before I took my shower.

While I was in the shower he said, "Oh you got it like that?"

I replied, "Not really, it's just because of my job. I get to meet and help people, so it's who you meet." I did know the right men, because I was a sex therapist on the side. Some men hired me to teach their wives certain skills or council them as a couple.

"Well I'm impressed," he said as he buttoned his shirt.

As I put on my dress I said, "I don't care to impress you or anyone. I live a beautifully blessed life and all I care about are my actions and how I treat others." I said thinking I'm not really being nice to him.

"I didn't mean to offend you." He said holding his hands up in surrender.

"You didn't. I just want you to know who I am and where I stand." I tried to sound polite, but he was getting on my nerves.

"I see now that TNT stands for your whole persona," he laughed.

"Well if you say so," I said rolling my eyes. This dude was getting on my nerves by the minute, but the sex was so good.

"Come on; don't be like that, I was just kidding." He said grabbing me.

I sighed, "Man I'm hungry and it's causing me to be annoyed." Truth is he was getting on my nerves.

Could that statement have irritated me that bad? We talked for four hours the night I met him. I knew then he didn't have any money because I paid for everything, but I still enjoyed him. Maybe I am just hungry because I get mean when I'm ready to eat. As we rode we didn't talk much. We valeted the car and was greeted by my friend Jack, arm in arm he escorted us to our table. Blair's mouth was open as he saw a couple of famous people. He kept tapping me on the shoulder saying, look that's such and such. That was fine until he said, "I'm going over to speak to..."

I smiled at Jack and whispered, "don't do that, please be quiet and don't embarrass me." We sat down and I leaned over. "These people pay for peace when they eat here."

"I pay money to watch them I have a right to get an autograph." He arguably said.

I thought this is it, the sex is not worth it. I put my head in my hands to cover my shame. He reached over and grabbed my hand and kissed it saying, "I was joking with you. I didn't know you were going to take it serious."

I rolled my eyes. "Let's just order." I slowly pulled my hand back. "Do you see anything you like?"

"Yes, but these prices are crazy." He said looking shocked.

"Look I brought you here and I want you to enjoy yourself. Order what you want and forget about the price, because I'm paying to hit that tonight." I smiled thinking about what

I was going to do to him.

"Now that's the lady I fell for in four hours." He said smiling.

"Oh, so it wasn't the sex?" I whispered. He held my hand and said, "No that just sealed the deal." He kissed my fingers and continued speaking. "While you're playing, I was about to buy you a ring tomorrow." We smiled. The waitress came over and took our order when she brought out the starters and drinks. "Do you like it so far," I asked. I told Jack what I wanted as he escorted us in. Like a kid he said, "Yes, this is really nice."

"I'm glad you like it," I said smiling. We enjoyed the rest of our meal and the ride home was much better as we laughed all the way back.

Well as I said before, "An even swap ain't no swindle," so he dropped them drawers when we got back. Every time I had sex with Blair I was sprung all over again. Because I don't want this book to be on the porn shelf I will not go into detail about our three months together. We had a sexlationship because all we ever did was have sex in the six months I spent with him and very little talking.

After three months I had gotten tired of Blair, as usual, but he had been working harder in the bedroom each time. During our first three months Blair and I had some form of sexual encounter at least twice a day and four to five on the weekend. The night before my two week business trip I told Blair I couldn't come over. I had to get this man out of my system.

Blair called me the day I was to come home and asked if we could have dinner, his treat. I couldn't resist because this dude was like crack. I had been out of town for a couple of weeks and needed a fix. As soon as my plane landed that evening I got in my car and headed for Blair. I thought after this I would leave him alone. Blair had filed for divorce when we first met and he was ready for a serious relationship, but I don't do those. As I drove to Blair's house that evening I had a weird feeling in the pit of my stomach. Before I could ponder why, I was distracted by a car driving erratically up the street. I pulled into a drive way but before I could put my car in gear to back out a second car came flying up the street. I rolled my window down so I could hear better and counted to ten before I tried to back. My phone rang, "Hello." It was Blair asking me to drive my car tonight and pick him up at the corner. I was about to make my second turn to get to his street when I saw him walking toward me with a bag. He flagged me down, so I stopped and he got in. As we passed his street I could see blue lights so I asked, "What in the world is going on?" I didn't wait for a reply before continuing. "I almost got hit by two speeding cars and police in your neighborhood, this is unusual. I pray everything is alright."

"It was probably some kids having fun, but some people got into it and my neighbors called the police. That's why I called you because I didn't want you to drive into that mess." He was monotone and looked straight ahead. For some reason I knew he was not telling the truth, but what the heck. It had been a couple of weeks and I needed some. "So where would you like to go?"

He mumbled, "Anywhere but here right now." What?" I asked pretending I didn't hear him. "I want to spend some time with you in a place we can be free." The last weekend I spent over there was ugly because his ex-wife came over and caused a scene. He hid me in the bedroom and calmed the situation down. After that I told him we would get a room for the weekend. Blair was not allowed to come to my house, so we only fooled around at his because of his crazy ex-wife. I don't think he even knows where I live. Only a few select men knew where I lived because I had several stalkers. I didn't want my "special projects" or three month flings' women on my door step. Blair's parents never knew I was there during the week because I always came after nine o'clock and parked my car down the street and Blair would meet me to walk back to his house. There was a separate entrance on the side of the house we used. "What do you mean?" I asked a little puzzled.

"So my baby can scream her little head off." He said leaning over to kiss me. "You are the loud one, always screaming into a pillow." I laughed. "Whatever, let's get a room tonight." He said. I could hear the plea in his words. "Are you okay, because you look a little different?" I said.

"I am good. Are you really hungry, because I want to get a room for the weekend? I want to go to Motel First." He inquired. I had to refocus after that. I playfully said, "Hello, how are you I'm great and how was your day Blair?"

"I'm sorry baby. How are you?" He held my hand. "I'm great, but it was a day."

"I'm good. Are you sure everything is good?" I said looking concerned. "Yes." He smiled but I could tell he wasn't. "Then why is your phone going off like that?" I said pointing to his phone. "My ex is giving me the blues." He looked at his phone. "Wait this is my sister." He started talking in code while he was on the phone with his sister. He told her he would call back. "Everything is going a little crazy." He nervously smiled. We pulled up to the hotel and he said, "Where are we?"

"The hotel, man I was not staying in that crap you suggested."

"But my mon ...." I put my hand over his mouth before he could turn me off. I wanted and needed some. "This is my treat; we haven't seen each other in a couple of weeks." I said slowly removing my hand.

"I had already called ahead for the room and the meal; which would be brought to the room once we've checked in." His phone went off again. "You take care of that while I check us in and once we are in the room turn the phone off."

The bellman unloaded our bags and followed me into the hotel while the valet parked the car. I checked in and texted the room number to Blair. I went up to the room and tipped the bellman. I always carried a bag of cleaning supplies with me to a hotel so I could clean the room, so I started in the bathroom. I pulled the spread and the top sheet back on the bed to make sure the sheets were clean (clean sheets in a hotel/motel have a distinct smell). I sprayed everything down with a disinfectant spray (they rarely change the spread in most hotels or motels so I bring my own). Thirty minutes later there was a knock on the door and I thought it was Blair, but it was the food I had ordered. I tipped room service and closed the door. As I turned around my phone rang. "What room are we in?" Blair asked.

"804. They just brought up the food." I said rushing off the phone. "Okay, I'm on the way up," he said. "Forgive me for being rude."

"I understand, because that's life." It worked out just right because I wanted to eat first. I had no sexual control when it came to Blair. When Blair got to the room he started coughing. "Didn't I tell you to take it easy on that spray the last time, you're gonna kill yourself one day. All that damn disinfectant."

"Shut up and open the terrace doors." I said pointing to the door.

As he walked past he grabbed me around my waist with one arm and with an unusually strong passionate strength he kissed me. "Baby I didn't realize how much I missed you until this very moment." He said through kisses. "I told you flattery will get you everywhere. I've missed you too, you sexy thang you." I smiled as I slapped him on the butt.

We scarfed down enough food to satisfy our stomachs because we were both ready. I stopped eating first and ran and took a shower while he put up the food. Blair was dressed and ready when I came out (had on a condom and was naked). He wanted me in my usual required position, but this time I laid on my back and spread my thick red thighs far enough for him to hear the dinner bell ring. He came running to his sweet potato pie. He ravaged me as if he was starving and this was his first and last meal. I reached my peak faster than ever as I screamed out from the center of my being. This caused him to jump up and thrust himself into me as hard as he could. He had never acted like this before. He caused me to slide further and further into the headboard. Suddenly thrusting faster he screamed out, "Alisha will you marry me?" Because I stay in character I said, "Yes daddy yes!" When I said those words he gave me his essence and passed out. I got up, washed my hands and turned on the TV and ate some more. Twenty minutes later he rolled over got up and went to the bathroom. I had already closed my eyes by this time and the TV was watching me. I felt someone standing over me and opened my eyes to Blair. He was on one knee with a ring. In my mind I thought, what the hell? "Blair what are you doing?" I asked rubbing my eyes.

"This is why I wanted to have dinner with you." He sat on the bed. "Alisha I love you and it took those two weeks for me to realize what I had found." I thought he wasn't in love with me. He was horny and found a woman with a high sex drive that stayed ready at all times, with no need for foreplay and willing to go for hours. That's the truth with some men or most men in my case. They fall in love with my sexual ability or they love to hang out with me, but once a man has sex with me I confuse his emotions. I'm the best twenty percent woman in the world because I will never love you, but I will play the role to perfection. I was once told I was an 80% woman playing the role of a 20% woman and men could see my value and wanted more. "What is that?" I asked squinting.

"A woman that loves God, loves me unconditionally, and is just as if not more beautiful on the inside as she is on the outside." He smiled at me. I thought, dude for the past three months all we've done is screw and I didn't ask details or questions about what's going on in your life, so how could I love you? Guess I'm going to have to pull crazy girl back out to run him off. Wait, think about it Alisha the sex is good and he is a gentleman, any woman would want a man like him. What do you have to lose, go ahead and try it? I held my hand out and said with a smile, "Don't disappoint me." He kissed me on the forehead and jumped in the bed and slid on a condom as he commanded me to mount him. I straddled him and for the next two hours we changed positions until he couldn't hold back anymore. That went on all day Saturday and by Sunday we needed a break. Neither one of us went to church. As soon as he turned his phone on Sunday morning his phone rang, it was his sister, "Mama isn't feeling well and if she doesn't get any better after breakfast I'm going to take her to the hospital."

"How long has she been feeling like that?"

"Since Thursday night, but I talked to her doctor on Friday and he said we should watch her closely for the first week, but if she stops eating bring her in or take he to the hospital." His mom was on a new medication. On the weekends the other siblings would take the parents to their house since their father got sick, but his mother had been at his sister's house for the past few weeks and his father was in the hospital.

"Which hospital?" he asked.

"Where dad is." she replied as he stood up.

"Okay, I was about to get ready to go see him anyway." He said looking out the window as he sat down next to me. "Why did you have to turn off your phone, is crazy Nikkei stalking you again?" I could hear her laughing through the phone. "Why don't you just divorce that woman?" Blair jumped up and walked into the living room and onto the terrace of the suite closing the door. I got up and took a shower. "She got the papers Friday and now she's mad." He said to his sister. "She came over to the house, so I hid." He said looking into the room. "Man, you better get a restraining order." She said becoming serious. "That's not the bad part; while she was there old girl came up." He sat down in the chair and rubbed his head. "Who Alisha?" his sister asked. "No Cheryl." He said abruptly. "Who is that?" she questioned looking puzzled. "The lady you met last week." He said in an annoyed way. "I thought you were seeing Alisha? Wait, isn't that the lady whose son plays on your team?"

"Okay, Alisha went out of town and I was thinking she didn't want me anymore." He said standing up in a distressed tone. "Cheryl called a few months ago and asked if I could help her, so we've been dating on the down low for about six months. I've been having sex with her for the two weeks Alisha was gone." He leaned back on the rail.

"You are stupid. I thought you wanted to marry her." She said disappointed.

"I am, because she said yes." He smiled.

"Does she know you have a wife and a girlfriend?" his sister asked sternly.

"No," he quickly answered. "Why would I tell her? I broke it off with Cheryl and the divorce will be final thirty days after Nikkei signs the paper." He peeked into the room. "Look, it took me sleeping with them to realize what I had in Alisha and she's drama free." He said turning to enjoy the view as he smiled. "We'll see how drama free she is when she finds out

about your wife and girlfriend." She smugly
said. "Wait, why does she think you're
divorced?"

"She saw the papers when we first met and I
thought it was over with Nikkei, but I had to
be sure first." He said looking into the room
before continuing. "I forgot to send them off,
but two weeks ago Nikkei wanted to work it
out and a week later Cheryl wanted more." He
said as if he were searching for support from
his sister. "I have feelings for all of them, but I
want to spend the rest of my life with Alisha."

"Here's some advice from a woman and as
your sister that loves you. Tell her now before
it's too late." She commanded. Walking into
the room he said, "I will, we are going to see
dad today so I might stop by your house."

"Okay, have a good day and be careful." She
said full of concern. "If I take mom I'll call you,
bye."

"You do the same. Thanks for the advice. Love
you, bye." he hung up as he entered the bed
room.

Blair walked into the bedroom with a
strange look on his face. "Are you okay?" I
asked. Blair would later tell me when he
looked at me he felt like it was his duty to
protect me because I look so innocent and
precious. "Yes that was my sister." He said as
he searched through his bag. "My mom isn't

doing too well."

"Is it serious?" I asked putting on my shoes. "I don't know." He said as he retrieved what he had been searching for and walked into the bath room.

He stuck his head out the door saying, "Would you like to go to the hospital with me to visit my dad?" His dad had surgery a little over two weeks ago and would be released next week. "Okay, how's he doing?" I said without looking up. "He says he's ready to come home." Blair laughed. "That means he's fine." I replied with a laugh. Blair took a shower and got ready. After we checked out Blair drove to the hospital. On our way there we stopped and picked up something to eat, he always made me eat breakfast.

When we got to the hospital, his daughter Staci was in the lobby. She ran over and with a big smile as she hugged him, "Hi daddy." It sounded as if she were singing, but the look on her face change once she noticed me. "Mom is up stairs with granddaddy." She said giving me a nasty look. Turning her attention back to him as she continued. "I came down here to get him some chocolate." "Hey precious now you know he doesn't need any chocolate." He said walking off as if I wasn't there. "Who is she?" she questioned. He acted nonchalant as he replied. "She gave me a ride here because my car is messed up." The truth was Nikkei and Cheryl beat his car with a baseball bat and a tire jack after they flattened his tires. While yelling at him they got into an augment and sped off before the police got there. He packed a bag, snuck out of the house, ran up the street, and hid until I picked him up. "Is she that woman mama told me about at your house?" she looked at him in disgust. "No," he said rubbing her back. "That woman was stalking me I broke up with her weeks ago." He lied.

"But I thought you and mom were trying to make it work, so why did you give her divorce papers?" she asked bewildered.

"I love your mom, but I don't think we are right for each other anymore." He said hugging his daughter. "Why because of her or the other one?" she question in anger.

"It's because I want a different life with peace and less arguing." He said looking her eye to eye. "I deserve a chance to chase my dreams and a woman that would support me, but not berate or belittle me." He calmly said.

"But daddy, mama loves you and wants to make it work, give her a chance." She pleaded. "Let's talk later." He said looking around, "did you drive or ride with your mom?"

"I drove because I'm going back to school when I leave." She said anxiously.

"Okay let's talk when you give me a ride home precious." He said kissing her on the forehead. "I'll be up in a minute."

Blair's family didn't care for Nikkei, but tolerated her because of Staci. While Blair was still with her, they kept quiet. Staci turned to get in the elevator as Blair turned and walked over to me. "Baby, please forgive me, but I didn't want to break the news to my daughter like this." He said holding me.
"I understand, she's young and your divorce is just over three months old so don't..." the elevator doors opened and Nikkei stepped out mouth first. "Hell nawl, I know you didn't bring this home wrecking ho up in here while our poor father is lying on his death bed." I knew then why this man wanted out and at that moment so did I. Blair began to walk me toward the door when Nikkei, screaming and cursing, started charging us. Someone called security and Blair turned around and raised his arms to protect me. I thought this witch with a capital B done ran up on the right one, but I knew that was ignorant. It would not only make me look bad, but more importantly my (at the moment) man. I had built a certain character or reputation and fighting was something I was good at, but it could only be used when there were no witnesses and in self-defense. I just kept walking and security

ran in and started to arrest Blair. The front desk clerk let them know he was not the aggressor, nor did he strike her back. He was trying to protect that woman that ran out the door.

I walked back in as the police were pulling up. The police questioned Blair first and let him go see his father. Then they questioned the person at the information desk, Nikkei, and then me. When it was over Nikkei was taken into custody. I went home thinking about what the officer said, "They're still married and he has a girlfriend." Suddenly it hit me; the car speeding away, police at his house, having to drive my car, and picking him up on the street. He was having issues with Nikkei, but why did he lie to me about it. Why would he ask me to marry him if he can't trust me? I drove to his house and left his bag on the front steps. I ignored his first ten calls and then I blocked his number. He began texting me apology after apology, but I deleted each one. I was feeling some kind of way, but couldn't pin point it. It was a feeling that seemed to be familiar, but I had not felt that in a long time. Did I really care about Blair or was I just hurt by another failure? Did his actions affect me or is this how the girl friends or wives feel? Well, I don't like feelings and he is not the one to start with.

His daughter took him home. He explained to her that he wanted to marry me and that it was over between him and Nikkei. He said he would never try to make it work again. He hugged his daughter and told her he would always be there for her, but never would he step foot in that house again. For two hours he tried to contact me, but no response.

Later there was a knock at his door. With a big smile he ran to the door, but his heart sank looking at Cheryl with a teddy bear and a bottle of his favorite liquor. "Come in," he sadly uttered. She made them some drinks and once he got drunk, he took her into the bedroom, covered her face and pretended she was me. It didn't work, so he drank until he passed out broken, replaying in his mind the image of my final glance once I found out the truth.

He awoke in the morning thinking it was all a dream, but when he turned to look at the woman next to him, the contents of everything he swallowed last night came rushing back up. He made it to the bathroom just in time. He stumbled over to his phone and called me, but it went straight to voice mail again. He got dressed and went to work. For two weeks he moped around going to work, drinking himself to sleep. His sister came over to talk to him. "Blair you can't live like this." She talked as she cleaned bottles clothes and glasses up off the floor and table. "But I love her and she won't talk to me" he slurred. "Didn't you say she was a contractor?" His sister walked over to him. "Yes, but that doesn't matter." He fell back and stretched out on the sofa. "Yes it does. I could call her and get her to give me an estimate on the basement," she said with a smile. Blair jumped up and said, "Call her right now."

"You need to give yourself a few days to clear up that drunk smell you got going on. I will call her tomorrow to come over on Saturday and you can have the house." She said holding her nose. "We will fix up a romantic dinner and roses, but use the guest room only. Don't be doing the do all over my house." She said as she dreamed about her own fantasy.

Melinda, Blair's sister, went to work on the plan. She had set up a meeting for 11:30 on Saturday morning and now the romance. Blair's sister had never known her brother to act this way over a woman, so this one had to be different. Most of the women he dates come with a warning label of drama. They bust his windows, key his car, hide in bushes and show up at his job. I never did anything so she knew her house would be safe.

The big day had arrived and like clockwork I was early for her appointment, Blair had warned his sister of that. She was at the door and before I could ring the doorbell it flew open. "Hello Ms. Coleman, come in come in," she said shaking my hand. She cheerfully expressed as she led me toward the basement. "Before I get started, what are you going for?" I asked pulling out a note book. "What do you mean?" she asked looking puzzled. "Is this going to be a work area, a playroom, movie room, or extra living space?" I asked with a smile. "Well let's go down and you tell me how much space I have for each and then I will make a decision." I was thinking she was one of those, her husband wants one thing and she wants another. "Okay, let's go to the future project." Halfway down the stairs she turns around because she heard the phone and runs back upstairs, closing the door. I walked down the stairs, but before I could find the switch I heard a familiar voice. "You are so precious to me that I can't go on without you." I turned on the lights to see Blair on his knees with a single pink rose. I don't really care for flowers, but I love pink. "Please forgive me. All I wanted to do is protect you, but in my selfishness I thought I might lose you and made some poor choices." He stood up walked over to me and grabbed my hand. "Alisha you are such a beautiful woman and your inward beauty gives off such innocence. I felt I had to protect you from my mistakes and poor choices." I knew this Negro was full of it, but he had me at the one knee and pink rose. It showed me that we did have more than sex and we did do more than just have sex. That was the moment my desires started flowing so I started kissing him. He stepped back, "I have to tell you everything."

"No I don't want to hear it until after we have sex, you got any condoms?" I asked.

"Yes, upstairs my sister said we are restricted to one room." He said with excitement in his eyes. I dashed up the stairs. "Which one and what are you waiting for?" I said looking back. "I'm right behind you," Blair said almost knocking me down to get the door open. We ran to the room pulling off our clothes and he went for his sweet potato pie. I pushed him down, put on a condom and mounted him before he could say a word. He gave up his essence unusually quick and returned to his pie. This lasted for only an hour because I had to get back to work. He asked me to put the ring back on that I had mailed back to him and he talked. He told me everything about his wife, girlfriend and the result of dumping them after a two week affair while I was gone. I realized that I would never marry Blair because he needed to be reassured too much and I can't live in that drama. I know everyone has a different love language, but Blair had one that would cause him to cheat. Blair had always told me he would never cheat on me because he never had a relationship like ours with anyone. I will cheat with a man, but I would never cheat on my man and I don't want him to cheat on me. I know it sounds crazy, but I have distain for cheaters.

For the next few weeks we were good because the sex stayed constant, but by the end of the month he had to go. Like I said, he has to be reassured, so by the third week it was easy. I got him to go back to his wife. They are still trying to work it out in separate homes, playing boyfriend and girlfriend, and his wife is still not having sex with him. Blair says he is a better man for knowing me, but he still needs to be reassured. Blair and I had this conversation that year.

Blair asked, "If I divorced my wife would you marry me?"

"I already gave you that answer," I said with a sigh.

"I'm talking about now," he said.

"I can't trust you," I said bluntly.

"Alisha I wouldn't cheat on you." He said as if he was pleading for me to believe him.

"But you did," I said annoyed with him.

"That was different. I didn't think you wanted me anymore and I was horny, so I slept with

Cheryl." He took a deep breath. "I wanted to be sure that I had tried everything with Nikkei before I ended an 18 year relationship.

Blair forced me to cuddle, kiss and do things I hated to do, but he made me better for the next man.

8

My Best Friend

Christian T Ponder III, the preacher and my oldest friend. Tommy was short for his middle name Thomas. He was a fourth generation Preacher/Pastor and was the first man in his family that didn't marry the woman chosen for him. A decision he would regret later. Tommy and I became best friends in elementary school. Our grandmothers were close and we played together almost every day growing up. Christian's wife, Natasha, was the tall slim model type. According to his family she had a jezebel spirit and she was not welcomed as a daughter-in-law. Christian's chosen wife, Lisa Porter, on the other hand was a big part of family gatherings and stayed single waiting to be with Tommy. My friend was a good guy, or should I say a virgin until he met Natasha. She's had his nose wide open until I came back into the picture. The women, except Ma Carrie, in the family pushed Lisa on him until he actually said, "I do to Natasha."

Lisa was a beautiful woman, but she was settled and dressed like she was sixty or going to a funeral after high school. She had a body to die for. I guess that's why they made her dress like that or she was hiding secrets. She was the oldest of the girls, but the second child in her family. Natasha was the youngest of three and the only girl; can you say spoiled and irresponsible? Christian, Thomas, or Tommy is the oldest of four; two girls and two boys. Everyone looked up to him, blames his for his sibling's poor behavior, and has higher expectations for him and he hates it.

Tommy is that guy that will give you his last, loves everyone, and will help anybody. Tommy wanted to travel the world, eat exotic foods, and experience different cultures. That dream was cut short after his senior year and he had to attend an Ivy League school. We were going to attend the same college, but his family had plans for him and I moved away. I never met his wife, nor did I attend the shot gun wedding to save their name. He was forced to marry her quickly in his senior year of college. Tommy was excited at first, but after two years she hated being the wife of a preacher and the thought of being a first lady was out of the question. She started doing her own thing openly, so Tommy was devastated. Almost five years after they had been together,

I finally had quality time to give my best friend.

Tommy's family tolerated me for four reasons: I was not a threat to their plans for Tommy's wife, my grandfather was a preacher, they knew my family, and they watched me grow up. Whenever I went home to visit I would always attend Mount Zion American Methodical Evangelist Church South just to see Tommy. He was not like them and that is why he married Natasha; rebellion. I didn't really care for his family. They were stuck up and felt superior to others. I tolerated them for his sake. I was home for six months for a little peace and rest, so that meant no work or men. Tommy was an extremely intelligent guy, but he would not get his Doctorate; rebellion again. Tommy hated the way his family wanted to control his life, but it was a generational tradition kind of thing. Tommy and Natasha had no children because she refused to be tied down. Natasha was a spoiled little rich kid whose parents were excited about her union with Thomas. He was the opposite of the mess she would bring home. Natasha's father wanted to set him up with a job, but my buddy Thomas refused because. Like past generations, his path was ministry. Natasha went on lavish trips with her mother so much that she stopped having marital relations with Tommy, his words not mine.

I arrived on a Saturday and Tommy's brother Marcus picked me up from the airport and took me to their parents' house. Everyone was there preparing Sunday dinner. It was a tradition for them to prepare dinner as a family and everyone had an assignment. I asked if I was needed anywhere, but I knew the weekly assignments had been given out for the year. I would not be allowed to help, but God forbid if you didn't ask even if you knew the answer was no. Lisa was given the duties of a wife, because Natasha wouldn't do it anyway and she hated Sunday dinner so she would rarely show up.

His mom and grandmother, Ma Carrie, made a fuss over me and hurried back to their assignments. Everyone else gave the normal pleasantries. "Where's Tommy?" I asked looking at Ma Carrie. Lisa corrected me by saying, "If you mean Thomas, he's at the church with Senior." She turned up her nose. Senior was Tommy's grandfather and Tommy was about to be given the okay to Pastor Mount Zion American Methodical Evangelist Church South. His grandfather would retire as Bishop and his father, Christian, would take over that position. They had four churches, east, west, north, and south, Papa was ordained at south but attended north after retirement. A family member always held the position of Pastor, while the senior member held the office of Bishop.

I walked into the living room and Tommy burst through the door screaming, "Lisha where is my Lisha." Once he spotted me he grabbed me and spun me around saying, "I've missed you so much." As he rushed me back outside, Lisa jumped up and rushed to the door exclaiming, "Thomas you didn't tell us what happened today?" Lisa hated my guts because of our relationship and thought I was threat to her. She would try to cause issues between us every time I came home, but Tommy would laugh at her desperate attempts to kill our friendship. Tommy waved her away as we jumped in the car and rushed off.

Ma Carrie said, "Baby you might as well forget it 'cause that boy can't hear nothing when that girl first gets to town." She gave a laugh as if she was the only one that got the joke. She went on while turning up her mouth. "He probably ran off to tell her about that no good wife of his." She smiled as she talked about us. "Them two been like that for years and it ain't gonna stop now."
"But don't you want to know what happen with him today?" Lisa said plopping down in

her chair. "If he was my husband I wouldn't stand for that so call friendship." His mama looked up and asked, "What are you saying sweetie, do you think they are more than friends?" She stared at Lisa until she replied. "Well, look how he was carrying on and acting like he done lost his mind," she replied carefully.

"If I had anything to do with it Alisha would have been his wife 'cause that girl was the only somebody that could tame him." Ma Carrie said with a slight chuckle as she reminisced about the two of us. Lisa rushed out of the room. Tommy's mother called for his sister to go after her. "Mama C, why did you have to say that? You know that girl loves Thomas."

"Honey you know that boy don't want that tired child sitting over there looking old as me." Ma Carrie laughed and looked at Lois so she knew to end the conversation.

Once Tommy got to our spot by the lake he told me everything that happened for the past few months with his wife and cried in my arms. I comforted him as usual and within twenty minutes Tommy was back. "Alisha, how's life treating you out there, why haven't you been home in almost two years?" Quickly he interjected, "The real reason not the answer that just shuts people up?" Tommy knew me well.

"Life is great, everything is going great." I smiled. "I was out of the country with a male friend okay."

"Alisha Coleman I know you are not having martial relations and you're not married?" Tommy said shaking his head. "Well you're not doing the do and you are," I replied with a laugh and punch to his shoulder. He replied with a smile saying, "That is not funny at least not right now." We continued to talk about our life until the sky was black and our hearts were empty, revealing all of our secrets. It was midnight and he had to preach his first sermon as the Shepherd of the flock in the morning, so on the way home he asked if I would sing Senior and Pastor's favorite song with him tomorrow. I agreed and we headed to his house for some much needed rest. This is a man that I loved and I was beginning to hate his wife.

I showered and readied myself for bed, before my eyes closed there was Tommy standing in the doorway with pleading eyes. I motioned him to the bed and he curled up in my arms, like he did when we were kids, and drifted off to sleep. I quickly followed. The knocking on the door startled us. He ran down stairs to Lisa waiting at the door offering him breakfast and a ride to Church. She was so busy trying to appease Tommy, that she didn't see me walk into the kitchen. Lisa was shocked to look up and see me. She expressed her shock and dismay. "Thomas, you are a man of the cloth and married! How could you have allowed your flesh to be tricked by this jezebel?" She pointed at me with her nose turned up.

"What do you mean Sister Lisa?" he said calmly. Her tone softened as she said, "I mean how could you have relations with this harlot?"

"I haven't had any type of relations with her," Tommy said as he fixed his plate.

"Then why is this this woman in your house?" Lisa questioned with her hands on her hips. She stared at me as I laughed. "First of all you will respect my friend and guest because she is more welcomed than you are in my home." Tommy said walking toward her. "Why would I be having sex with Alisha, she's my best friend and she means the world to me." He looked at her for a response.

"That's why you would and I am going to report this matter to the board." She said gathering her belongings. I responded. "Lisa before you leave I just have a few questions for you." I said walking toward her. "Who was it that aborted Billy Hawkins baby in the 9th grade, or helped some guys rape an 11 year old girl, or better yet gave the entire special teams gonorrhea?" I scratched my face and smiled. "I thought that would get your attention, so before your self-righteous behind start calling people out check your closet, shake your own tree, and check the mirror to see where your heart is. I'm sure its revealing the true nature of you." By this time we were face to face. "You see God is going to check your heart and those old lady clothes won't hide the true you from God. It might trick man because they see in the natural or their own holiness instead of the spiritual, with the heart of the One that knows all." I stepped back smiling and grabbed a piece of toast before I said. "Good morning, I will see you at Church later today." Lisa ran out of the door cursing me and Tommy. Tommy looked at me in shock "What just happened, are you alright?"

"I'm fine, go get dressed or you'll be late," I said and he ran upstairs to change.

Tommy came back and grabbed me asking," Was she in on it?"

I pulled away saying, "Tommy I will talk about it later. Please go get dressed." With that line of questioning over we got dressed and headed to the church thirty minutes later.

When Tommy and I were younger we would sing "Amazing Grace" every time we had a bad or rough day. Our parents overheard us singing, so we sang that and many others as a duet until we went to college. On our way to church I started singing "Amazing Grace" and Tommy fell right in with me, but a look of concern was on his face. We arrived at the church with his family waiting on him at the door to the Pastors office. He opened the door and a brand new robe was hanging in front of him. Before he could thank them, Senior rushed everyone out.

We entered the Sanctuary from the front entrance and we were ushered to our seats. Lisa gave me a stare and turned up her nose as she rolled her eyes. Marcus asked, "Why isn't Lisa barging her way into the family space today?" It was as if no one said a word because everyone found a fixture within the Sanctuary to capture their thoughts. When Tommy walked up to the pulpit everyone clapped and some even cheered for joy over the new appointment. The Praise Team began to sing as the choir joined in with them. At the end of the prayer Tommy let the congregation know we would sing the sermonic selection. The Church knew me well and some older members remembered our duets on Sunday mornings and welcomed the surprise. The time came and he instructed the piano player to play "Amazing Grace" and we began to sing. Tommy realized what I was talking about earlier so his compassion and love for me came forth. It was as if he was reminding me God has blessed you and God will never leave or forsake. The funny thing is at that moment I was praying for a restoration and change in my mindset because I knew my life was torn, but I love the life of freedom that I lived; which was fleshly. At that moment my flesh and spirit were at war as I sang. The result of us singing was causing a shift in the atmosphere and people in the congregation became joyful. People were speaking in tongues, prophesying, declaring over others, and just like fire the congregation was slain in the spirit. Never before had our singing caused a revelation, but a change was coming in the lives of everyone within those walls that would also affect the people around them. That was the first Sunday that a traditional word did not come forth from the pulpit. Before we got up to sing, Thomas gave a history lesson on the song and scriptures that supported the grace and mercy of God upon a people that deserved punishment. His last words before we begin to sing, "The grace and mercy of a loving God sent forth a part of his Glory, Jesus. He knows how weak our flesh is, so we could never make it without the love and support of the Father, Son, and Holy Spirit. Now relinquish your selfish ways, repent, and believe as you pray for others. Delight yourself in God while seeking the Kingdom first in your life. Loving one another always, including those unsaved. Don't be envious or jealous and forgive those that hurt you, so that you may be forgiven. It is time to walk like Jesus; living like our sent example Jesus, being ambassadors of God." Tommy has always had a healing and peaceful effect on people when he counseled or preached to them, but this was different. I felt a shift in my spirit and I tried to keep my cool. A new me would emerge one day, but I kept fighting it because of fear.

On the way to Sunday dinner the ride was peaceful and silent. Tommy held my hand to our destination. Before we got out of the car we shed tears. Tommy and I were so close that we didn't have to use words to communicate in times like this, but we always supported each other.

We walked in to Ma Carrie saying, "Here is the dynamic couple of God." She raised her hand to introduce us. "You babies were awesome." Kissing us and patting Tommy on the back. "God used you to bless and be blessed today maybe soon you will see what I see." Tommy's mother Lois said, "Stop it mother so Thomas can bless the food." Tommy's maternal grandfather died before he graduated from high school and his paternal grandmother died after he graduated college.

Senior was the father of Bishop Christian II or Chris. Ma Carrie was Lois's mother. Ma Carrie and I were the only two that ever called Thomas "Tommy" because everyone respected or was scared of her, we were never corrected. Ma Carrie always wanted Tommy and me to get married, but the family had other plans, so she never opened her mouth. Tommy and I thought it was absurd for that to happen. She secretly hoped that Tommy would never marry Lisa, even under pressure, because she knew her heart and secrets.

Tommy blessed the food. This was a tradition passed down for generations. He was the newly appointed Pastor, so he gave the blessing. Only Pastors gave the blessing on Sunday and it was in rotation. Conversations started flowing about the service, daily life, and so forth. Total silence fell over the room after Marcus said, "Where Lisa at and how is it that she's not bombarding her way in as usual to our family dinners?" He looked up and down the table for an answer before saying, "Well I'm glad she's not here and this is the beginning of a new tradition those seated here now." His statement was said with a matter of fact look. Marcus did not care for Lisa, nor did the other siblings or family members. That was a newsflash to me. I knew how Marcus and Tommy felt, but no one else wanted Lisa around, except his mother. Tommy's mother didn't care for me being around now, because I was a distraction for him and she wanted him to marry Lisa. Within the silence Ma Carrie made a joke and the room relaxed and the flow of conversation started again.

When dinner ended Tommy was debriefed by the Elders and Preachers, which they did every Sunday. When a newly appointed Pastor preaches for the first time all of the preachers in the family attend to give a critique, or a good, bad and ugly report. Tommy had done a good job, even though he never preached a word today. A message was given and people were touched, causing them to come to the altar. After Tommy's debriefing everyone said their good byes and the house was beginning to clear.

Ma Carrie called me into a back room and prophesied over me. I had seen in the spirit everything she said, but again I bottled it up and pushed it out of my mind. As soon as she was about to speak, Tommy walked in and gave confirmation to what she had already said. We gave our hugs and good-byes and went to our favorite hangout as kids.

Tommy was excited about today and told me he wanted to divorce his wife. "Alisha, first my wife stopped having sex with me, but now

I don't want to touch her because I don't know who she's been with." He looked up as if to catch a glimpse of a thought. "You told me not to marry her because she was my first and I was whipped." He had a sudden revelation. "Is that why you didn't come to the wedding?"

"No Tommy, you had a last minute shotgun wedding because of a fake pregnancy and I was traveling," I said pushing him." Now that was the first time I've heard of the bride being forced to marry, but the groom is willing." I exclaimed with a chuckle.

"Alisha, that's why I love you," He looked at me. His eyes were saying something so I quickly averted my eyes. "I have never met anyone like you." Tommy held my hand and kissed it. "You know you spoiled it for other women because now they all have to live up to the Alisha code." I pulled my hand away. "Natasha got me drunk and sucked my, well you know. Forgive me for being so graphic, but you were right about her from the beginning and I didn't listen." He held his head down in shame.

"That's because your nose was wide open." I laughed and pushed him to lighten up the mood. "I can understand how a woman can break a man and cause him to make foolish choices." I said lifting his head up. "You are human Pastor, so stop beating yourself up." I said with a smile as I playfully shook his shoulders.

"Alisha," he said with a long pause as if there was more, but the thoughts from his head had not reached his mouth. "Let's go home, it's getting late." He said standing up.

We joked and laughed all the way home. After that first night I stayed in my grandparents' house, well my house. That's where I would stay during my visits. After three days I got a single pink rose every other day until I left. My heart would ache each time I opened the box and saw that single rose.

Tommy and I were inseparable for the next two months and then the phone call. There was a loud banging at my front door, to my surprise it was Tommy and he had been crying. I escorted him into the kitchen and asked if he wanted anything, but he didn't. After a few moments he started pacing and mumbling; I got up and walked into the family room. I knew that is where he would end up once he was ready to talk. After ten or fifteen minutes he came in and sat down next to me saying, "My wife has been rushed to the hospital due to complications." I didn't open my mouth because I knew he was not finished and I figured she was having some type of plastic surgery. "Complications during a medical procedure, A PROCEDURE!" he yelled standing up. "She had a procedure to rid an issue," he begun to pace saying, "What issue you ask? My wife, whom I haven't had relations with in over two years, was aborting another man's child. My wife has been gone for almost six months and I get a phone call to tell me she's in the hospital." He sat down as if he had a revelation. "I know I have to go because it's my duty as her husband and my responsibility as a Man of God but..." After his last statement he took a deep breath and said, "My flight leaves in the morning, will you take me to the airport?"

"Of course I will. Come on lets go back to your house and pack, but I'm driving." I said snatching away his keys and he began to laugh.

We finished packing and put the bags in his car. We went into his man cave to relax as we talked. Before we knew what was happening, Tommy and I were kissing. We had never kissed, not even a peck. He started to caress my body and with each touch my body ignited with passion. Before I knew it I was caressing his manhood with my tongue. As my mouth was filled with his throbbing lust for me, I gently caressed the tip of his love with my tongue. He thrust his desire deeper in to my love and glided further with each thrust, until he exploded with passion. I savored each drop carefully as to not waste anything he gave me. As he pulled me up to gently kiss me once again, we allowed the passion to rise again. He carefully placed me on my back and spread my legs to search for his longing desire. He gently caressed my lips with his tongue until they separated and gave way to the eye of a flowing passion. He caressed me with the tip of his tongue, causing me to cry out his name and plead for more. Tasting every drop of my pleasurable desire, I pulled his head deeper in to my pleading lust. As he got closer, the essence of me became closer. I arched my back, allowing him to have the pure sweetness of my lust that his tongue had been searching for. He slowly guided his rising lust into my pool of desire. We both gave way to a buried passion that had been screaming to be released for years. Our essence mixed, ending in a long awaited dream that finally came true. We lay in each other's arms, but were awakened from our dream by his ringing phone. It was his father-in-law calling to let him know he found a flight and paid for the ticket. Tommy had less than an hour to get to the airport. With barely enough time to wash off our passion, he dashed into the shower, changed, and we were out the door. He was on his way to see about his critically ill wife. I was his partner in this forbidden lust that was hidden for years, taking him to his final destination. This was the first time in our lives we sat in an awkward silence until we said our good byes during his descent from the car.

I called his father to let him know about the departure and why. As soon as I hung up, my phone rang and a familiar voice said, "I love you. I've always been in love with you. You were my first and only choice, never forget that." The voice was gone, nothing but silence until I heard the horn blow for me to move. I drove back to his house and cleaned any evidence of my presence and locked the house up.

Everyone knew she was sleeping around on him, but he refused to let her go until now. That day he faced the reality and essence of love not just given, but received and given back to him.

Tommy was tormented with such guilt because of his lustful actions. When he was with his wife, he pretended she was me until the dreams and pretending got harder to control. His desires and longing for me to be his wife grew. During his first encounter with his wife was, while he was drunk, he called her Lela. That was a name he use for me when he was aroused and needed relief. Natasha would always ask who she was, but he would always say he didn't remember. He would cry out Lela whenever he was about to reach or reached that climatic moment with his wife. Tommy was so ashamed of his actions because she was his wife.

Natasha never wanted to marry Thomas, but her father was about to cut her off and her mother helped her devise a scheme to force Tommy's hand. In college Natasha was a party girl that slept around and her father was tired of supporting her. She met Tommy and lied about her age and started dating him. After two months of dating her plan was ready. She spiked his drink and had sex with him. Natasha was not going to really get pregnant, but she knew his family would not allow him to have a bastard child. Natasha's mother was Lilith, but the father called her Lillie because she was beautiful. She was an older version of Natasha. Her father, Philip, loved Tommy like a son and hated the way his daughter walked all over him and felt a little guilty.

When Tommy got to the airport, Philip was there to pick him up in a limo and took him to the hospital. Tommy was quiet during the ride. All he could think about was me and wishing that he was still with me. Then guilt for his actions, resentment toward his wife, and his love for me started swirling around in his head. Before they arrived Tommy turned to Philip and said, "Once your daughter has fully recovered, I would like to sit down and have a talk with you." Philip already knew what it was about. He knew his daughter was sleeping around and that the baby was not Tommy's. She bragged about not having sex with her husband. Philip patted Tommy on the shoulder and said, "We don't have to talk, I understand and if you need anything I'm here for you." He shook Tommy's hand. "Thank you for coming. I know you didn't have to, but you're a good man. I am a blessed father and man just knowing you."

Immediately Tommy's thoughts' went back to how he betrayed his vows and God by giving in to his desires for me. "I wouldn't call me good," Tommy humbly mumbled more to himself than Philip. When Tommy walked into the room Lilith turned up her nose as did Natasha with an unsettling question. "What are you doing here?" She sat up in bed. "I didn't call you or ask you to come!"

Tommy replied, "I'm glad to see that you are well." He turned toward her mother. "Mother Lilith I see all is well with you."

Her mother said, "Thomas please leave, can't you see your presence is upsetting Natasha." This happened for several days and Tommy would go back to the hotel until the fourth day.

Philip walked in while Tommy was there and Natasha screamed, "Daddy get him out of here. I don't want to hear that Holy God mambo jumbo."

Philip looked at Tommy and patted his back. "Thomas I apologize for my daughter's rude behavior. Come on let's go get some coffee?"

"That would be fine sir, thank you." As the men walked down the hall Natasha's lover rushed by them and entered her room. Philip walked Tommy to the limo and said, "This is the best divorce lawyer in the world and he's waiting on you to get the process started." He said handing him a card. "Thomas my door will forever be open to you, so don't hesitate to use it." Philip reached inside of his pocket. "Here is your plane ticket. My driver will continue to escort you until your departure." With a hand shake the men parted ways. Tommy immediately called Senior and told him everything. "What should I do Senior?" "Thomas, are you sure this is what you want?" Senior was surprised it had lasted so long. "Yes grandfather this is what I want," Tommy said, "Ok I will speak with your father and the board before I make a decision. Keep the faith, I love you Thomas." The fear was gone and Tommy had arrived at the lawyer's office. Tommy took a deep breath and walked into the building and headed for the 19th floor. As he opened the door he was greeted by a cheerful receptionist. "Hello Mr. Ponder, have a seat. Mr. Michaels has been expecting you.

Mr. Christian Ponder is here to see you Mr. Michaels." After five minutes Michaels came to the door and called Tommy back. "Mr. Ponder I have drawn the papers up in your favor. You keep the house and all of the belongings except any family air looms or personal belongings of your wife. You keep the vehicles, the local bank accounts, credit cards that are in your name only, a cash payment of 200,000, and an alimony payment of 10,000 a month until you remarry." Thomas could not comprehend all the information. He thought it was not really over and he had to pay for all the years of suffering with her. Confused Tommy said, "What did you say and how much will I have to pay her?"

Michaels said with a smile, "No Mr. Ponder she is the spouse with the assets after your marriage, so she has to continue to keep up your life style."

"But I'm a simple man." He replied still confused.

"I understand and if you had not been you would be getting more." Tommy sat back in the chair and listened in disbelief. "In two days a moving truck will remove her items from the premises, the house will be deeded into your name paid in full, as well as the vehicles. Do you have any questions or would you like to have someone else look at the divorce decree before you sign it?"

"No I can read over it myself," Tommy said slowly.

"Okay, I will leave you to it." Michaels stood to leave. "Here are some sticky notes for you and if you have any questions, Mark White will assist you or dial 813 for me. Thank you Mr. Ponder." He said shaking his hand.

"Thank you, but call me Thomas." Tommy sat in disbelief and then an unspeakable joy fell over him as he thought, "I can't wait to get home to surprise Alisha with the news." Tommy sat down and looked at the papers. "Okay slow down, the final decree will not happen for 30 days." Tommy signed the papers and headed for the awaiting limo.

While at home I had packed and said my good byes. Marcus took me to the airport. Less than two hours later Marcus picked Tommy up from the airport. He told Marcus. "Take me straight to Alisha's house."

"Okay which one?" Marcus said.

"Take me to her grandmother's house, because I want to surprise her" Tommy said overly excited.

"Okay, but she's gone." Marcus said shifting the car into gear.

"Is she at our house?" Tommy said with sadness.

"No I mean she went back home, her plane just left." Marcus said looking up.

"What. she's gone, but I..." Tommy silently sank down in his seat. His thoughts began swirling around in his head. Is she upset with me after all these years, did I take advantage of her the other night, was she reliving the pain, did I lose my friend forever. God help me, help us, help her! "Nooooooo!" he screamed out. Marcus jumped, "Warn me the next time you want to yell out like that. Where do you need to go because your car is at Mama C's?" Everyone else called Ma Carrie Mama C. Tommy and I call her Ma Carrie because when I was little I thought that my Grams was saying Ma Carrie, but she was saying Ms. Carrie and it stuck. When they arrived Tommy walked into Ma Carrie's room and said, "She's gone. I think I've lost her and I'm finally free." Ma Carrie hugged him and they prayed.

While waiting to board the flight my phone rang, it was Ma Carrie. "Alisha baby I couldn't say this in front of everybody, but Tommy loves you. That boy has loved you and has always wanted to be with you, but he was scared. After all that happened to you years ago he felt guilty because he couldn't protect you and he holds that guilt in his heart. You became a different person and wouldn't let anybody in child. He was just so happy to have a piece of you, so if being your best friend was as good as he was going to get, he gladly accepted it. I guess he just became satisfied with a piece of you, which was better than none of you. Honey that boy wants more and both of you deserve it. You don't have to say a word, but don't give up on him and take that peace. I'll keep praying for both of you and know that Mama C will always love you." The phone was silent. I tried to keep my composure and throw the thoughts of my past and purposed failures one after the other out of my mind. For the first time I thought, why do I set myself up to fail? In a way I knew it is unhealthy with these unavailable men and go nowhere relationships? Before I could ponder my own thoughts I looked up in to the eyes of Brice Chauncey McNabb asking, "Are you okay?" I had no idea who he was or what to say at first because he was so beautiful. When I came back to myself I said, "Yes." Another trap was being set to distract me. "Well the plane is boarding and you seemed to be in another world." I purchased a ticket and had no idea of where I was going, but I was running as usual. "I just left my home town so I was thinking about old times and something that I would never get back." I said with a chuckle.

"I know that feeling," he smiled, "as a matter of fact we are in the same boat." He grabbed my carry on and talked as we boarded the plane. Brice made his way to me during the flight and we talked for the entire two hours. He told me he was having problems with his girlfriend without directly telling me, so we made plans to meet at his hotel for drinks and he would get me a separate room.

9

My One Week Stand

Brice Chauncey McNabb, the confused jock (quarterback) that fears what others may say about his Puerto Rican fiancé. Brice grew up in a small town trailer park village. He was an awesome football player and a natural as a quarterback. This allowed him to have the best education and he took full advantage of it. Brice was intelligent but insecure, so he only took opportunities that were readily available to him. Brice had a degree in communications, with a minor in engineering and a Masters in Mechanical Engineering. He loved talking and building things. I met Brice on a flight which was supposed to be home after a devastating revelation. I thought he would be the perfect project to take my mind off of Tommy. Brice was intelligent and interesting. He loved working with his hands. He was intrigued with the fact that I had the ability to build. I could tell Brice was arrogant and conceited, but insecure because I smelled it dripping off his every word. This man was making my stomach turn and I was wondering why. What was happening to me?

Okay Alisha, shake it off and keep your head in the game.

Brice and I met at a hotel, ordered room service and had sex. After we were done I retired to my room. Okay, I said it like that because have you ever had sex with a man that looks at himself in the mirror as he is doing the do; that's Brice. He was an okay guy just stuck on himself and he reminded me of a song by Al B Sure. The whole time we had sex all I could hear was "I can tell you how I feel about you night and day" and I was singing the chorus ohohooh ohoh. This was a struggle because after he left I was thinking about what happened with Tommy and then if Mikael would ever come back and changing my life to completely serve God. I was in a lukewarm place and God was about to spit me out. My phone rang and it was Tommy, so I ignored it. I couldn't take hearing about his wife at that moment.

Two hours later there was a knock on my door. "Who is it?"
"Room service," I opened the door, Brice was standing there with roses and a huge 'I'm Sorry' teddy bear.
"What is this for?" I laughed.
"You didn't enjoy yourself and unlike most women that fake it, you didn't." He laughed aloud and said, "Hell, you called me out.

When I looked into your eyes I saw
disappointment and shame. That was a gut
punch and I wanted to ask if we could try it
again please?" He said pouting.
"Come in here." I expressed my joy by
playfully pulling him into the room. I was glad
I did because for the next few moments all I
did was think about pleasing Brice. Even
better Brice would be a better lover to his girl
and start getting some self-esteem. I am so
vain that I always have to be better than the
man I'm with and I hope he has those same
characteristics. Brice was tit for tat and we
were exhausted, but he stayed in there in
between saying, "don't move and be still or I'm
about to... okay you can move now," so he
wouldn't have an orgasm.

After our pause and start session, Brice
ordered room service. We ate and he fell
asleep. I went out to the terrace and read
some of the text messages Tommy sent before
that night. Everything else I deleted. I was
wrong for going that far with Tommy, he was
my friend and I loved him more than anything
on earth. As I gazed up at the stars I said a
prayer for his marriage and asked for
forgiveness. Tommy was the only man I
allowed to get that close to me and now I have
destroyed it. I was too scared to hear what he
had to say, so I would delete or erase the

messages. When I looked up Brice was standing behind me looking up at the stars. "It's a beautiful night."

"Yes it is." I said giving him my full attention before saying. "Are you thinking about Eva?"

"Yes, I miss her." He said stepping out onto the balcony. "She dumped me a few days ago." He sighed and leaned on the railing. "That's why I came here for a week to get my mind right."

"What happened?" I said before I caught myself, "If that's not being too personal."

"No," he turned toward me. "She dumped me Sunday. She said I was ashamed of her."

"Well are you?" I asked.

"No!" he turned back around. "It's just that the area I grew up in had a lot of Hispanic people and the guys would treat them bad."

"So what does that have to do with you?" I asked puzzled.

"Well my brother dated a girl named Maria and they beat him pretty bad. Maria and her family had to move away. I fear what my fans might say," he sighed as if he were defeated.

"Your fans, 'F' your fans," I said standing up. "She is a person and not a thing or something to hide. Whoever did that to your brother is sick. Two things I hate are liars and racists. They are weak cowards that can't do anything unless they are in a pack like animals or the other person is smaller and weaker." I said leaning next to him.

Well my mom warned us not to date outside of our race after that. She thought we might get attacked or something." He said standing up looking for approval.

"So your mom knows about her, right?" I looked him in the eye. "Did you tell Eva about your brother?"

"No, I would not want to scare her," he said shamefully.

"Tell her, I'm sure she's had to deal with a lot of that," I reassured him.

"But she won't answer my calls," he said throwing his hands up.

"That's why I got the bear huh?" I laughed.

"Yes, I wish it was that easy," he smiled

"You're going to be here this entire week right, so do you really want to keep having sex with me?" I asked.

"Yes and hell yeah!" he exclaimed.

"But you're paying for this room." I said.

"Hell yeah, I can't be seen staying in a room with you and if I can stay in that thang for a week Ima go for it." He cheerfully picked me up.

"Let's make a plan to get your Eva back." I smiled. I thought, since I lost my friend maybe I can help someone else mend their relationship.

Brice wrote down everything she loved to eat, her favorite color, and her work schedule. Brice talked about her likes, dislikes, and everything in-between. When we finished my room looked like a marketing board room. My phone rang, but I ignored the call again. Brice looked at me "Why are you helping me mend my life, but you won't fix your own?" I was taken aback. "What are you talking about?" "That guy has called you at least thirty times since I met you and you won't answer, respond, or check his messages. You just look at your phone, sigh, and stare out into an empty space as if you lost your best friend." "I made a mistake and had sex with my best friend. He's the only man I love and he's married. The bad thing is once I have sex with a man after three months I push him away." I blurted out before I realized it, but I regained my composure. "Why?" he asked picking up my phone. "I mean, why push them away?" "It's a long story as to why, but I become detached. I can't allow myself to ever love or trust a man." After I said it I thought, what is wrong with you this is business.

"That's fucked up because you are such a caring and compassionate person. Living like that is a waste of such a beautiful woman and your extraordinary talent." He smiled.

I chuckled. "Thank you, but that was lost as a child and it's too late to change."

"I know we are sinning, but you prayed with me about my future and my family, hell you even prayed for those knuckle headed folk in this world. That means you have a faith that is above my natural understanding. If you have faith that God will help them, why is it that you don't believe He will help you?" He shouted at me. I had regained my focus so I said, "Can we get back to you now?"

He sat on the bed and said. "Yes. But I was just saying have faith in God for you and not just everybody else. Ok what's next?" Brice had given confirmation on what God has been dealing with me on and I didn't want to face it. By the time we finished planning, praying, and fellowshipping our week was up and the plan was ready and without sex.

I took an idea from a man that caused me to want a normal relationship.

"Okay Brice, starting tomorrow I want you to send her favorite color to her in an assortment of flowers. The card should be personal but don't put your name on it. Send her a single rose or her favorite flower in her favorite color to her house twice a day. Send it with the personal card. Twice a week send her favorite color in flowers to her office and the personal card." I talked as I wrote the plan.

"What do you mean by personal?" he said confused.

"When you look at her what do you see, what made you fall in love with her, or what makes your heart leap when you think about her?" I asked.

"I love the way her eyes twinkle when she sees me." He smiled.

"Stop, this is not about you Mr. Vain and Selfish. This moment is about her, so stop at: I love the way your eyes twinkle when you're happy."

"Can I call you before I write on the card?" he said desperately but smiling.

"Yes Brice. If she is still ignoring you, step it up. The next week do the same things, but this time send her favorite flowers in her favorite color with a card describing the most memorable moments of your relationship with a single flower. Don't send anything that references sex." I said holding up my hand and shaking my head.

He said, "but what if she doesn't respond?"

"If she doesn't respond the first week she's really upset with you, but after the second week if you don't get a response she never loved you." I started writing again. "Once she responds your first date should be at your house with your family. Like a big family celebration."

"My family can be embarrassing," he laughed.

"It doesn't matter. Before you go to bed tonight order those flowers and call your family starting with your mom and tell them about her. Tell your mom everything and tell everyone else you want to marry her and would like to invite them to meet her," I said as I put the final note in his book.

"But, what if they won't come to the celebration?"

"Tell Eva what happened as a child and why your family feels the way they do over a private but romantic dinner." As I was talking I got an idea. "If some are willing to meet her, invite the few but let her meet them after the dinner. If your mom comes alone have a private dinner with just the three of you." I looked up and Brice had a confused look on his face. "Yes Brice, you can call me, but I am writing everything down step-by-step." I said with a smile.

"Thanks Alisha, but tell me why I can't talk about sex?"

"Because the average woman has issues with her sexuality and doesn't understand that men are visual creatures. Sex is their motivation, just like cuddling and remembering important dates are a woman's." I knew it was deeper than that because sex is a beautiful thing that should be shared in a marriage only, but I was so off I gave up on that reality.

"Why did you turn your nose up as you said that?"

"Because if women would respect, admire, and give it up to their husbands the way he likes it on a regular basis, there would be no need for me." I shook my head.

"But men love women like you because all you want to do is screw and walk away." He looked serious. "Being with you is almost like being with me because you knew everything I wanted and I didn't say a word. You forced me to step it up because you didn't fake it and most of all you fuck extremely well...where was I going, oh yeah. You screw with no insecurities or need for confirmation. I didn't have to hold you or tell you anything. You enjoyed pleasing me, which made me want to please you more. Most of the women I screw are trying to be my woman or my wife. You are not like other women, so you screw and move on without commitment or attachment. Then you try to help a man mend his relationship. Ain't no other woman doing that, they want the man for themselves." He shook his head. "Alisha you are a rare gem and there is a very lucky man out there waiting on you. It's your turn to be as pleased just like the men you deal with."

"How, did you know that about me?" I said feeling exposed.

"Because I'm a good judge of character and you have a good heart and, even though it's been damaged, you want to help others.

Granted it's a little weird. Actually its fucked up the way you do it, but it's your way and if it works for you that's good." Brice grabbed my hands and leaned forward to kiss my forehead. "Alisha a woman like you deservers so much more and I ask that you allow yourself a forever after." He started getting ready to catch his flight home.

That day I decided to allow God to guide me so I stopped having sex or dating until God revealed me to me.

10

My Beginning To The End

Malcolm Diablo Maldad was my first in
many things. I met Malcolm when I was hired
to do a special project with his company. He
fit most of my requirements and he was 6'4'
so the tall part was good. But he had a
protruding belly which meant he was out of
shape, but there was something about him.
Malcolm has three siblings and was raised in
the Midwest, but moved to attend college. I
met Malcolm on a Tuesday morning because
he was assigned as my contact during the
remodeling project. We worked together well.
He would take me out for lunch during the
day and in the evening with his friends.
Malcolm had a wife, Lealtà, he said he didn't
cheat on her, so that meant he was safe. I
believe what people tell me until they show me
different. Malcolm was charming and a
gentleman. We worked long hours the last two
months of the project and I began to notice
him as a man. By this time I had gone without
any type of sexual contact for over two years
and he started to affect me. Malcolm didn't

wear his ring, so I had to think of a ways to stay away from him until the project was over.

I was asked to do a second remodeling project with my crew, but it was not with Malcolm and I was glad. He saw me on the job again and asked if I would hang out with him and some friends. I loved hanging out with him and his friends. Malcolm and his co-workers hung hard and my non-drinking behind hung with them, even though they teased me about not drinking. This time would be different because it was at his house. When I got there I would find out his wife was not at home.

I went to Malcolm's house that evening with the impression that he had other people there. He lived in the Arboles Montaña subdivision. When I pulled up I called, "Hey Malcolm I'm at 5300 Arboles Trace, is that the correct address because I don't see any cars?"
"Yes, a couple of people had to work late, but they're on the way. Come on in the door is open."
"Okay, I'm parking now." I parked on the street of his house because I didn't want to be trapped in the driveway. I walked up the driveway and into his house. I thought for a man at home alone he lived pretty well. "Hey I'm glad you made it, but if one more person calls and cancels it's just you and me." He

said sipping on a drink.

"Well I'm going to play a little pool until they get here." I said pointing downstairs towards his pool table.

"Cool, I would love to show an amateur how to do it." We walked down stairs.

"Dude I dated a pool shark and he taught me some skills." I said with a sly grin.

"Put your money where your mouth is." Malcolm said as he took another sip.

Malcolm and I were having so much fun that I never realized how late it was or that no one showed up.

"Hey try this, you'll like it." I took a sip and he was right.

"This is good." I looked at him sideways handing him the drink. "Is alcohol in it?"

"No." He said and pushed the drink back towards me. After three sips my head started spinning.

"Did you put something in my drink?" Malcolm knew I didn't drink, but he kept trying to get me to try his drinks that tasted like it was a non-alcoholic tasting concoction. I guess, unknowingly I gave in. Tonight would be one that I would come to regret in a few months.

"If you can't drive, you can stay here with me." I was attracted to Malcolm so I knew I couldn't stay, but I was not thinking straight.

"I need to sit down." I said stumbling over

nothing.

"Come on I'll help you." Malcolm helped me to the smaller sofa in his living room, as I lay back he sat down next to me. "Are you okay, you want some water?"

"No I just want to close my eyes for a few minutes and then I'll leave." Malcolm would always brag about being a patient man because sooner or later he would get what he wanted and tonight that would be me.

"Are you comfortable?" he asked pulling a blanket over me.

"I'm good." I retorted as I turned to get comfortable. "I just need a blanket." I was so out of it, but he played along.

"I'll bring you one and I have a t-shirt you can put on too." He said as he stood up.

"Thanks," I said covering myself with the blanket I already had but didn't realize it.

I thought because he was such a tall man his shirt would be like a dress on my 5 foot 130 pound frame. Not thinking the t-shirt wouldn't provide any protection while I slept. "Where can I change?" I said trying to stand-up. The alcohol had caused me to lose all sense of precaution and now he had me where he wanted me. I got up and stumbled to the bathroom. After I changed I sat back down on the sofa and covered myself with the blanket. Malcolm came back into the living room, sat down next to me and turned on the TV. I hadn't noticed that he had changed. I lay back on the sofa and stretched out. Malcolm started massaging my feet. In my head I was saying stop, but my mouth never relayed the message and I drifted off to sleep. In my dreams I felt soft kisses on my neck. I opened my eyes with a moan. "Malcolm you're married, stop." I slurred trying to push him off me.

"I'm a very patient man and I'm willing to wait, but in the end you will cum." He kissed me on my neck. I don't like to mix business with pleasure, but this man was making it hard. I closed my eyes again.

Now I thought Blair, the math teacher, was the best I ever had and couldn't do better. We would entertain several different positions while he enjoyed the sweetness of my pleasure. But Mr. Malcolm, with his three positions, was about to teach me something the teacher never could. Between my flexibility and his skill level, that protruding belly became a non-issue.

I awakened to soft kisses on my inner thigh. Before I could respond Malcolm had emerged his tongue deep into the sweetness of a forbidden and lustful pleasure. I had never felt that level of sensation before causing me to give in to the beautiful pleasure. This man knew how to give a woman what she desired and most of all how to get her there fast. As I pulled him closer I had given myself up to his pleasure. Little did I know how much I was about to give this man, all he needed was an opening. Malcolm picked me up and carried me into his bedroom. He laid me on his bed and once I felt his throbbing passion, mixed with the essence I had already given him, I cried out in pleasure gripping him tighter and tighter with each invigorating thrust. As the intensity of his movement grew, my cries increased. His name echoed in my ears as the words bounced off the walls. With every moan he gave in the crease of my neck to give it to him, I would release my essence to him over and over until he fell over panting for rest. Once he rolled over I could see the evidence of a lustful gripping passion. Evidence I had never left on a man before. That night we saw the sun, moon and the stars. The next morning I got up early and went home to change for work. My phone rang, "Hello" I answered.

"Hey Alisha, I hope you enjoyed yourself" I could hear him smiling.

"Yes I did," I smiled.

"You kept trying to hold back on releasing." He sounded serious.

"No I didn't," I said coyly.

"No, you couldn't once I told you to give it to

me. You surprised me because you released so hard and strong. Hey you put a lot of scratches on me too."

"I told you it's been over two years, so forgive me I've never left marks before." I said a little embarrassed.

"I want you to spend the next two nights with me," he said.

"What about your wife?" I questioned.

"Don't worry about that, you just worry about being pleased." He commanded.

Lealtà took a lot of business trips and visited her parents often because they stayed in Malcolm and Lealtà's house in the Midwest. Lealtà's oldest daughter from a previous marriage lived in the house with them. Malcolm and Lealtà would float from state to state depending on their job requirements, but their home was in the Midwest.

When I got home I picked up the white box and threw it in the corner. After last night I was unconcerned with its contents or the card. Before that night I would always put the pink rose and card in a scrap book, marking the page with the date and time I received it. From that day on every time I saw Malcolm at work he smiled at me while I avoided his glance. Around lunch I received a text. "I hope you packed a bag because ima tear dat ass up."

We spent the next few nights after work in bed and only got up for two reasons, water and the restroom. Malcolm and Lealtà went on a two week vacation a month later. That following week he went on a business trip. We talked until his battery died while he drove to pick her up. He tried to call once a day, but texted me several times about how much he missed me and couldn't wait to get back. Malcolm called me every time he could sneak away from Lealtà.

During Malcolm's first week back we had sex for five to six hours every night and enjoyed each other again before going to work. We couldn't get enough of each other. Every evening consisted of us taking a shower and hopping into the bed. We would talk, have sex, talk and have sex until the wee hours of the night. On Malcolm's first night back we had dinner at my favorite spot. That first night back in bed he told me his secrets and by the third night I knew his deepest darkest secrets. That Friday the alarm went off for work, so we got up and got ready as usual. When I walked into the room Malcolm was sitting on the bed. "Baby, I'm tired and I have to meet my wife today. I don't think I'm going in. Do you have to go in today?" He said with pleading eyes.

"Let me call the foreman." I turned over and

had a short conversation with the foreman. "No I don't." I smiled.

"Good, open up. I want to take my time and taste every part of you," so he slid to the floor. "Alisha I love tasting you." He moaned.

"I love the waaaa..." Before I could finish he had pulled my legs up and embraced every part of me until his tongue was satisfied. He pulled me closer to the edge of the bed and enjoyed the delicate sweetness of my desire. I released the source of my sweetness, engulfing him with my full essence as he enjoyed the lingering flavor. I cried out from the pit of my belly as he caused me to convulse in pleasure. I fell to the floor as he retired to his side of the bed. He turned over to go back to sleep. Before he could close his eyes I rose to my knees, but he stopped me. "Baby I don't like that, so you're wasting your time." With his hand on my forehead I smiled and said, "I'm the best."

"I've had friends tell me about women that could, but it's never good." He said shaking his head.

"Can I try?" I pleaded.

"Yeah, but it's not gonna work or be good." I he leaned back and dropped some warming gel on my tongue. I slowly massaged the thickness of his love until the fullness of his love reached the back of my throat. When I swallowed he screamed out. "Muthfuka what in the hell are you doing to me!" He beat the side of the bed as I continued to massage his swollen pleasure until I could no longer hear the echoes of his screams bouncing off the walls. Malcolm filled me with the pleasure of his essence. "What the hell was that?" He asked as he pulled me toward him for a passionate kiss. "My difference," I whispered in his ear as I lay beside him.

"Alisha I love you. Baby I wish I could be with you forever." I smiled as he wrapped his arms around me. We slept until his phone went off. Groggy Malcolm answered the phone. "Hello, I over slept." Malcolm pulled the clock closer and sat up. "Okay, Lealtà I'm getting ready now." They were supposed to meet up at a couple's retreat for the weekend. I knew to be quiet until he got off the phone, so as soon as he hung up I rolled over. "Is everything okay?" I said rubbing his chest.

"Yes my wife has been calling for two hours." He said getting up.

"Two hours, how long have we been asleep?" I said jumping up.

"Four hours. Shit I have ten missed calls!" He exclaimed, While looking at his phone.

"Dang I guess we wore each other out." I laughed slipping on my clothes. "I thought you were leaving before lunch to meet her." I said kissing his chest.

"But it's almost three now and it's a three

hour drive." Malcolm finished packing as I continued to dress. Malcolm pulled me close so he could kiss me before we went our separate ways.

On my drive home I began to ponder my relationships, thinking about love and the things I wanted. As I pulled into my driveway I could see the white box, but it seemed bigger than usual. I got out of the car and for the first time I prayed, "Please don't be two." I shocked myself when I heard the words fall from my lips. Am I willing to give up all hope to be with Malcolm? I picked up the box and walked in to my house and the phone rang. "Baby I miss you." He said sadly.
"I miss you too." I said pouting.
"I won't be home until Tuesday because she wants me to go with her to see her parents." He said annoyed.
"Okay, I hope you have fun." I said with a sigh.
"I'll try, but I already miss you and I'm still tired." He laughed.
"I wish I was in your arms." I pouted again.
"Alisha, I don't know what you've done to me, but I feel like we've been together for years." Malcolm said slowly and a bit shocked.
I began to smile, "I was getting a little worried because I feel the same way."
"Alisha, I believe I've fallen in love with you."

He announced suddenly.

"I love you too Malcolm," I said with excitement.

"You have my heart and in there you will be my wife." He promised.

"I've never believed in this, but I believe you're my soul mate." I said with hope and confidence.

"I am and we will forever be together," he agreed before pausing. "I'm sleepy and need to focus on the road."

"Okay bye," I sadly said.

I took a shower, brushed my teeth and fixed my hair before I lay down. Within minutes my phone rang, "Hello" I said still sleepy.

"Hey Lisha," he said all excited.

"Tommy?" I said. Not fully awake to catch the joyful voice.

"Yes it's me, come down stairs." He said impatiently.

"What?" I asked still confused.

"Go down stairs but stay on the phone." He instructed.

"Okay," I got up and walked down stairs.

"Tommy I'm down stairs." I said looking around.

"Open the door, I sent you something." I heard him smiling through the phone. I unlocked the door, but remembered the box. It was

from Tommy, so I turned to get the box and
someone grabbed me from behind.
"Surprise," he exclaimed.
I screamed, "Tommy, oh my god Tommy." I
turned around and hugged him.
"Alisha, I've missed you." He said picking me
up and kissing me. "I'm sorry for anything I
did to hurt or take advantage of you." He said
as his eyes we searching for a response.
"Tommy you've never hurt me, you could
never do that." I hugged him again.
"Let me take you out to eat." He paused and
looked at me before asking, "Why are you in
your robe?"
"It's a long story." I blushed before turning my
focus back on him. "Tell me, how is
everything?"
"Ma Carrie sends her love and my mom keeps
trying to play match maker with me and Lisa."
He laughed.
"I talked to her yesterday and she didn't tell
me you were coming." I said pushing his
shoulder.
"It was top secret." He laughed. Suddenly his
facial expression changed. "I have to ask you
a question and be honest with me."
"Okay Tommy, what is it." I asked as we sat
down.
"Was it Lisa?" his eyes pleaded for an answer.
"What are you talking about?" I asked
standing up to avoid his eyes. I knew what he

was asking me, but I didn't want to talk about it.

"Never mind I should've never brought it up." Tommy looked at me and gave me a big hug. "I came to spend the weekend with you and ask your opinion." He said leading me back to the sofa.

"Yes you can stay and what is it," I asked.

"Where's your boyfriend?" he asked looking around.

"He's out of town." Malcolm and I made a decision not to have sex with anyone else. I knew if Tommy thought I was single, we might end up in the bed.

"I'm having relations with Lisa." He said in a muffled voice.

"What?" I said shocked as anger crept up in my eyes.

"I've been having sex with Lisa and she wants to get married." He said with sadness.

"You are having sex outside of your marriage." I said in shock. "Didn't you learn your lesson the last time?" I said getting up.

"Yes I tie up the condom and flush it." He exclaimed. I thought about my best friend with the epitome of evil and I cringed. "Does that bother you?" He asked as he saw my eyes flicker with disdain.

"How can I tell you who to sleep with?" I said with annoyance. "You're married, that's your wife's job."

"Alisha, I'm not. I got a divorce the last time you were home." He said holding my hand.
"What?" I said in complete shock. We had not talked in a couple of years, so I never knew. Ma Carrie didn't tell me and I never brought him up when we talked.
"Yes I was coming home to ask you to be with me." He said pulling me back towards the sofa.
"You were what?" I asked because I was thinking about him being divorced.
"Alisha, I know you love me and I'm so in love with you it's crazy." Tommy got down on one knee. "I want you to be my wife." He said pulling out what I thought was a ring.
I wanted to say yes, but he was with Lisa and I was with Malcolm while waiting on Mikael.
"Tommy I love you, but I can't say yes and drop my life." I stood up as I rubbed my hands together.
"I know but I want you to know my desire is to spend the rest of my life with you." He placed a necklace around my neck as he spoke. "I'm not giving you a promise ring, but this necklace as a reminder for you. I will diligently work on making you my wife." He kissed me on the forehead.
I smiled because I didn't know what to say. Tommy broke the ice, "come on let's get something to eat." I stood up and remembered the box. Why was it bigger than normal?

"Come on sleepy head and get a move on." I went upstairs and got ready. When I picked up my phone I saw a text message. It was Malcolm telling me he loved and missed me. I ran down stairs "Hey Tommy, where would you like to eat?"
"I've already planned out the whole weekend so a late dinner is next. I have the place programmed in my GPS." Tommy thought anything after 6:30 was a late dinner.
"Well, alrighty then let's go." As we walked toward the door I took another look at the bigger than usual box and walked out the door.

That morning Tommy made breakfast and went into details about his divorce as we ate. Afterward I fell asleep in his lap on the sofa as we talked and he watched TV.

For lunch we went to one of my favorite places to eat, well because I like to eat I have a lot of favorites. When we walked in the owner was at the entrance. "Hi Alisha, I haven't seen you in a while." Hugging me he said, "Julian and Donna are here. I'll let him know you're here." He said as he walked towards their table. Julian and I would eat there all the time but he introduced me as his cousin. Donna, his mother, knew who I was but everyone else including his father thought I was a distant cousin on his mother's side.

Donna always liked me because I caused a change in her son, but supported his marriage to Rasheda. I guess the work I did for her helped too. "I didn't know you were a celebrity," Tommy joked.

"I'm not, I counsel people while assisting them in restoring their lives and mending relationships." I said proudly before laughing.

"But I thought you were a contractor and put your master's degree aside." He said looking puzzled.

"No, I do both and once I complete this last project I am a contractor in name only and focusing on my practice." I said wiping my forehead. Charles was my very silent partner and he let me lead because as a female minority owned small business we got a lot of contracts. I saw Julian before he saw me. As he walked up I said, "Hi Julian, how are you?"

"I'm well cousin Alisha. How are you?" he smiled.

"I am well. This is Tommy I mean Thomas Ponder," I said pointing at Tommy.

"Well I finally meet the infamous best friend and partner in crime." Julian replied with a hearty laugh as he shook Tommy's hand. "We just sat down, would you like to join us?" He said leading the way.

"Julian, Tommy just got into town and we have some catching up to do." I knew how Tommy was about his time with me and didn't want to seem rude.

"Okay, but Mother would love to see you." He said looking sad.

"I don't mind sharing Alisha and it would be nice to meet some of your friends." Tommy said. Julian put his arm around Tommy's neck as they walked to the table. He was telling Tommy the made up version of how I became his cousin. We ordered as Tommy and Julian sat and talked like old friends, including us briefly. Donna and I talked about life as she showed me pictures of the grandkids. By the time lunch was over Julian and Tommy had made plans to play golf on Sunday. "Hey Thomas, maybe we can get her out there for a game." Charles had taught me to play golf, but Julian and I played all the time perfecting my game, so I give him the credit for teaching me. I gave Donna a kiss and hugged Julian as we parted ways.

As we drove off Tommy out of the blue asked, "So, how long did the two of you date and when did you start playing golf?" The question was a surprise.

"Tommy we are friends and I started in grad school." I laughed.

"I saw the sparkle in his eye when he talked about you." Tommy laughed. "Why didn't you tell me?"

"Tommy, Papa said you had that same sparkle and we never dated." It was my turn to laugh.

"Well, he has it bad for you. That's what happens when a man spends quality time with you. We're sucked in by your eyes." Tommy said caressing my face.

"You're silly Tommy." I brushed it off and quickly changed the subject. "What's next?"

"Tonight we will have dinner and a movie, but not in that order." Tommy looked over at me while we were at a light. "Put that phone down. That's not going to make him call you." Tommy commanded.

"What are you talking about?" I tried to look innocent.

"You've had a death grip on that phone since we left. Look, if he is working he'll call when he's free." He said looking straight ahead. I wanted to tell Tommy the truth but I couldn't.

When we got to my house I took a nap while Tommy unpacked his golf necessities and returned some calls. While I was asleep I dreamed that I was getting married and as I walked down the aisle to my awaiting groom Malcolm, he smiled at me. I looked at my husband to be again and it was Mikael. When the preacher told me to place the ring on his finger I saw Tommy. When I kissed my husband his face changed again and again. Seeing the faces of all the men I had sex with I woke up screaming in a panic. Tommy ran in, "Alisha baby is everything okay." Tommy held me as I lay back down. "Alisha what's going on, you've seemed distracted since I got here?" he said full of concern.

"I'm okay; I just had a bad dream." I said in deep thought, but it was more like a confused nightmare. I thought what is God trying to tell me?

"Baby close your eyes and go back to sleep." He said holding me close. I closed my eyes and fell asleep.

Tommy woke me up an hour and a half before the movie was to start. "Hey your phone vibrated." He said as I rushed to find it. "I looked and it was a message from Malcolm." I began to smile.

"I told you he would call." Tommy said walking back into my room. "Now come on sleepy head, let's go." I got dressed and we got in the car. "What's wrong with you Alisha, you seem different?" He was still concerned. I couldn't see what others saw. During the past month that I've been with Malcolm there was a difference in me, but people couldn't put their finger on it.

"How"? I asked confused by his question.

"You've been asleep all day and you hardly ate your food at lunch or touched your breakfast." Tommy said as he examined me when we stopped at a light.

"Tommy I've been putting in a lot of hours and

I was too tired to eat." I said sitting back in my seat. Knowing I had been up with Malcolm all night was the reason.

"I've never known you to push away food and you look pale." Tommy said with an over exaggerated expression.

"Tommy I'm tired." I said. "That's why I'm ending my career as a contractor because it's been wearing me out."

"Okay Alisha but I'm keeping an eye on you while I'm here." I turned to the side and fell asleep.

When we got to the theater Tommy had to wake me up. "Alisha we're here."

"Okay, so what are we going to see?" I said sitting up.

"It's a surprise," he smiled. We walked in and Tommy bought the tickets and then we went to the concession stand. "I want some chocolate covered raisins, a large popcorn and two white cherry Icee's"

"That will be $15.75." Tommy paid the guy and we went to theater eight. The commercials had already started when we walked in. All I wanted to do was sleep and I couldn't understand why. Tommy would get excited during action movies. I knew he would tap me throughout the entire movie and keep me awake, but he didn't. He didn't notice that

I had not touched my Icee or opened my raisins.

After the movie we went to dinner. I had perked up a little by then. We dined at a place I had never been to or heard of, but the ambiance was good and the food was even better.

"I guess you were right, you look much better" Tommy said.

"You know me Tommy; I've been putting in overtime on every job." I considered my relationship with Malcolm to be a job. I scheduled all my counseling sessions after work and before seven so I could get to Malcolm, before nine.

We had small talk and laughed during dinner. He paid and we walked to the car. "Well you can spend all day relaxing tomorrow while I play golf with Julian." Tommy said as we walked back to the car.

"That sounds like a good idea." Tommy opened my door, but I ran around him to the grass. "Alisha, are you alright?" Tommy exclaimed with a look of disgust and panic on his face.

"I am now," I said as I got into the car. Tommy got in and started the car.

"Alisha, I just want to say that was disgusting." He looked at me and asked, "What in the hell is wrong with you," as if he were demanding an answer.

"Nothing," I said confused myself.

"Are you anorexic because you have lost some weight?" He said looking at me as the traffic stood still.

"No." Annoyed I said, "Tommy can we change the subject?" Tommy was upset and didn't talk to me anymore in the car. He thought I was hiding something. We pulled up in my driveway and Tommy looked at me. When we walked into the house Tommy questioned me. "Alisha, I love you and you are my friend, so what's going on?" He pleaded.

"Tommy I must have eaten something or it's just the strain I'm putting on my body." I said fearful because I didn't know what was going on.

"Do I need to stay longer?" He asked walking behind me as I went up the stairs.

"Tommy, this is the first time that's happened and I need some rest." I said.

"Okay, I leave Tuesday afternoon, so if you don't feel better by Monday please make a doctor's appointment." He said with a sad smile. "I'll do that just for you." I smiled as if I were pleading.

I took a shower and prepared for bed. I started wondering why I was feeling so blah and wanted to sleep and not eat anything. I fell asleep and after midnight my phone rang.

"Hello."

"Hey baby," he said cheerfully.

"Malcolm!" I sat up in bed.

"How is my baby?" he said.

"I think I'm exhausted because all I want to do is sleep." I replied with sadness.

"I went to sleep two hours after I arrived on Friday and all day Saturday." He said in a reassuring tone.

"I guess we wore each other out." I laughed.

"I guess, so are you coming over on Tuesday because I'm off until Wednesday." He asked with anticipation.

"What time Tuesday?" I said because I was not feeling up to it.

"After one, but I'll call you when I'm on the way. I gotta go, love you babe."

"Love you too, bye." After we hung up I had to make a run to the bathroom. I brushed my teeth and went back to bed.

That morning Tommy cooked breakfast. He was dressed and ready to play golf. "Good morning sunshine." Tommy was cheerful and full of energy. I really disliked him at that moment for waking me and turning on my light. I yelled, "Tommy cut the light off!" I put the pillow over my head and mumbled, "Good Morning."

"Alisha you look bad." He said walking toward me. "I am not going to play. I'll call Julian right now." He pulled his phone out.

"No don't do that. I was up late talking to Malcolm, so I'm tired." I said from under my pillow.

"Okay," He said kissing the pillow. "I fixed you some breakfast, but call me if you need me." Julian blew the horn and Tommy raced out the door. I turned over and went back to sleep.

Tommy came back five hours later. "Alisha, are you okay?" He asked walking into my room.

"Tommy I don't feel too good," I said holding my stomach.

"That's it, come on I'll help you get dressed." I got up and put on some sweats and he took me to an urgent care clinic near my house. Within an hour I was in and out but I didn't like the results. "What did they say?" He asked.

"I have a stomach virus." I mumbled.

"What should I do?" He asked holding my arm as if I couldn't walk.

"Take me to the pharmacy so I can get this prescription filled." I said as I got in the car. We drove to the pharmacy near my house and I went in. Tommy called Ma Carrie while I was in the store. "Ma Carrie how do you treat a stomach virus?" Tommy whispered.

"Tommy did you get up there and get sick

before your meeting?" she fussed.

"No ma'am it's not me its Alisha." He anxiously said.

"Well don't be kissing on her or you'll get it too." She paused for a moment. "She needs rest and liquids that's only if she can hold'em down."

"Thanks Ma Carrie, I'll call you later, here she comes." He whispered and quickly hung up. I was walking to the car slow as I grimaced with each step because I wanted to puke.

Tommy jumped out of the car to help me.

"Alisha, I don't know why you didn't let me go in for you."

"Tommy I need to move." I said sitting in the car. "You know how I am."

"Yes like Papa T, stubborn." We laugh and went home.

When I got home I took the medicine I was given and went to sleep. Tommy sat at my bedside until I woke up. "Hey beautiful," Tommy had a big smile on his face.

I smiled back, "Hey Tommy." I looked around. "Have you been sitting there the entire time?"

"Yes, I was concerned about you." He said visually examining me.

"Thanks Tommy, but I'm okay just sick." I said getting up.

"Malcolm called you twice and you have several text messages." He said handing me the phone.

"So you answered my phone?" I said and smiled.

"No I silenced it when it rung." Tommy walked toward the door. "Are you ready to eat?"

"Yes I'm starving." I said scrolling through my phone.

"Ma Carrie told me to give you liquids only." He replied.

"You called her," I said and smiled with compassion. "Tommy I want some food."

"Ok, soup it is." He walked out and down the stairs.

"Pork chops smothered in gravy." I yelled.

"Soup or soup, those are your choices young lady." He ran back to say.

"I'll have soup." I conceded and sat down.

"I will be back," he ran down stairs.

While he was gone I checked my messages. Malcolm left me a message letting me know he almost got caught and would call me when he got close to the house. I had four clients that wanted to confirm or set up appointments. The texts were from Malcolm asking me what's going on and where I was. I finally loved a man the way the world says you should. Malcolm was all I wanted and vice versa. Tommy came upstairs with my soup and my phone went off. It was a text from Malcolm. "Where are u?"

"A friend had to take me to urgent care."

"Are you alrite?"

"Yes we'll tlk when you get home 2sday"

"not coming home going back with her driving home 2gether. She leaves next week 4 trainin"

"k wll wrk it out. call me."

"Never thought I miss us so much. Love u"

"Love u☹"

I had to go another week without him. I was so consumed with Malcolm that I forgot Tommy was in the room. "Alisha did you hear me?" he raised his voice.

"Huh, what," I asked unfocused.

"Are you going to eat in the bed or on the chaise?" He said calmly.

"Thanks Tommy, I'll eat it on the chaise." I got up and sat in the chaise and Tommy massaged my feet. "Tommy you are so good to me." I smiled.

"I told you I was going to make you mine forever," he smiled and winked.

"Well you're working wonders right now," I sighed and finished my soup.

After I ate we went down stairs to watch a movie. I walked into the living room and that familiar box that suddenly changed shape was all I could see, but tried to ignore. "You need to open it." He said nudging me.

"What?" I asked as if I didn't know what he was talking about.

"You know the box is from Mikael and they

are pink flowers." He said turning up his mouth. How did he know I was fixated on that box, was it that obvious?

"I didn't want to open it while you were here." I said.

"Alisha he is not a threat to me. That man made a big hoopla about marrying you and disappeared a month before the wedding without as much as a goodbye," He said parading back and forth.

I couldn't tell Tommy I still wanted to marry Mikael and wished every time I saw the box he was telling me he's coming back, well before Malcolm blew my mind. "Okay Tommy, I'll open the box." I said looking at it. I slowly walked over and picked up the box. I sat down to open it and Tommy's phone rang. "This is my Dad I'll be right back," He walked out the door. "Hello," was all I heard before he closed the door behind him. I took a deep breath and opened the white box. The inside was lined with pink and silver paper. I removed the paper and saw a CD. When I picked up the CD I saw three pink roses each one darker than the next. I picked up the card. *My faith has grown stronger and my love for you greater.* I flipped the card over and it read, **Play the Cd.** I put the CD in and cried. Before Tommy walked back into the room I dried my eyes and turned off the TV.

"What was in the box?" Tommy said as he walked in.

"Three roses and a CD" I replied.

"Well, what did he say?" he asked impatiently.

"That's none of your business." I said smiling.

"Oh, I thought we told each other everything." He retorted sitting down.

"Tommy you hated Mikael from day one." I exclaimed.

"Because I knew he was a coward and would hurt you." Tommy proudly said.

"Well you don't have to worry about that now." I reassured him.

"Baby, whether you're my wife or still my best friend I will be concerned about your happiness." He said hugging me.

"Dang, who's calling me oh..."Tommy pulled out his phone and walked outside to talk. I put the roses in the scrap book along with the Cd. "I only have three..." I thought.

"You only have three what Alisha?" Tommy said startling me.

"I have three more months on this project." I lied.

"Good, why don't you come home for a visit?" He said sitting down. "You can put your degree to use at the church and privately."

"Tommy I don't want to move back home." I quickly replied.

"You don't want to be the first lady?" he asked snuggling up to me.

"Tommy, I've never wanted to live there and it has nothing to do with being the first lady." I sighed.

"So if I marry you I would have to give up my position as Pastor?" He asked as he sat back to get a better look at me.

"Tommy please, we haven't even started dating." I said full of annoyance.

"That's your fault. I tried but you rejected me." He exclaimed.

"Tommy you can't expect me to drop my entire life and jump just because you got a revelation years later." I said in anger.

"Oh here we go again, my wife. Alisha I cheated on her with you in my mind and the week I filed for divorce." He put his arm around me. "Baby I've always wanted you, but because of that summer you wouldn't let me in. I love you and because of that, forgive me. Mikael is a threat because I want you to be my wife, but if you choose him I'll still be here." I threw my arms around Tommy because that was the first time he was honest and he put my needs first. Tommy and I talked about taking it slow and then we got ready for bed because he had a long meeting the next day.

We had dinner Monday night because after his meeting, on Tuesday, he had to rush to the airport. I had a meeting Tuesday morning that was supposed to end at eleven, but it lasted through lunch. My phone started going off. I wanted to check it but I had to present some facts I found out during the meeting. I rushed through the minor details, but gave time for the important details of their questions. I made a point to let them know I would email some facts because of the short notice I received. Once the meeting was over I checked my phone, it was Malcolm letting me know he was at home, so I rushed over. Before I could knock, he snatched the door open. He picked me up and swung me around into the house. We never made it into the bedroom. Malcolm threw me on the living room floor and pulled my pants off. He penetrating the steaming desire caused by being in his arms. Our essence exploded, causing him to cry out my name as my cries melted away in his pleasure. "Damn I missed that." He said putting his arm behind his head. "I was about to go crazy." He pulled me closer. "I missed you so much Alisha." He kissed me.

"How do you think I felt, but I have to leave. I have a client in about two hours." I rested on top of him and gave him a big kiss.

"Well you need to open up so I can finish what we started." He rolled me over and spread my legs.

"We need to tal..." Before I could finish, he

buried his face between my legs. I was giving up my essence before I knew it. "Malcolm we need to talk!" I cried out.

"Okay," he retorted as he grabbed the back of my head and cried out as I succumbed to his demands. As he screamed and cried out I grinned at the power I had over him during this moment. He gave in to the pleasure that encompassed him from head to toe and relinquished his remaining essence to the pleasures of my love. I jumped up and showered so I could meet my client. "Malcolm we have to talk when I get back." I said running into the living room.

"Okay baby but it's going to be hard." He laughed. "I will call you in five minutes." I said as I kneeled on the floor and gave him a kiss before I ran out the door. As I drove off, I saw a car pull into his driveway. When I turned my on ear piece I called him, "I can't talk my wife just walked in." I left Malcolm lying in the floor with my panties on his chest. What was she doing there? I thought she wasn't coming home until the weekend. I texted Malcolm, "I need to talk to you now!!!!" I knew he wouldn't respond, but he needed to know I was serious.

I turned my first house into a personal counseling center/clinic. I had a room for me to sleep in, the counseling room and a room for married couples. My den was my office, the sitting room was for teens, the living room was the waiting room, the dining room was the kid's room, and the kitchen was just that, but I also used it as a role play or therapy room.

I arrived with ten minutes left. I breathed a sigh of relief. Since I've been seeing Malcolm my time has become strained because we have to sneak in our time together, whenever we could. My client arrived and my phone rang at the same time. "Hold please." I said to the caller while I escorted her into the office. "You can have a seat in my office Mrs. Miller." I walked into a back room. "Malcolm," I whispered.
"I can't talk long. I ran to the store so I could call you." He quickly said. "I think my wife suspects I'm cheating." I could hear the nervousness in his voice.
"Did she say that?" I asked trying to keep my voice down but thinking of course she does.
"No. But she walked in and I was lying in the middle of the floor naked with panties on my chest and your residue all over me. I hid the panties before she saw them, but I called out your name because I thought it was you. When she tried to kiss me I turned my head and she wanted to know why," he said.
"Does she drive a light blue BMW?" I asked.
"Yes, but how did you know?" He sounded

alarmed. "She was pulling up as I was driving off." I said.

"Did she see you leave out of the house?" He quickly asked.

"I don't know."

"Shit, what did you need to tell me, because I gotta go."

"I'm pregnant."

"Fuck, are you sure?"

"Yes, I went to the doctor yesterday."

"What the fuck?" He paused. "Is it mine?"

"Yes, why would you ask?"

"Hell I don't know where you been. You could be trying to set me up."

"The first time we had sex did you use a condom?"

"No, you said you hadn't been with a man in two years. You're not on the pill?"

"No I'm not on the pill because I don't have sex, remember. I don't know you like that. Why would you...oh my god. I asked if you put on a condom and you said yes. You accuse me, but you knew I was drunk. You did that crap on purpose."

"Look I don't know you and I'm denying everything. You need to get rid of it."

"No I'm not doing that, but you can go on about your business. We will be alright." I hung up and walked into the office with my client. I had two more sessions and then I could wash this day off of me. After my last client I locked up and sat in my car. Before I knew it I was crying. I wiped my face and pulled myself together, before I pulled off. I called Tommy. "Hello."

"Hey Tommy, are you busy?"

"No, but let me close the door. I'm at my parents' house. Are you alright?"

"Yes and no. I'm pregnant by a married man." I blurted.

"Alisha, baby I'll marry you and raise the child like it's my own."

"Thanks Tommy, but I need to work this out." I told Tommy everything that night from what happened on that summer day, in college, with Mikael, Terrance, and everything in between, ending with Malcolm. "Alisha, why did you go through that by yourself?" Tommy started crying, "I am so sorry I didn't protect you that day, but I thought Lisa really wanted me to be her boyfriend. She stood me up that day, so I was crushed. That evil...I'm sorry Lisha."

"Tommy that day was not your fault, so that blood is on the hands of those involved."

"I was supposed to help Papa T and Grams protect you and I failed all of you."

"No you didn't because of you I am still here. I love you Tommy, but I need some rest."

"Lisha come home until things get better."

"Tommy things are about to get better. Even in my wrong, God keeps me. After we sang

Amazing Grace that Sunday my life has been changing and those past hurts are being healed as God does a new thing in my life." "Good night Lisha."

I arose early that morning to give myself time to feel better. When I got to work to my surprise the first person I saw in the break room was Malcolm. "Good morning Malcolm." He walked out and never acknowledged me. Jason asked, "What's up with Malcolm, he's been rude and nasty all morning." "I don't know I just got here" I said looking surprised. Carol waved us closer and whispered, "He bit Charlie's head off for overlooking the plans he wanted and he sent Neil home." "Well I don't know," I said as I turned to walked out. Jason said, "Maybe you could talk to him he listens to you." "Not this time Jason. You saw what he did to me." I went to our make shift offices so I could check the progress of our work and the time frame so I could see how long it would be before I started showing. Darn, we had over fifteen weeks to go and that's if they don't make a sudden change that causes us to redesign a whole room. Shelly ran up to me. "They're having an emergency meeting right now and you need to get in there." I walked over to the board room for the meeting and the senior production officer, Alonzo Avery, was there. I was thinking what now, I just talked to him. I walked in and we all said good morning. Alonzo started the questioning, "Ms. Coleman it has been brought to our attention that the plans for the outer rooms will need an upgrade in less than two years. Because you are using the green reinforcements instead of black, is this true?" He waited impatiently for my response.

"Yes Mr. Avery, but I brought this matter to your team lead two weeks ago." I opened my file. "I was told because of the budget we had to work with a less expensive reinforcement." I handed him the document. "I looked into areas that we could be cost conscious about and I wrote a report and passed it on to your project lead." Handing him the report I turned to Malcolm. "Before passing it on I discussed the matter with Mr. Maldad and gave him a copy."

"Ms. Coleman, do you have any signed documentation that supports your claim?"

"Yes." I pulled out two signed copies of the proposals and handed them to Alonzo. I've worked with Alonzo before, so he gave me a heads up about the paperwork, but he didn't tell me about the meeting.

After the meeting Alonzo pulled me aside, "what's up with you and Malcolm?" he whispered.

"What do you mean?" I asked.

"Did you step on his toes or something?" he said looking around.

"I don't think so, why?" I looked at him.

"He called George Russell last night and told him some things about you that I know aren't true." He whispered even lower.

"Like what?" I said curious.

"Look, have dinner with me tonight and we can talk." He said turning around to check his surroundings.

"Okay, call me with the details." I said playing it off.

Later that day my foreman pulled me aside. "Alisha, what is going on?" He said throwing his hands up. "The guys are being fired left and right because of safety violations. I know for a fact that these allegations are not true."

"Okay let me...who's doing this?" I asked

"Malcolm," he said shaking his head.

"Okay, tell all the guys to take the day off with pay while I straighten this out." I gathered up my stuff and walked to my car. As I drove off I called Alonzo. "Hey you what's up?"

"Are you still at the site?" I quickly asked.

"I'm headed to my car now." He said.

"Meet me at the Rivers End for an early lunch. My treat," I said smiling

"Okay, I'm on my way." Alonzo got there ten

minutes after I did.

"Hey Alisha this is a mess. What's going on between you and Malcolm?" he asked before he sat down.

"I'm pregnant by him and he's trying to force me to get an abortion. So he's trying to destroy my credibility on the job." I blurted.

"Well he's actually hurting himself because when George called me I couldn't believe it. You skimming money and taking short cuts. I couldn't tell you about the meeting, but I could tell you to have the proof because I was the one investigating."

"Thanks Alonzo. I told the dude it was over and I won't contact him again, so why is he doing this." I sat back folding my arms.

"I can't believe you gave that joker a chance but not me." I liked Alonzo, but I was done with available men when we met. "Believe me Alonzo it was not like that." I told him what happened that night. "Alisha we had a lady in our northern division get fired and I found out later that she was seeing Malcolm."

"I can't believe I let my guard down," I said folding my arms.

"Alisha I know this may be inappropriate, but I still want to.... never mind."

"Alonzo when I finish this project I'm done with contracting. The end of this project is in less than six months now, so ask me again later." After lunch we hugged and went our separate ways. We had less than four months left on the project but because of the change we now have almost six. I was sick after lunch. I called Charles to let him know about the extension and why. He knew I was giving up the business side and day to day activities, but I would still be a partner.

I had four clients to see that day so I went directly to my clinic after lunch. I arrived an hour early and set up the room for my struggling married couple. She had issues with freedom in the marriage bed and he was on the verge of cheating, but his wife didn't know. When I consult married couples I always gave them a separate session so the spouse can be honest without backlash later on down the road. I was almost done setting up when I heard the doorbell ring. I thought who could this..."Who is it?" I asked.
"It's me Malcolm." I opened the door and he had a big bear and some candy. "I'm sorry Alisha."
"Malcolm, I don't have time for this. What do you want?"
"I want you." Malcolm didn't know I knew what he had done or that I was friends with Alonzo.
"Oh really, because this morning you tried to throw me under the bus by getting me kicked off of the project."

"Baby, it wasn't me that threw you under the bus. Alonzo called me and asked about the reinforcements."

"But Malcolm you knew I brought...you know what, never mind. I have clients coming, so I don't have time for this."

"Can I kiss the baby."

"What?" I was thinking the baby that's not yours and you told me I had to kill.

"It's the evidence of our love."

"Malcolm, I have to go." Malcolm kissed me on the neck and walked out. I threw the candy in the garbage and put the bear in the children's room with the things that needed to be cleaned. I continued to set up, when my phone rang. I was about to curse and then I thought, mood swings already? Darn it's a restricted number, "Hello."

"Hi Alisha," the person said.

"Hello, may I ask who this is?"

"I just wanted to hear your voice." When they hung up the doorbell rang.

I opened the door for the Chesterfields. "Hello Mr. and Mrs. Chesterfield come in and let's get started." I escorted them to the therapy room. When Meredith was a child her mother would always say, "Good girls didn't have sex," but she forgot to say unless they were married. This caused her to be uncomfortable in the marriage bed. We had gotten to a point that she was starting to feel uninhibited to the idea of passion in the bedroom. I really liked this couple and this was their last session as a couple, but Meredith wanted to keep seeing me one on one. She had some things she needed to learn before her husband's birthday. Their sessions would last for thirty-five to forty-five minutes depending on their progress. Tonight the session only lasted twenty minutes. I wasn't surprised because it should've ended last week but she wanted to have one more session. I saw the last of my clients and was done before five, so I crashed at the clinic for a few minutes before going home. Malcolm thought I lived at the clinic because I would sleep there some times. I walked out of the clinic and Malcolm was sitting on the porch. "Alisha we need to talk." I was startled, "Malcolm, about what?"

"The baby, Alisha what else would I want?"

"Malcolm you were clear about your feelings and I am walking away from you."

"Alisha I can't be in the child's life and you know I don't want to keep doing that."

"If you choose to see your child that's fine, if you don't that's fine. I will have a man raise this child as if the child were his own."

"No you won't have another man raise my seed."

"You are married and have a family already."

"I know, but that belongs to me."

"You're talking crazy."

"I know you set me up, but I'm willing to take responsibility."

"Malcolm this is your fault. You tricked me and got me drunk. You decided to have your way with me and when I asked if a condom was used you lied to me about it. No this is your fault." As I turned to walk off Malcolm grabbed my arm. "Alisha, I am in love with you and my wife knows about us. I don't want to have another child, but I want to continue to see you."

As I tried to pull away I fell off the porch. "Alisha!" Malcolm said in a panic as he ran to me. "Baby, are you alright?" I shooed Malcolm away.

"Yes, I just hurt my finger." When I tried to stand up my hand gave way, causing me to fall back down. "Damn it," when the words flew out Malcolm shook his head as if his hearing was distorted. I was in so much pain I wanted to keep cussing. The neighbor, Mrs. Steinberg, saw me on the ground and asked, "Alisha, baby are you alright or should I call the police?" I forgot about the 6 foot 4 man standing over me as I lay in pain on the ground. "No, Mrs. Steinberg I'm alright. I just slipped off the porch."

"All right Alisha I'm here if you need me. I told you about wearing those too high heels." She sat down on her porch as Malcolm helped me into his car and we drove off. She lived there before my grandparents bought my house. Mrs. Steinberg was black and her husband was Jewish so they had it hard. My grandparents readily accepted them and they stayed friends until my grandparents died. Her husband passed two years before they did.

Malcolm took me to the ER and I was there for over two hours. He was not the man I had seen earlier that day and I was falling for him again. Malcolm was with me when they checked the baby. He seemed more excited than I was. When he first saw the baby his eyes filled with tears that never fell and he kissed my hand. "That's the result of our love Alisha. Baby I'm sorry for trying to hurt you." "That's okay Malcolm." The words flowed out of my mouth and my brain screamed at me. What the hell you need to wake up, have you lost me completely. I was so overjoyed at that moment and couldn't think straight. "I am going to do everything to help you raise our child." I thought; see he is sincere about this. There was a part of me that didn't trust him and I couldn't understand why.

When Malcolm pulled up in my driveway he helped me to the door. When I tried to open it he took my keys and opened the door. I forgot

I sprained my wrist and it hurt to use my left hand. Malcolm's phone was ringing, "Hey baby." Malcolm said as he kissed me on the cheek. "I know, but I told you I've been drinking. Let me sit for two more hours." He hung up the phone and started kissing me. "Malcolm stop, you need to go home." I said pushing him back. "I'll go home once I know you're okay." He kissed my hand. "Now go get ready for bed." I wanted to tell Malcolm this was not my home, but something in the pit of my belly wouldn't let the words come out. I took my shower and got in the bed. "Baby, can I make this day up to you?" he asked kissing the palm of my hand.

"How Malcolm, look I just want to get some sleep." Malcolm snatched me to the edge of the bed and pulled my legs open. I moaned in anticipation of what he was about to do. Once Malcolm buried his face into my burning desire, I grabbed his head and pulled him closer as I tried to fight off the action of the day. I thrust my hips faster and faster, so I could sink into the sensation of his pleasure, before releasing my uncontrollable desire as his reward. Malcolm turned me over and thrust his thick and awaiting desire into my sweet essence. He exploded as he grabbed me around my waist, causing him to give up his essence without warning. Malcolm helped me into the bed and rested beside me, quickly falling asleep. He was awakened by his ringing phone. "Hello," he said in a low groggy voice. "Baby I pulled over and fell asleep in the car. I'm on my way."

"Shit," Malcolm said jumping up and putting on his clothes. "My wife went to the bar looking for me."

"Be careful," I said with a strained look. "She knows about you, so I have to come up with a good lie." He kissed my belly and my cheek before dashing out the door, so I went back to sleep.

When I got to work the next day and the buzz around the office was about Malcolm's wife looking for him last night. Everyone that worked with Malcolm hated him because he was a butthole. Shelly walked up to me. "Did you hear about Malcolm's wife going to Cindy's house looking for him?" she said smiling.

"No," I said in shock, "but how did everybody find out?"

" She was having a dinner party and Neil was there. You know Neil hates Malcolm." She whispered.

"Isn't this going to make it worst?" I asked.

"No because Neil got promoted last week and this is his last day. I can just see her now with those curlers in her head and a robe on," she balked.

"You do know his wife is a top executive at her company, so that's hard to believe." I said in her defense.

The truth was Malcolm's wife had come to the dinner party expecting to see Malcolm because they were invited. When she got there they told her he was at the emergency room with her. Malcolm lied to me again he told me she went to the bar. I thought about the things I heard about Malcolm. Suddenly, I became a little fearful, so I had my doctor test me for every STD there was. After explaining to her the circumstances she understood. Malcolm didn't come to work that day. He had taken some time off. Malcolm had not called or texted me in days, so I just went on with life as usual. Almost three months had passed and still nothing from Malcolm, but Tommy called every day and Alonzo took me out every weekend. Malcolm returned to work, but I rarely saw him and the gossip silenced after a few weeks. I had not heard from Malcolm in months.

Tommy hadn't called all day and Alonzo had to leave on an emergency business trip on Thursday, he wouldn't be back until Wednesday. I drove home that Friday a little sad. As I pulled in to my driveway, I saw a man standing on my porch. My god is that Malcolm, but the joy soon faded as I remembered he didn't know where I lived. I got out of the car and walked up the steps. "Excuse me sir, how may I help you?" This tall gorgeous man turned around and dropped to one knee and said, "Alisha, will you entertain the thought of getting to know me again so that one day I can call you my wife." He handed me flowers that consisted of pink and white roses. "Mikael," I cried before everything went black.

He was the last thing I remembered before I opened my eyes on my sofa. I woke up to his smiling face and dancing eyes that sparkled every time he looked at me. "Alisha I'm back." "But Mikael, I betrayed you. I'm pregnant." I looked down in ultimate shame.
"Baby, that doesn't matter to me unless you're married. You are my wife." I hugged him and cried, "But the baby."
"You mean, the baby I'll raise and give my last name whether we're married or not." I loved that man so much and I realized that I wanted to make it work. "Mikael are you back for good?"
"No not yet, I wanted to spend the weekend with you. I will be home for good within the year."
I didn't know where all of this love and joy was coming from, because this man walked out on me and didn't look back. I know he

sent flowers, but the hurt of opening a box and all I saw was a single rose crushed me day after day. Was I so lonely and crushed that I was willing to settle for anything. "Come on let's go out to eat."

I ran upstairs and took my nausea medicine and we went to eat. We went to Mikes Sports & Wings because they had the best wings in town and that was our spot back in the day. We walked in and grabbed a table. I excused myself so I could use the restroom. "Alisha!" I stopped and looked around because I thought I heard someone calling my name. I turned and started walking when someone grabbed my arm. "Alisha, it's me Blair." I turned and gave him a hug.

"Hey Blair, how are things?"

"Great, I'm celebrating my divorce with some of my boys. I got the final decree in the mail today." He said as he pulled the paper out of his back pocket. "Remember what you said?"

"Blair I'm here with someone, so this conversation needs to end."

"Okay it will end out of respect, but I'll call you." I walked into the ladies room shaking my head. There were a couple of ladies in there talking. "Yes he's good in the bed, but his pockets are empty."

"What difference does it make, girl he's a man and he's single."

"Girl you're right, if I can get him to live with

me the next step is marriage."

"That's how I got his friend. Girl, Blair is in need of a strong woman that loves him."

"You're right. We've been dating for a while now, so I guess it's time to live together."

"Come on before that desperate Noel tries to get her claws in him."

"Yeah, did you see the way she was all over him?" They left as I was walking out of the stall. I washed my hands and went back to the table. I saw Blair as I walked over to Mikael. "Hey baby I thought I was going to have to get a search party to find you in this crowd. Let's just get our food to go."

"Okay, that sounds like a great idea." Mikael waved the waitress down and told her we wanted it to go. "So, who was that guy over there you were talking to?"

"What guy?"

"On your way to the restroom, is he the baby's daddy?"

"No I dated him for a couple of months a while back."

"Oh ok, so did you sleep with him?"

"What?"

"I was just wondering, never mind I was being jealous because I've been gone and I thought you were waiting on me."

"Did you wait on me?"

"I'm a man. I have to relieve myself, but I always wore protection and got tested. You taught me that." The waitress brought our food, so Mikael paid and tipped her.

When we got back to my house we talked about when we dated, Papa T, Ma Carrie and Grams. He told me that he talked to Papa T every week and was at the funeral. I had fallen asleep. "Hey baby, you need to take a shower and go to bed."
"You're right. I can't sleep on the floor right now."
"Yes, both my babies need to be in a bed." I went upstairs and took a shower while he set up in the guest room. When I came out of the restroom he was standing in my room with his pajamas on. "Alisha I had an idea, why don't I come back in a few months to help you set up the baby's room?"
"That would be nice," I said as I smiled. He walked over to me and put his hand on my stomach. "How far along are you?"
"I'm about 16 weeks or four months." Mikael picked me up and carried me over to the bed. "Baby I don't care how inappropriate this is or how it looks, I miss all of you." Mikael swirled his tongue in the midst of my passion. As he pushed me back onto the bed and caressed the resulting flavor from the source of my desire. He caused me to release my essence, becoming speechless. He entered into my passion filled desire with skill. He searched for

my hidden essence, causing him to go deeper until he convulsed. Crying out my name he released the fullness of himself to me by giving up his essence. He rolled over and fell asleep. I pulled off the condom and covered him while he slept. I lay there looking at the ceiling I thought about what I had done. Suddenly, my phone rang. "Hello."

"Hey Lisha sorry about the late call but I had a lot going on since last night."

"What's up is everything okay?" I walked out of the room.

"Baby you have enough on you as it is."

"Thomas if you don't...."

"Okay okay Mama Lisha. When I got back home I broke it off with Lisa. Well, now she's pregnant and told my dad if I didn't marry her she would tell the whole congregation. You know my family and their deal with image, but Ma Carrie ain't having it. She told him no. I told him it's not true and to do a DNA test first, but he has set a date for us to get married or I step down as Pastor."

"What are you going to do?"

"I'm going on a six month sabbatical at the end of our church quarter and not tell a soul."

"Tommy, what if they replace you?"

"Alisha I have more than enough to retire on after the divorce settlement and alimony. I need a break and if I'm going to be your husband, I need to see the world not just this little town. How are you and my baby?" I knew I couldn't tell him about Mikael right now, even though I was having doubts about him. "We are good, but I'm sleepy so I'll call you tomorrow."

"Not tomorrow I'll call you because your name keeps coming up, Good night my love."

"Good night Tommy."

That morning I got up and made breakfast. "Good morning Mikael."

"Who were you talking to on the phone last night?"

"Tommy," I said looking at him puzzled.

"Why, is he the baby's daddy?"

"No, I told you who the father was."

"Then why are you talking to another man while I'm here?"

"Tommy is my best friend."

"Not if we're going to be together. My woman doesn't have male friends."

"Mikael you've changed, what's going on?"

"Look, I've seen how y'all are and you ain't gonna play me."

"Have I ever played you?"

"Yes, I come home and you're knocked up with another dude's baby. What kind of lowdown shit is that?"

"Mikael I didn't know if or when you were coming back, so how did I play you?"

"You should've waited on me; no other man

should have had you. I sent you flowers and kept up with you and this is the thanks I get. Shit, your womb violated by another man's seed. But to show you the kind of man I am, I'm willing to raise it and give it my last name because I love you. I spent a lot of money on you."

"Well guess what Mikael I kept up with you as well. Let me see if I have this right. You married Keira and then you had five paternity suits against you and you are here because you just found out Keira lied. The little boy wasn't yours and I told you that from day one. Now all these years have passed and since your son is not your seed, I'm supposed to be excited because the now famous Mikael Brats is burned out and realizes the woman he left all those years ago was the only good and true thing he had...you hurt me, but I never stopped loving you."

"I think it's time for me to go hell, I can see when I'm not appreciated. If you were so much better than me why did you let me fuck you last night? Be gone, I can do better."

"I never said I was better and no one should think more highly of themselves than others because we are all saved by grace." He stopped on the stairs and turned to me. "Don't get holier than thou on me, because when a man tries to do the right thing he fails and in the end gets hurt." As he turned to go upstairs I said, "When it's done in your own will you kill your future, so we have to let God lead us. You found a wife and she was right, but you lost it when you let me go." Mikael rushed down the stairs and out the door.

I was so upset that I started cleaning up after he left. I cleaned I spoke the scriptures I remembered aloud and prayed. I prayed for everyone I hurt and all those that hurt me. People faces would appear, so I prayed for them and my indiscretion. The sky had become dark in the midst of my praying and cleaning, but I had one last room to go. I walked toward the guest room as my heavy heart begun to ease. I opened the door and pulled off all the linen and throwing them into the hall. I replaced the linen and dust the floors and furniture. Then the familiar, but smaller, white box caught my eye. I walked over and opened the box. Two tightly closed rose buds were nestled in the box on top of a card; *my heart won't let me stop loving you.* I sat on the edge of the bed and cried. I got up a few minutes later and finished cleaning. I went into my room and lay across my bed. "I need you Papa and Grams. I've made such a mess of my life because I couldn't let that summer day go." Later that night I received my first of many texts from Malcolm. We met at the clinic that following weekend, but all he wanted was sex so I ended it.

A few months had past and my belly was big enough for the world to see. Tommy was preparing for his secret sabbatical and Alonzo was the picture perfect mate. On a beautiful Saturday morning I awakened to my boyfriend in the kitchen making me breakfast. I got up and dressed for our Saturday morning ritual; which was getting the baby's room ready. I walked down stairs. "Are you sure you're just six month?" Alonzo laugh. "You know this is a big baby."

"Well I can't wait until we have another one." Alonzo had not revealed his secret to me yet.

"Well let's make it through this one first, Daddy."

"Have you talked to Tommy today?"

"No, he hasn't called me yet."

"Isn't he leaving soon because I want him to see that belly before he leaves."

"Ha-ha, he'll be here next weekend."

"Good so are you going to eat this morning or will I have to force feed you?"

"I am going to eat. I want four pieces of bacon, a spoon full of grits, and two eggs with cheese."

"Okay queen of my heart and what would you like to drink?"

"That passion fruit drink you make so well."

"Stop trying to butter me up because I don't feel like making it."

"Pretty please Lonnie. If not for me do it for the baby." I said playfully pouting.

"I knew you were going to do that," he said as he turned toward the refrigerator. "I made it last night because you do that every week."

"Well because you know I'm going to do it, you should have it ready anyway." I smiled as he walked over with my plate and kissed me. After we ate breakfast we started working on the baby room. Alonzo and I were not married yet, but he bought me a ring a couple of months ago to eliminate any questions about me being pregnant and unmarried. After we completed the work on the nursery we had to get my clinic ready for the baby. That was a busy weekend and the longest. I slept all day Sunday after we got out of church.

On Monday I had two new clients, so I rearranged my schedule so they would be the only appointments for that day. I went into work early that morning and left by noon because my first appointment was at one. When I got there Mrs. Steinberg told me she had to run some woman off last week, because she was taking pictures of the house. I thanked her and after some small talk I went into the house. I kept the door unlocked if I was in the clinic, but Alonzo didn't like it so I started locking it in the evenings. I walked in and prepared the clinic for my clients. At 12:45 my new client had arrived. She was already sitting in the waiting room when I walked from the kitchen.

"Hello Ms. Willis, I'm Alisha Coleman. Can you give me a synopsis on the issues you're having?"

"I see you're pregnant." She said sitting on the edge of the sofa. "How far along are you?"

"Yes," I smiled rubbing my precious cargo, "I'm a little over six months and walking is getting harder." I said with a chuckle.

"Well are you sure you're just six months, or is the father of the child a big man?" She said standing up.

"Yes, but that is not always the case." I started to get a funny feeling in the pit of my stomach after that question. I walked over to the window to open the blinds and let in more sunlight and spotted the tail of a light blue car. I turned around and asked, "Ms. Willis what seems to be your issue or were you referred or...?"

"No, I got your card out of my husband's pocket because I wanted to know where he disappears to at night. I've seen your number in his phone dating back over six months, so is that my husband's baby?" she pointed.

"Ms. Willis I have no idea who you husband is." I franticly said knowing I was lying.

"So, you sleep with that many?" She pushed me saying, "Malcolm Maldad is my husband." She screamed at me as I lay on the floor. "Ms. Willis...I mean Mrs. Maldad, I am not sleeping with your husband." She pulled a big envelop from her purse and started throwing the contents at me. "Then why is his car in your drive way?"

I tried to stand. "But Mrs. Maldad I'm not in any of those pictures and neither is my car." "But your number is in his phone when I found out about the woman he was cheating with," she said as she slapped me. I hit speed dial on my phone when she pushed me to the floor the first time. "Mrs. Maldad I am not having an affair with your husband, but I worked with him on a project at work." I said as I got up off the floor again. She charged me screaming "He said he's in love with you and wants to help you raise the baby!" I jumped over the ottoman and she fell to the floor. As she got up from the floor she said, "I'm going to kill you and that bastard."

"If you do, then you won't have him either." She fell to the floor and cried, "What am I supposed to do? He sleeps with everybody, but you were the only one he wouldn't stop seeing."

"Lealtà, I'm not sleeping with your husband anymore and forgive me for hurting you." I said sitting next to her.

"Why did you get pregnant?" she asked looking at me.

"I didn't do it on purpose," I said in shame. I told her everything that happened the night I got pregnant. She cried, "He has been cheating on me for years and he's always disappearing after work."

"I could recommend a good counselor for you," I said rubbing her back.

"No, I want to use you because if you can get my husband to act like a fool, you must be good at what you do." She laughed.

"That is unethical and I can't do it." I said in a calm professional tone.

"Let's do this. We will meet me once a week for lunch and you pick up the check."

The door flew open as a man yelled, "Alisha where are you?"

"I'm down here," I said waving my hand as he ran over and helped me up.

"Are you okay, what about the baby?"

"We are fine daddy."

"Baby you scared me." Alonzo said as he dropped to his knees. "I didn't know what to do or who to call or if I needed to call somebody." He was talking in such a panic that he didn't notice her at first. When he breathed a sigh of relief he noticed her. "Mrs. Maldad what are you doing here," he said looking around. He noticed the room and the

apparent struggle that must have taken place.
"What did you do," he questioned as he looked
at her in disgust jumping up. He quickly
turned back to me. "Baby, did she hurt you?"
He was asking when suddenly the pictures on
the floor caught his attention. "Why is his car
parked in front of your house?"
"Alonzo it's not what you think." I said trying
to stand.
"After what that man did to you and you're
still dealing with him?" Alonzo yelled before he
turned and walked out.
"Alonzo please," I said as I ran toward him
and reached out. Suddenly a sharp pain went
across my stomach. I grimaced and held my
stomach. Lealtà jumped up and ran over to
me. "Are you alright?"
"Yes." I said while standing erect. "I just
moved too fast. Why don't you give me a call
later because I need to straighten up."
"I'm going to stay here until your last
appointment leaves so you go lie down, while I
straighten up."

My second appointment wasn't until four
and I needed to lie down. After I helped
straighten things up I called Alonzo, but my
calls went straight to voice mail. I told him
what had happened and I had not seen
Malcolm in months. I called Tommy, but he
didn't answer so I took a nap. My phone rang

at five minutes to four, it was my second appointment for the day and they had to cancel at the last minute. I told Lealtà they canceled. We hugged and I apologized again and she left. Ten minutes after she left my phone rang again. "Is it too late for me to come in?"

"Well I am closed and I won't charge you for the late cancelation."

"But I need help now." After the day I had maybe this will take my mind off of it.

"How far away are you?"

"Two to three minutes," they said.

"Okay, come on."

I walked toward the front door and the bell rung. I opened the door and it was Malcolm. "Since you won't see me, I thought I would make an appointment. Why was my wife here?"

"No Malcolm, you need to leave."

"I have a right to see my baby."

"When she gets here, but you can leave now."

"Did you call my wife?" Malcolm pushed his way in, "Why was my wife here?"

"Malcolm leave or I'll call the police." I pulled out my phone and he slapped it out my hand. I started screaming and he grabbed me by the mouth so that my screams would be muffled. He forced me into the waiting room and started loosening his belt with his free hand.

"You thought you could just leave me? I'm going to remind you of why we fell in love." Malcolm started undressing himself with one hand as I kicked and made muffled screams through his hands. After he pulled up my dress he ripped my panties off. Malcolm snatched my legs open as he out his weight on my chest, while keeping his hand over my mouth. Malcom positioned himself between my legs as he started to ram himself into me he heard a noise outside. Malcolm pushed off me and ran out the door. I got up and decided not to accept any more new clients until after I had the baby was born. I picked up my broken phone and headed home. When I got home I could tell Alonzo had been there, but was long gone because his car was gone. I took my shower and got into bed. Before I turned off the lights I saw that Alonzo's things were missing. I jumped up and checked the bathroom and then his closet. I sat down on the bed as if I had been defeated and cried. I lay back and cried myself to sleep.

It was about one o'clock in the morning, but I never heard a sound. Alonzo was beating my door down and calling my name. He opened my garage and kicked in my door. He was calling my name as he ran upstairs as fast as he could, but I never heard him. "Alisha. Alisha baby, where are you?" he cried.

When he opened my bedroom door he ran to my bed. "Baby, are you alright." I turned over and couldn't make sense of what he was saying. I reached out and caressed his face. "Alonzo what's wrong."

He couldn't talk. All he could do was kiss me on my head. "Where's your phone?"

Tommy called him because I was not returning his calls and my phone was going straight to voice mail. "Malcolm broke it." My speech was incoherent so Alonzo couldn't understand me.

"What?"

"Malcolm broke it when I tried to stop him."

"Tried to stop him from what?"

"Coming into the Clinic."

"Why was he at the clinic?" he demanded.

"He wanted to see his baby. Alonzo, why are you wet," I asked.

"Baby I'm not wet." He said lifting my head.

"Why did he want to see the baby?"

"Because I wouldn't respond to him, so he tricked me." I slowly said.

"Baby how did he trick you, what did he do?" He questioned franticly.

"Alonzo you got the whole bed wet." I said feeling the bed.

"Alisha, look at me baby please. Are you alright?" He ordered desperately.

"Alonzo, stop getting me wet." I said as I touched his hand.

"Baby, is your..." he snatched back the covers "Oh my God Alisha be still." He pulled out his phone and dialed 911. He turned me over on my back and then ran down stairs to open the front door. He ran back to the bed room yelling, "Alisha, baby how long have you been pushing?" He was so hysterical he asked the wrong questions. The 911 operator calmed him down and coached him every step.

"Alisha, how long have you been cramping and how often are they coming?"

"I'm sleepy."

"Alisha, baby please. I don't see anything. Yes she's six months or twenty eight weeks." He heard a rumbling. He yelled out, "I'm upstairs in the bedroom." He picked me up and carried me down the stairs. "Sir we are taking her to North Memorial so follow us in your car." Alonzo jumped in his car and headed to the hospital. He had forgotten to call Tommy, but less than five minutes after he jumped into his car the phone rang. "Hello."

"Hey, is she alright?"

"Man they are rushing her to the hospital."

"Is the baby okay, what happened?"

"I found her in the bed incoherent and her water had broken, but I think she was just sleepy."

"How did...is the baby due?"

"No and it was Malcolm. Between him and his wife they..."

"What did they do."

"She tried to fight Alisha and he tricked her and broke her phone, man I don't know for sure."

"What did he do to her?"

"I don't know man I couldn't understand her. If I had not walked out…I hope my baby is alright."

"Just calm down, I'm on the next flight out. It's not your fault." Tommy hung up and called Ma Carrie, "Pray for Alisha, they rushed to the hospital because her water broke. I'll call when I have more details. I'm catching the first flight out."

When Alonzo got to the hospital they rushed him up to my room. They had me ready to push. Alonzo held my hand as the nurse walked over to calm him down. "Do you know the sex?"

"Yes, it's a girl," Alonzo said with a proud smile.

"Have you picked out a name?"

"Milagro Vida Coleman, I mean Avery"

"That's Spanish."

"Yes because she's a miracle of life."

"Well Mr. Avery, get ready to meet your daughter." He felt a proud nervousness.

"Okay Mrs. Avery push," Alonzo held my hand tighter. "Give me one more big one on the count of three. One, two, three, push push

push push push push." We got her, "Waaa!"
"Congratulations you have a....oh my god she
stop breathing. How far along was she?"
"Between twenty-six or twenty-eight weeks," a
nurse said.
"Get NICU in here stat." The doctor walked
over. "Your baby is fine, but she's tired and
not fully developed so we need to get her to
the neonatal intensive care unit."
"We're going to get you cleaned up so you can
see the baby." Alonzo called Tommy and told
him what happened.

Several hours later Tommy arrived and
went directly to the hospital. "Hey mama, how
are you?"
"Hey Tommy, I'm good thanks for coming."
Alonzo was asleep in the chair. "Hey Tommy
what time is it?"
"It's nine. Have you seen the baby?"
"I haven't, but Alonzo did."
Alonzo woke up and walked over to the bed.
"Hey baby, I have to head out I'm going by the
house and pick up a few things. I called the
job for you and I'll pick you up a phone. Glad
you made it Tommy." Alonzo walked out of the
room.

Tommy and I talked and laugh and talked
some more until two hours had passed.
Malcolm walked in, "Alisha, baby I just heard
you had our baby. Where is she?"

"Malcolm please leave."

"I have a right to be here to see my daughter."

"You can't because you don't have a daughter, my husband does."

"Hello Mr. Maldad." Malcolm turned around he became nervous and stumbled over his words. "Hel-hello Mr. Avery," he said as he turned.

"Malcolm, I didn't expect to see you here." Alonzo said.

"I heard she had the baby, so I wanted to see her."

"I didn't know you knew Ms. Coleman so well or is it the father you know?" Tommy had to hold back his laughter. "Did you bring any flowers or a card?"

"No, I just wanted to see a good friend."

"Ms. Coleman and I have been friends for years and I've never heard of you as being her friend."

"I just wanted to check on you Ali....Ms. Coleman."

"If she was your friend, wouldn't you call her by her first name?"

"Well, I have to get back to work. Have a good day." He left so fast he almost ran.

We all burst in laughter.

"Hello, Mrs. Coleman-Avery we have some documents for you to sign."

"Okay."

"Which of you is the father, because I need

your ID so you can sign the birth certificate?"
Alonzo ran over and signed the paper work.
Tommy looked disappointed, so I grabbed his
hand and gave a little squeeze. "I'm going up
to see the baby." Tommy walked out. "Did you
go see her again?"
"Yes and she's beautiful. When we finish I'll
take you up stairs."

When Tommy got upstairs Malcolm was
coming out of the room in a huff. "Tell her I'm
the father of that child and she will have my
name."
"What Evil?" Tommy said, "I bind you in the
name of Jesus." Tommy walked into the room.
Twenty minutes later Alonzo and I went
upstairs. I spent every moment I could in the
NICU until I left the hospital. Tommy went
home and Alonzo was there every day.
Malcolm would come early in the mornings to
avoid Alonzo. We were a happy family and
were open with our relationship once the
project was done. Malcolm's wife hadn't set up
a lunch date yet.

God had started doing a new thing within me,
but I didn't realize how new that thing would
be.

11

The Story Of Me

I was raised by my grandparents Tobias and Marie Coleman who were devout Christians. My mother had me when she was fifteen. One year I researched our last name because I was searching for my identity. In English our name meant, someone who gathers coal and in the Latin version meant dove. Since that one summer day I wanted to fly from that small town like a dove. I think like me my mother wanted to fly away like a dove from that small town too. She had just turned fifteen and a silver-tongued dude from up north talked her into following him up there with the promise of marriage and big dreams. She snuck out late one night and they caught a train heading north. He told her they would get married. Well six months later she came home as Grams says, "With a belly full of baby." The man was ten years older than my mother. The only big dream she saw was that big pipe dream he used when he knocked her up. The story they told everybody was that he died in a car accident and because my mother was underage, she couldn't legally change her name without a proper marriage license. My Grandparents wanted to protect her because the saved folk wanted to crucify my mother. I was her only child. Ma Carrie told me, "I tore up all her inside female parts." I had no idea what that meant then or what it means now, but my mother could not get pregnant again. Apparently my mother was gullible because every man that came to town she would run off with and come back home looking more tattered than the last. I was four when Papa said my mother couldn't take me gallivanting around the world anymore, so they raised me. The last time I saw my mother I was eight or nine. Papa, Grams and Ma Carrie became my parents and my support. Grams took care of Ma Carrie when she was younger and later in life they became best friends.

I believe I was ten when my mother died, she looked older than Grams and she was still in her twenties. My mother was the youngest child of seven. Papa saw that as a sign from God as completion. She was that surprise baby that you didn't think you had in you. The way I talk proves I've been around too many old people (Okay back to the story). My mother had two brothers and four sisters. My favorite was Uncle Junior, he was named after

Papa. Mitchel was named after Papa's dead baby brother. The girls were Martha, Sue, Maggie, Aunt "The Original Baby Girl" Cindy, and my mother Sabrina.

The first two weeks of the summer break Tommy and I spent almost every day together, until that one summer day. My Mother died, so during the last two months of school I received special treatment. The popular kids didn't like me for that and since my mom was looked down on in that town it was unheard of. My grandparents were well respected because Papa was a Preacher and Grams was a Missionary. My grandparents live a righteous life and that's how I was brought up. I knew God very well through my grandparents, but I didn't have a personal relationship with God.

Lisa was the ring leader of the popular kids and because her family had money she was betrothed to my best friend, Tommy. This was not publicized, but it was just how they did things in this small town. Tommy was groomed to be a Pastor and she was groomed to be the first lady. She hated me as well as her family and Tommy's mother because we were so close. Lisa wasn't just popular because she had money she was popular because she was having sex with older boys. She was the easiest girl in the County, but because of her parents everyone looked the other way.

Lisa was a very pretty girl and Tommy had the biggest crush on her so when she asked him to take her to the movies he jumped at the chance. We had plans to go fishing and tadpole hunting like we did every Wednesday, but that would change. Tommy came by as I was on my way out of the house to meet him. We always left early, so we could be back before it got dark. I told Tommy that day I hated him and would never speak to him again. He ran up the road and I cut through the trail behind my house. I walked to our favorite spot, but I didn't feel like fishing or catching tadpoles. I pitched a few rocks before I came back home.

On my way home as I walked through the open field I saw Lisa walking on the path. I thought she left my friend at the movies by himself. I kept walking until I felt like someone was following me, but before I could turn around I was dragged into an old shed. I kicked and screamed so much that they called in reinforcements to drag me into that shed. Lisa ran up to the door and told me to stay away from Thomas or I'll regret it. I spit at her. She was so angry that she started hitting me and I laughed. She got so angry that she ripped off my clothes and told the guys to enjoy me. There were six boys between the ages of 16 and 20 and three girls our age. Everybody grabbed me and held me down, I fought until I was out of breath but they were still energized. The third girl ran and hid when the first boy penetrated me. The first boy got on top of me and I never felt such pain in my life. I screamed bloody murder. When the third boy penetrated me my screams were no more. By the time the last boy penetrated me, I had lost all feeling mentally and physically. The all ran off laughing, but Lisa laughed as she stood over me and poured whiskey in my mouth and on my body before they ran off.

The pain was excruciating and I couldn't move. I lay in the dark naked, cold, and alone. In the distance, I heard Papa calling me and then I heard Tommy. I could barely move so I stretched out my hand to find a rock, stick or something. I reached out and found a bottle so I threw it as I tried to scream. They didn't hear me, so I searched franticly for something within hands reach. The voices got closer and then I heard Tommy calling me, "Alisha is that you? Alisha, oh my Go...Papa T come quick!" I heard a man say, "Oh my God, not my baby!" before everything went silent.

I woke up in the hospital with Grams, Papa, and Ma Carrie praying. Tommy was standing at the foot of the bed. "She's up Ma

Carrie." Tommy yelled as he ran to my side, "Lisha, how you feeling?" Ma Carrie snatched him away from the bed. "Boy let them go first." Grams was kissing on my as Papa stood behind her with red eyes. The only time I saw Papa cry was at my mother's funeral. Papa always said don't worry about it give it to God, so I thought he was the bravest man in the world. I also wondered, after that summer day, why would God allow that to happen to an innocent child.

The police chief came in and Ma Carrie made Tommy leave. "Isn't that Sabrina's child, well this case is closed." He said closing his note book, "Girl, tell your grandparents who you were in that shed with drinking and fornicating." He turned toward Papa. "Look its simple. She was in there with some boys and things got carried away. She's a product of her mama." Papa got so angry he almost hit the chief. "Since you won't find them I will and when I do, they'll be sorry." Papa turned to leave. The Chief said, "Now Tobias you can't go around beating up little boys." Papa walked out. I sat up in bed and whispered in the Chief's ear and he shot out of the door like he had seen a ghost. "Baby, what did you say to him?"
"I told him who it was." Grams and Ma Carrie walked closer to me pleading with their stares.

"It was Lisa, his two sons, his three nephews and the Judge's son, but she set it up."

"I never liked her and they want my Tommy to marry that little witch." Ma Carrie viciously said while folding her arms.

"We can't tell Tobias because he will kill'em and end up in jail." Grams said looking shocked. She flopped down and she covering her mouth in disbelief.

"Well, what are we going to do?" Ma Carrie exclaimed.

"Pray," Grams said holding her head down in shame and regret. "God will make them suffer for such a horrible act."

"I mean, besides pray," Ma Carrie shouted. "I want to kill'em now and ask for forgiveness later."

"Ms. Carrie you can't talk like that, you're the mother of a Pastor and kin to the bishop." Grams said in a hush like manner.

Nothing was ever done or said, but the boys disappeared. I had changed. I would only sit in my yard and it was almost four months before Tommy could make me laugh. The next school year the girl that ran never came back to school. They said she went crazy, but she told what she saw and her family moved out of fear. All the boys were gone either to the military or with family in other states. Lisa and her female partner, Leslie, were the only ones left. The first day of school they came over and started picking on me. I got up and walked away, so Lisa made Leslie keep a look out while she beat me up. That say I beat Lisa so bad she was out of school for a week. Nobody said anything because everybody knew Lisa had something to do with my attack, but no one could prove it or was scared to tell.

During high school I would study and read, but I never hung out or drank. Tommy would come over because he always wanted me to go to parties with hm. Soon Tommy started hanging with the popular kids until our junior year because that was college application time. In our senior year when the letters started coming in we both got into the school we wanted. I had a full scholarship. At the end of the year his parents broke the news and officially announced Tommy and Lisa as a couple. Lisa didn't go to college because she saw no need for school. Tommy and I left town and spent a month on the road. We caught it when we got back, but we had fun.

When I was about sixteen, I studied the art of sex and the pleasure points of a man. I would read all day and quizzed myself the following day because I wanted to conquer men and cause them to be weak. That summer day they didn't just take my innocence, but a part of me that I didn't know was missing until I gave birth to my daughter. A pure love was missing and that only came from a relationship with God.

12

Alisha Lives

A few months later my little miracle of life came home. Alonzo was the happy father and I was in awe of his love. A few days after she was born we filed papers so he could legally adopt Milagro. Malcolm fought us until he realized how much he would have to pay in child support. We had already hyphened her name to Coleman-Avery. A week after Milagro came home it was official and Alonzo was Milagro Vida Coleman-Avery's father. We loved being parents, but the marriage proposal did not come.

Alonzo had been married for almost twelve years when he was in a horrible car accident. Alonzo came out good except for two things, he couldn't have children anymore and he had issues in the marriage bed. Alonzo had two girls ages 5 and 4 with his wife. A few years ago she left him for the children's father. Alonzo's wife had been cheating on him with his best friend from high school. She was his high school sweetheart and they married right out of high school. Alonzo was heartbroken and now he fears being hurt. He told Tommy, "I love her and would marry her tomorrow, but what if she leaves me?" Tommy tried to explain that there is no guarantee that a relationship will last forever, but if God is in it things will be okay. Alonzo and I broke up a month later, but we parent our little Miracle together.

During the first month of our break up it was hard because Alonzo didn't want things to change and neither did I, but I wanted to get married and he was scared. Alonzo is the perfect father. I loved Alonzo because as my mate he could do no wrong, but I wanted a home and he wanted a security I didn't know how to give. Alonzo was the first man to fall in love with me for me, once I became a woman. Alonzo wanted to have sex with me but he was scared I would run off sooner.

Blair, my sex driven math teacher, called me two months after our complete break up and we went to dinner. Blair told me how he wanted to settle down and get remarried. We talked for hours about his kids and how he had chosen a different path. After ten minutes he sounded like the teacher from Charlie Brown. All I could think about was Alonzo and what he was doing with Milagro. He had taken her to see his mom and stayed for the weekend. When I got home, early I must say, Alonzo was sitting in the kitchen. "Did you have fun on your date?" he asked sarcastically.

"No," I said pulling off my shoes. "What are you doing over here?" I asked looking puzzled.

"What, I can't come home early?" he said standing up.

"Yes, but your mom lives an hour away and this is not your home, remember." I said annoyed.

Alonzo walked over to me and put his arms around me. "Baby, the truth is I couldn't sleep knowing you were with another man." He kissed me on the forehead and I melted. "I don't want to share that part of you."

"Alonzo you're making this harder than it needs to be." I said walking away.

"Baby I love you." He yelled.

"Just not enough to marry," I said walking upstairs.

"That's not fair." He quickly replied running behind me.

"No, this is not fair." I said as tears fell down my face. "I thought about you the whole time I was on this date and I come home to you in..." I threw my hands up and turned towards the bed room to get undress. Alonzo pulled me closer and started kissing me as he picked me up and carried me up the last two steps. He placed me on the bed and began his journey to a path he had traveled so well. As I cried out in a familiar pleasure, he began to do something he had never done before. I had never had the pleasure of his throbbing passion. I felt the oversized pleasure of him and as I rose from the bed. Arching my back before he could continue the unchartered journey, he spilled his essence. I quickly repositioned myself to give a never before felt pleasure. Alonzo stuttered and convulsed while trying to pull away and pull me closer at the same time.

"Alisha I want you to be my wife, but I'm more fearful now than I was yesterday. I did this to secure my position with you, but now you have my head spinning." He said placing his head in his hands.

I rubbed his back to comfort him. "I don't understand Alonzo, are you saying our first time having sex was because you were jealous?" I got up to put on my clothes and walked out of the room. "Baby it's not like that," he said running behind me and trying to put on his pants. "I've always wanted to make love to you, but as you can see I'm extremely sensitive." He said grabbing my hand.

"Is that your issue from the accident?" I asked contorting my face.

"Yes, I can't control my outcome or how fast it happens because I'm so sensitive." He slowly said looking embarrassed.

"You mean to tell me the only issue you have is...Okay Alonzo you taught me something, but you marred it at the same time." I pulled him into the living room to sit down. "I have more to offer than what is between my legs, but I'm not worth marrying."

"No baby you are, but I'm just scared." He fell to his knees. "Baby, you are excellent at what you do and that frightens me even more."

"I don't get it, so I'm going to bed." I stood up to walk away.

"I can't explain it, but I'll leave." He looked back with a sadness I had never seen before. "Alisha, give us another chance."

"I will not date you without you seeking professional help, so drive safely and kiss Milagro."

"You can counsel me." He pleaded.

"No I can't, it's too personal and I may steer you in the wrong direction because of my own emotions." I said looking away. Alonzo walked out the door and my heart sank. For the next two months we were parents only.

A month later as I sat at home alone, I became sad and cried out, "Lord what is wrong with me? You sent me Mikael and he did what he thought was the right thing. Then you sent Blair but he was a cheat. Tommy was next and he's closed minded and scared to see the world. Then Alonzo came with a fear that can never be comforted. Is this my punishment or my revelation, should I move on or be still? Lord I can't do this without You. Forgive me of every sin I've committed against You Father, the children you've created, or myself because I didn't realize I was worthy. In Jesus name I lift these prayer, petitions and concerns unto You, Amen.

A few weeks later I went home to visit Ma Carrie and Tommy. He picked us up from the airport. "Hey where's Alonzo?"
"We broke up for good." I said sadly.
"Are you ok?" Tommy asked with concern on his face.
"Yes, because Alonzo picks up Milagro every other weekend and a few days during the week." I said trying to fight back my true feelings. "How are you?"
"Lisa left town because the real father came forward. I stepped down for a year to go on my sabbatical. I realized I was closed minded and needed to see the world. I still haven't given up on us either." Tommy looked at me with a big smile.
"What are you talking about, either?" I asked confused.
"Alisha, you have had that necklace on since I gave it to you. That tells me in your heart there is a hope for our happily ever after."

354

Tommy reached for my hand.

"Whatever Tommy," I said, but he was right.

"Okay, well I leave tomorrow so until then you belong to me. You can see Ma Carrie when I'm gone." He joyfully announced.

"But, Tommy if you leave I have no reason to stay." I said slowly.

"Go see Ma Carrie when I leave and drive my car until you leave." He commanded.

I conceded, "Okay let's go home."

It was like old times; Tommy and I laughed and talked all night. He played with his god-daughter until she fell asleep. Late that night Tommy came in my room and whispered in my ear. "I love you and this will remind me of what's waiting at home." I had no idea what Tommy was talking about. Until he caressed my buried desire for him, releasing everything he searched for. Then he glided into that desire. Releasing himself of the passion that burned so deep for me and fell asleep.

Milagro woke up for her bottle, but Tommy was already there ready to feed her. I got up took a shower and walked down stairs to make breakfast, but Tommy had already prepared it. I ate, cleaned up, and he walked down stairs with Milagro. "I packed the car, so all we have to do is strap little mama in. I will be out of the country for at least six months." He talked all the way to the Airport, but I was speechless. I thought it was wrong for not stopping him last night. I felt confused as I dropped him off and gave him a hug. He kissed Milagro and disappeared through the gates.

After I dropped Tommy off I went to see Ma Carrie. "It's about time I get to see Marie's great grandchild." She said walking toward us. "You know this would do their heart proud to see this, so is Tommy gone?"
"Yes ma'am, we are coming from the airport." I sighed. "He told me yesterday was his time with the baby and I could come see you after I dropped him off at the airport."
"I know I spent the week with him before you came and that's all he talked about you and Millie."
"Ma Carrie her name is Milagro." I corrected her by mistake.
"Well y'all young folk come up with these names that can't nobody pronounce, so I'ma call her Millie." She smiled pinching her cheeks.
"Yes ma'am. I like that, Millie." I said it looking up in thought.

That became her nick name. Alonzo's mom called her Millie too. Ma Carrie told me to come closer. "Baby, I can see your heart is heavy with confusion. Let me pray with you." After Ma Carrie prayed she spoke a prophetic word over me. I had seen in the spirit everything she said. "God does not want us to live in confusion, so relax He will show you. Just like John leaped in his mother's belly while in the presence ˊ ˪ Jesus, so will your heart in the presˊ ˪ce of your husband because you ˙ ˪st connected spirit to spirit. The follˊ ˪ng week Marcus took us to the airˊ ˪ ˪.

That afternoon Alonzo came over. "Bab... I mean Alisha I am so glad you came back earlier." He smiled playing with Millie.
"Why, did you miss Millie that much?" I couldn't believe I just said that. I was searching for recognition.
"Yes I did, but I have to fly out in the morning. I will be gone for a few months and I wanted to spend time with Milagro. I also wanted to ask you to take me to the airport," He said looking serious.
"Okay." I said sadly.
"Can I cook dinner for you?" he asked with a smile.
"I don't know." I coyly answered.
"Please," he got on his knees as if he were praying and wobbled over to me.
"Okay yes, so you can get up now." I went upstairs to set her room up for him and finished unpacking. When I came down stairs dinner was ready. We had Fettuccine Alfredo

with a butter parmesan sauce, a spinach salad with strawberries in a balsamic and honey vinaigrette, and ended with bananas foster crepes for dessert. "This is why I didn't want to let you cook. How are you going to cook all of my favorites? Really" I said smiling. "I forgot one thing." He quickly jumped up. "What could you have possibly forgotten?" I asked surprised.

"The tropical smoothie and I made a batch that I put it in the freezer." He smiled.

"You make it hard for me to move on." I smiled looking into his eyes.

"That's the point. I don't want you too." He caressed my hand.

"Alonzo I can't sit around wondering what could've been." I exclaimed as I snatched my hand back.

"Alisha I started therapy last week. I want to be your husband so much so that I am willing to go against everything I believe in, so I got professional help." He excitedly announced. I smiled and thought this man makes me give in every time. We finished eating and I cleaned up while Alonzo played with Millie. I went to bed and let them have their fun. I awakened to the familiar Alonzo searching for a pleasure in a desperate attempt to make me stay, but this time rewarding me with an unfamiliar pleasure of his manhood greater than the first. He disappeared into the bath room to clean up before returning to Milagro as I rolled over for some much needed rest.

That morning I prepared breakfast. After eating I cleaned up and went upstairs to shower and change. I walked out of the bathroom and Alonzo was in my room. He was standing there in every sense of the word. "Baby, are you going to give up on us?" He said walking over to me. He threw me face down on the bed. Without any gentleness, he thrust himself into my saturated passion causing me to cry out his name. He erupted into the man of my dreams. I turned to give him the honor he deserved as his essence filled me he convulsed in weakness falling to his knees. "Baby I'm so proud of you," I said as he looked at me still on his knees. I held his face and kissed him. "What are you talking about Alisha, I failed again." He said slowly rising. "Alonzo you walked in here and took charge twice in less than twelve hours." I smiled. I was so excited that I started kissing him. He slowly pulled my leg over his and I found myself entrenched in passion. My hips swirled around as I retreated, but quickly returned to the love that filled me. With each move Alonzo gripped me tighter until the strength of his squeeze matched the volume of his cry. In the nape of my neck he whispered, "I love you baby." I threw back my desire a little harder, so He yelled out breathless. "I've wanted you for so long, so you can't give up on us. I never thought it would be this way. Baby, I don't want to leave." With each confession his grip was tighter as he pulled me closer. "Alonzo, I love you." I held his face as I looked into his eyes. "Come on before you miss your flight."

For months I lay beside him longing for what he had just given me, instead of just the skillful pleasure of his tongue and now I didn't want him to go. My legs are weak in anticipation of the leap. I was hoping at that moment it would be him. I ran down stairs and looked him eye to eye again hoping to feel the leap. I was forcing the feel of the leap, but to no avail. I could hear a small quiet voice within me saying you're not ready. "I'm not ready?" I said aloud.
"Alisha what did you forget?" I heard Alonzo say, "Baby, are you okay?" he looked at me puzzled.
"Yes, you just blew my mind this morning." I said smiling.
"Did I really?" he smiled sticking out his chest.
"Yes, it's not how long the ship stays in the water, but how much it accomplishes while it's in there." I looked down and caressed his thick manhood. "Oh and the width, not the length helps the maneuvering when it comes

to pleasing me." He leaned over and kissed me. "Thanks baby. I needed that." We loaded the car for his departure and we were off to the airport in no time.

13

The Leap

I had just finished with my last client and I laid Millie down to finish some paperwork. As soon as I sat down I heard a knock on the door, so got up to answer it. I was shocked to see Malcolm standing there. He looked different, almost humbled and he had lost a good bit of weight. "Can I talk to you, please?" he asked. "Yes Malcolm," I felt sorry for him. I had never stopped caring about him or lost my appetite for his sexual skills. "Forgive me for being such an arrogant fool. I know I hurt you and I'm sorry. I think about our daughter and everything I've missed out on because I was not there for you or her. I heard you named her Miracle." He said as he smiled.

"We call her Millie; I like it because it means strength and determination."
"But where did Millie come from?"
"Ma Carrie couldn't pronounce Milagro, so she called her Millie and it stuck." He smiled with pleading eyes. "I divorced my wife. I moved here permanently, so if you and Alonzo are

willing. I would like to be in her life. I made a lot of mistakes, but I have dedicated my life to doing the right thing. I miss you. I miss your smile and your laugh. Hell, I miss the way you crinkle your nose when you're thinking and most of all I miss you in my arms. Alisha, I never stopped loving you and it was because of your kindness. I am a changed man." Milagro started crying, "Is that her, can I see her?"

"Yes, but wash your hands first." He walked into the room and his face lit up. I thought about his face when he saw the ultrasound and my heart melted. "She's so beautiful." He said looking up at me. "She looks like you."

"Well you can hold her while I make her dinner." I walked into the kitchen and prepared her food. Malcolm walked in and asked, "Can I feed her?" I thought this would be good, so I could finish my paper work.

"Yes, I put her in the chair. "Her food goes on the table because she will grab it and give her the bottle when she's done."

"Okay, thank you Alisha." I thought. What is he up to? I walked into the office and rushed back out thinking, are you crazy, leaving that man alone with your baby. After she finished, I laid her down. When I walked out Malcolm was cleaning up the kitchen. "Thanks for coming by Malcolm," He grabbed me and started kissing me. Every part of my flesh had given in, but my mind thought about Alonzo. "Stop Malcolm, I can't do this to Alonzo."

"He's doing it to you." He yelled.

"What?" I shook my head as if I couldn't hear what he just said.

"I have proof." He pulled out the pictures of Alonzo with another woman.

"Is this why you came here?" I yelled as tears flowed down my face.

"Alisha I didn't come here to hurt you, but you need to know the truth. This man doesn't deserve you and Milagro. You both deserve my last name I'm willing to marry you." He got down on one knee.

I yelled, "Get out! Get out Malcolm!" He stood up and walked toward the door but turned to say, "By the way she's pregnant." And he threw the package on the floor spilling the contents. I cried aloud and screamed, "Why did you do this to me Alonzo, why? I knew Malcolm was up to something. Lord what now?" I began to pray and I started to calm down as I crawled over to the package Malcolm had dropped. As I picked it up I thought aloud, "Pregnant?"

A month later I was sitting at the table thinking aloud, "Papa told me he saw the hand of God on me, so Alisha means protected by God. I know my life has been protected because I live in the peace represented by the dove. Instead of flying away from my reality I've learned to face it." I wrote my thoughts so that my prayers and petitions would be known as I continued to ponder my growth. I spoke my revelations aloud, "Alonzo taught me how to appreciate a man with the absence of sex. Rodney taught me what tenderness looks like when a man loves you. Charles taught me to be honest with myself. Terrance taught me what selfish, fleshly, unnatural love was. Tommy made me appreciate the innocence of love. Julian taught me how to fall in love. Brice taught me to never give up on love. Kelvin taught me about sacrifice. Mikael taught me the spiritual principles of love. Blair gave me the rawness of passionate love. But Malcolm gave me a keen awareness of making love. I realized that every man I had sex with was connected or tied to me spiritually, causing me grief and confusion. I still have nightmares of those that forced their ties upon me. The desire to be with Malcolm in spite of all he's done grieves my heart. I carry not only a sinful soul tie, but his seed. The revelation of why we should not have sex before marriage was clear. Now I'm tied to these men forever by choice. Now wait for what God put together, not who I choose to marry and to force God to approve. What God brings together no man can tear apart. If it's the two God saw fit to be together for His purpose.

One man encompasses a part of each type of love God knows I need and that man is...." Suddenly, the doorbell rang so I jumped up to open the door and my heart leapt when I saw...

Okay Your Wife Isn't That Good...

Follows Alisha with her heart leaping love but who is he? Has Tommy become the man that will lead a family or has Alonzo overcome his fear of commitment? Is Alisha ready to be a wife or did she allow her drive to push her into another man's arm's? The second book of the series will have you wondering, "What just happened?"

If You Are Together...

Follows Alisha through ups and downs, so has she returned to Malcom. Has she stopped playing with evil or allowed it to consume her. Wait, was this all a dream. Who did Ms. Daniels see in the bed with Alisha and where did he go?

Really!

Assist women on examining their actions and reactions, while reflecting on their heart condition.

- Have you been broken
- Do you fear success
- Do you love yourself
- Have you settled for the wrong mate

Made in the USA
Charleston, SC
30 October 2014